THE BULLET-CATCHER'S DAUGHTER

The two thugs crashed past me, clattering the curtain, thundering out to the storerooms at the back. Thus my first thoughts were with the Duchess, fearing she'd had insufficient start to reach the border, though it must lie very close.

Then I heard the clipped footsteps of the third man approaching. Hard soles to judge by the sound. New and expensive. He drew level with the booth, but instead of following his men out through the rear, he hesitated mid-stride and turned towards me.

I felt the fear gripping at my chest.

"Madam?" he enquired, leaning forward for a clearer view in the low light.

"I want no trouble, sir." I said, in the manner of a woman of the Backs. Hearing the tremor in my own voice, I felt certain he would also.

"Do you drink alone?"

"Would you keep my company, sir?"

"Don't trade wordplay with me woman."

"Then shall it be foreplay, sir?"

Beneath the table my hand shook. I placed my thumb on the hammer of the pistol, braced ready to pull it back.

"Who sat here with you?" he asked.

"A fine lady," I said.

"And?" He tapped his cane on the table.

"And a young gent, sir. He'd promised me business but you've chased him away."

ROD DUNCAN

The Bullet-Catcher's Daughter

BEING VOLUME ONE OF
THE FALL OF THE GAS-LIT EMPIRE

ANGRY ROBOT

ANGRY ROBOT
A member of the Osprey Group

Lace Market House
54-56 High Pavement
Nottingham
NG1 1HW
UK

Angry Robot/Osprey Publishing
PO Box 3985
New York
NY 10185-3985
USA

www.angryrobotbooks.com
All change…

An Angry Robot paperback original 2014

Cover art by Will Staehle
Set in Meridien by Argh! Oxford

Distributed in the United States by Random House, Inc., New York

ISBN 978 0 85766 530 0
Ebook ISBN 978 0 85766 531 7

Printed in the United States of America

9 8 7 6 5 4 3 2

CHAPTER 1

There was once a line marked out by God, through which were divided Heaven and Hell. And thus was chaos banished from the world. The Devil created lawyers to make amends. They argued the thickness of the line until there was room enough within it for all the sins of men to fit. And all the sins of women too.

THE BULLET-CATCHER'S HANDBOOK

Had I been a man, I could have strolled into that dark warren of narrow streets, blind alleys and iniquity, letting the steel tip of my cane tap out a leisurely report of my progress, receiving winks and catcalls from barkers and gamblers, gin-sellers and rowdy girls.

But the Backs is no place for a lady. By which I mean that no woman can risk the scandal of being seen there. Thus I strolled along Churchgate attired and disguised as a young gentleman. And from many years of practice, I was able to walk as one also, rolling the shoulders rather than the hips, maintaining a distance between my feet, occupying the centre of the road. Men fancy that they recognise a woman by dress, figure and face but it is more through movement that gender is revealed.

The further I advanced towards my goal, the deeper the potholes became. Deeper too were the shadows of doorways and arches, for the street lamps gave less light here, as if the grandees of the gas corporation wished to hide the lawlessness and sin that lay ahead. All of which worked for my benefit that evening. I do not willingly expose my disguise to brighter lights.

Skulking can attract the interest of the curious, however. Therefore I held my head and top hat high, creating the illusion of one in possession of confidence. The act felt easier thanks to the weight of my father's flintlock pistol, which bumped reassuringly against my leg.

On reaching Haymarket, one catches view of the border crossing itself. It consists of two identical sentry boxes, one on each side, wherein guards can shelter, and a wooden toll gate through which no goods ever pass. The deliberate symmetry does nothing to please the eye. On this October night, four flaming torches had been placed on stands across the road, each leaving a splash of yellow reflected on the damp cobbles.

I glanced up at the town clock and made some small show of checking my pocket watch, though covertly I scanned the road behind me for shadows out of place. Being so close to the border put me on my guard. And the meeting towards which I was making such cautious progress contained riddles yet to be answered.

Striding out again with that unnatural male gait, I crossed Haymarket and hurried through into Cheapside and then into that haven of smugglers known throughout the land as the Leicester Backs. With the rendezvous now close, I assessed the various decrepit figures propping up nearby walls, searching for one to enlist. My attention was drawn by a woman who stood apart from the others, huddled in a doorway.

She called out in a brittle voice as I approached. "Have mercy, kind sir, and spare a coin."

I saw now that she wore a curious assortment of rags and sacking. In one hand she gripped a bottle of back-alley gin.

"Would it be mercy to buy you more poison?" I asked, forcing my throat muscles open so that the sound would resonate at the top of my chest, giving my words a masculine pitch. Though I had practised this art for many years, my voice could only pass when I spoke softly.

"Blindness is a mercy, sir, for those who walk in the night." She held her bottle up for me to see and sloshed the inch of liquid that remained.

Nothing good would come of hiring her if she was already half blind from wood alcohol. I pulled a coin from beneath my cloak and flicked it up. Her head snapped towards the slight metallic ringing as it spun in the air and I began to think she used her ears, not her eyes. With a swift movement, I made to trap it on the back of my gloved hand.

"What say you?"

"Heads," she said, without hesitation.

"Heads for luck or heads for blindness?"

"For mercy, sir."

Removing my hand, I revealed the space where the coin should have been, but was not. Then with a deceiving movement of my other hand, I pulled it from the air. The woman's lips drew back into a grin, revealing the stumps of three stained teeth. I flicked the coin towards her and she snatched it, fleet as a snake strike.

"It seems you're not blind yet."

"No indeed, though I will work to remedy that with your good help."

"Watch for me as I go," I said. "Look for any other that may follow. I'll visit again on my return."

"Bless you, sir," she said. Then, as I walked away I heard her calling out, "May many buxom women bear you sons."

A bell jangled as I pushed the door and stepped into the warm closeness of the Darkside Coffee House. High-backed benches divided the room into a series of secluded drinking booths. Tables lay between them, on each of which guttered the inconstant flame of a small candle. A brass-mounted chromatic lamp adorned the shelf behind the bar. Its round lenses illuminated caddies of coffee, tobacco and hashish, but left the body of the room darker than the street.

I started to raise a hand to check the hair was still in place on my upper lip, but managed to stop myself halfway. The barman was watching me. Tilting my head forwards so the shadow of my hat brim lay across my eyes, I stepped towards him. "I'm here to meet someone," I said. "A lady."

"Aye." He turned a gilt-rimmed glass onto a matching saucer and started pouring thick Turkish coffee from a silver pot. "Was waiting on seeing who the lucky man would be."

"Where may I find her?"

Taking my money, he nodded towards the back.

Stepping between the booths I picked my way in the direction he had indicated. Sweet tobacco and hashish smoke mixed with the smells of bitter coffee and alcohol. Growing accustomed to the gloom, I could just make out the whites of eyes watching me. Here and there the bowl of a smoking pipe flared red.

The identity of this much-needed client had not been hard to ascertain. Her letter of enquiry had been phrased in that over-embellished prose so typical of the aristocratic houses of the south. An educated hand of swirls and serifs had written that letter. Heavy cream-coloured paper reinforced the impression. All spoke of money. But it had been the edge of a watermark that had narrowed my search to one estate.

It seemed that such a woman would be conspicuous in this setting, but when I reached the rear of the room and saw her, I marvelled at how well she had camouflaged herself. A coarse woollen shawl hung from her shoulders and a plain bonnet hid all but a few of her blond ringlets. Only when she reached out her hand did the shawl part and I glimpsed the jewel-green blouse she wore beneath, its full sleeves nipped in at the forearm by long, tight cuffs. Even in that gloom the colour seemed bright.

I took her hand, and made a small bow.

"Mr Barnabas?" she enquired.

There was a shifting in one of the nearby booths: a whisper of cloth as if a head had turned or a hand had reached to open a watch casing. I slid into the seat opposite her and placed my coffee glass on the table between us.

"You speak too loud," I whispered.

She leaned forwards, bringing her head close. "Please forgive me. But my mind has been racing. I did not think."

"If I hear the bell above the door, I may choose to slip away," I said.

As she composed herself, I examined the back wall of the coffee house and was pleased to see a curtain of glass beads strung across a recess. That I had not been able to see it from the bar made it an excellent route of escape, should one be needed. Store rooms would surely lie behind it, then a rear yard, perhaps a privy and beyond that the maze of hidden spaces and unwatched cut-throughs that had accidentally turned the Backs into a smugglers' paradise.

"Why did you come in person?" I asked.

"Your services aren't usually commissioned face to face?"

"I've never heard of an aristocrat of the Kingdom entering the Anglo-Scottish Republic by choice."

She folded her arms before her.

"Are you not the Duchess of Bletchley?" I asked.

"And if I am? The border lies not thirty paces behind me."

"But the embarrassment to your king should you be found?"

"A matter of no significance."

A matter of significance it was, though I let it lie. "Your letter mentioned a person missing. A loved one perhaps?"

"A brother. My brother. He's been gone three weeks."

"You must know I'm not free to cross into the

Kingdom. Even coming this close to the border is a risk."

"My brother has crossed into the Republic," she said. "He's not so much missing as out of my reach. And yet I wish to reach him."

"There are many private intelligence gatherers for hire," I said. "Men who are free to cross into the Kingdom if they wish. Why contract me? I can't even visit your home to question those who might have information."

"Your knowledge matches my needs," she said. "And I've heard that you are most reliable."

In my foolish vanity, her words made sense to me.

"Your coffee is growing cold," she said.

"How am I to find your brother?"

"I know where he is." She pulled the glove from her left hand, then reached inside with slender fingers and withdrew a fold of paper.

"I'll need payment," I said. "Gold, not some promissory note from the Kingdom bank."

"Gold you will have."

I reached out to take the paper from her, but stopped halfway. The air had shifted and I could smell the dank of the rear yard. Somewhere in the building a door must have opened. Or a window perhaps. I brought a finger to my lips, held my breath and listened. The low murmur of secret conversations in the Darkside Coffee House had fallen away to almost nothing. Keeping my head low, I peered around the high back of the bench. The barman was standing next to the open door, muffling the bell with his raised hand. Stepping in from the street were three figures, one wearing a tall top hat, the other two in cloth caps.

I grabbed the paper from the Duchess's hand, pointed towards the bead curtain and mouthed one word. "Go."

She was already moving, stepping towards the gap, her back towards me. So I ripped the false hair from my cheeks and upper lip then snatched the hat from my head, revealing the lacy head-covering beneath.

But as I was shaking out my long hair, the Duchess turned for a final look. For a fraction of a second she stood wide-eyed, staring at the woman I had halfrevealed myself to be. Then she was gone in a cascading clatter of glass beads and the thugs were charging towards the sound.

CHAPTER 2

There is no more complete and satisfying way for a man to disappear than for him to have never existed.

THE BULLET-CATCHER'S HANDBOOK

Illusion was my inheritance, fed to me on my mother's lap as the drowsy rocking of the caravan and the slow rhythm of iron-shod hooves lulled me. It was a ripe strawberry conjured from the air, or a silver coin caressed from my soft cheek by the touch of a loving hand.

As I grew, I learned that others built lives on stuff they fancied more solid. To them, illusion was a shifting mist they wished to define or dispel. But instead of shunning us, these people were drawn to buy tickets for our shows. At first they might choose seats at the back of the tent, as if embarrassed to be seen in our low company. But night by night fascination would overcome their better judgement until they were sitting on the edge of their seats in the front row. But the harder they clung to that which they thought solid, the further their gaze drifted from the moment of the trick.

The first great illusion given me by my father was the gift of being, when needed, my own twin brother. I learned by stages to move as he moved and to look as he looked. My voice would always be the weakest part of the illusion, but even this could be covered by misdirection. At a distance of twenty paces, under the deceiving illumination of the stage lights, my friends could not tell me from a man.

Of itself that would not have been enough. To create a great illusion one must combine several tricks. And so I learned the art of the quick change, taking every movement of the transformation and rehearsing it ten thousand times until I could walk across the stage, pass behind a cabinet and without breaking stride, or so it seemed, emerge from the other side as a man. For by repetition, the workings of the clock are slowed.

Mine was a secret nurtured. I practised it in windowless rooms. Even in the Circus of Mysteries, most did not know it. There had been but seven people who held the secret. With the Duchess's unexpected backward glance, there were eight.

The fast beat of footsteps crashed towards me from the front of the Darkside Coffee House. I repeated the mantra in my head and let my limbs follow the dance they had rehearsed. Lift. Unbutton. Swirl. Reverse the cloak. In the same movement, rip away the false coverings from my lower legs.

Breathe.

Click the release button and snap the cane into a parasol. Collapse and fold the top hat into a lady's purse. Pull the flintlock free from its straps. Grip it beneath the table.

Breathe again.

The two thugs crashed past me, clattering the curtain, thundering out to the storerooms at the back. Thus my first thoughts were with the Duchess, fearing she'd had insufficient start to reach the border, though it must lie very close.

Then I heard the clipped footsteps of the third man approaching. Hard soles to judge by the sound. New and expensive. He drew level with the booth, but instead of following his men out through the rear, he hesitated mid-stride and turned towards me.

I felt the fear gripping at my chest.

"Madam?" he enquired, leaning forward for a clearer view in the low light.

"I want no trouble, sir." I said, in the manner of a woman of the Backs. Hearing the tremor in my own voice, I felt certain he would also.

"Do you drink alone?"

"Would you keep my company, sir?"

"Don't trade wordplay with me woman."

"Then shall it be foreplay, sir?"

Beneath the table my hand shook. I placed my thumb on the hammer of the pistol, braced ready to pull it back.

"Who sat here with you?" he asked.

"A fine lady," I said.

"And?" He tapped his cane on the table.

"And a young gent, sir. He'd promised me business but you've chased him away."

The man stood tall again, drew a small cloth purse from under his cloak and shifted it in his fingers so the coins clinked within. The sound was similar enough in character to mask the cocking of the flintlock, yet not loud enough to allow the risk. I watched the purse as if transfixed.

"What did the fine lady and the young 'gent' speak of as they drank their coffee?"

I dropped my voice and leaned forward as if in conspiracy. "She was much insulted, sir."

"How so?"

"I couldn't say. But she was un-pleased to see me on the young gent's arm."

My voice was more level now. My heart still thudded fast but no longer jumped within my chest.

"Where is your hat, madam?" he asked. "That is not a hat."

"They call it a fascinator, sir."

"Then it is not a hat and you are not properly dressed."

"It passes in the Backs."

The thugs' footsteps were approaching once more from the rear. The curtain clattered as they side-stepped through. It seemed the Duchess had given them a run, for there was a bitter smell of sweat on them and a stormy anger on their faces. The man in the top hat took a deep breath and halfclosed his eyes.

"I fancy we have not the story complete," he said.

"Why, it's the truth, sir!"

"And yet..." He narrowed his eyes still further. "There is something about you." Turning to the more musclebound of his thugs, he said. "We'll need to question her more. See to it." Then he strode away, followed by the smaller one. At the door, the barman received the purse of coins and bowed. The bell jangled and they were gone.

The remaining thug regarded me with an emotionless stare. "Up," he said.

No time remained to think or to be afraid. I swallowed the bitter dregs from my coffee cup, then clinked it down loudly onto the saucer, cocking the pistol at the same moment.

I stood.

"Out," he said, violence just below the surface of his voice.

Men have died for not believing a woman would shoot them in the heart. So I chose instead to press the pistol to his groin. Obligingly, he froze. Then his gaze tracked down, ever so slowly, to the weapon in my hand. His expression might have been comical, but I had no doubt he'd break my neck as quick as clicking his fingers, and with as little effort, were my aim to waver.

"Out," I whispered, stepping forward, forcing him back towards the curtain of beads. In another two steps we were through and into the dank air of a storeroom. Of the room, I could see nothing save the pale rectangle of a second doorway some paces ahead. I accelerated towards it, pressing the muzzle hard into his flesh, not giving time for him to think of feinting left or right. The floor here was soft, uneven. He stumbled, just keeping his balance, as I pushed him backwards, through into a flagstone yard.

The privy stank, in spite of the cold. Brick buildings with overhanging roofs loomed all around. There would be narrow walkways near, some crossing the border to the Kingdom, others doubling back towards the Republic. I had no means of keeping the man off his balance for long enough to find my way.

I accelerated again. Trying to match me, he tripped and thudded back onto the damp stones, the breath knocked out of him. I was on him before he'd had a chance to inhale, my pistol close to his face.

Of the secret knot-craft of the escapists, I knew but a little. Enough, though, to secure a man's hands tight behind him in a loop of his own belt. "Take down your trousers," I hissed.

His eyes flicked to the turquoise inlayed stock of the gun in my hand. "That's a pretty thing. I'll point it in your pretty face one day. Then we'll see what you'll do for me."

I don't know if it was fear or anger that made me act. But I found myself shoving the muzzle of the pistol into his mouth and heard the grinding crack of metal against tooth.

CHAPTER 3

No matter what they or the law may say, there are people who want their money taken.

THE BULLET-CATCHER'S HANDBOOK

Bessie was once a hub of the Grand Union Letter and Parcel Distribution Company. Her long, narrow hull was topped with a coal bunker and three cabins that served as mobile sorting office and administrative base. Paddle wheels to port and starboard propelled her forward, while smoke and steam thundered from her tall brass funnel, flared gracefully at the top.

Then, in the Anglo-Scottish Republic's 155thyear, being equivalent to 1973 in the Kingdom of England and Southern Wales, the Grand Union Letter and Parcel Distribution Company transferred the last of its network to airship and the fleet of boats was sold at auction. Most were as good for bulk haulage as they had been when new and found eager buyers in the Bedford brick works to the south and the Staffordshire potteries to the north. But the hub boats, with their ornate oak-panelled sorting rooms lined with pigeon holes, each engraved with the name of a different parish, were good for no such industrial function.

When I first saw *Bessie*, her metalwork was tarnished and moss grew thickly in cracks on the deck. The hull rested low and lopsided in oily water. Yet, her simple lines seemed beautiful to me. Even before I saw the nameplate, I felt kinship.

On the morning after my escape from the two thugs and the gentleman in the top hat, I woke late. Sensing the strength and height of the sun through the curtained porthole over my bed, I rose quickly, pulling a pair of stockings from one of the pigeonholes on the wall. Then, from a wardrobe that must once have been an office cupboard, I selected a lavender grey blouse. The accompanying skirt, whilst unfashionably narrow in profile, allowed me the freedom of movement needed by one who must climb on and off a houseboat many times each day.

With the kettle rumbling on the stove in *Bessie*'s galley, I brushed and gathered my hair, applying a touch of powder to cover the redness of a graze on my brow. I must have caught myself on something during my flight, though I'd not been aware of the injury at the time.

In the distance I could hear the reedy notes of a concertina. The wife of the coal boatman was taking her morning break. She would have been up for hours already. I pulled a face at my reflection in the hand glass, concluding that the illusion of demure respectability would pass.

Thus arrayed, I emerged into the thin winter sunlight and looked down the cut to the barges and narrow boats moored aft to stern along the length of the wharf. My own small deck being clear of dew, I perched myself on the steering seat, placing my cup in its chipped saucer on the roof of the cabin and the Duchess of Bletchley's crisp ivory papers on my lap.

There were two reasons to believe her Grace would sever our brief relationship. First was the sudden and brutish interruption to our meeting. What sort of dangerous business must she think I dabble in to have such men on my heel? Second was the revelation that the man she had thought to commission was in fact a woman.

Unfolding the first of her papers, I re-read the message that had tempted me to our gloomy rendezvous in the Backs. The paper itself hinted at wealth. The message mentioned a missing person but did not indicate that any help had been sought from the constabulary or men at arms, from which I surmised some family shame or illegality must be involved.

When shame and wealth combine, money is always spent. My need on that account being so desperate, I had been tempted to the meeting despite its irregularity and possible danger.

Next I turned my attention to the fold of paper which the Duchess had carried concealed in her glove. In grade and texture it was identical to the letter. I raised it to my nose and inhaled the subtle suggestion of an expensive perfume. On unfolding it the previous night, I had expected to read an address. Instead I'd found the name of an institution.

Harry Timpson's
Laboratory of Arcane Wonders

Now, in the clear morning light, I experienced the same pang of excitement that had accompanied the first reading. I touched the words on the paper and wondered how much the Duchess knew of my past.

Lost in thought, I did not hear the sound of footsteps approaching. Startled by a sudden rustle of fabric close behind me, I stuffed the papers into the sleeve of my blouse.

"Miss Barnabus," came a brittle voice, "is your brother available this morning?"

Taking a deep breath to calm the thudding in my chest, I stood, adopted a passable smile and then turned to face the woman who had addressed me from the towpath.

"Mrs Simmonds, you gave me a start. A delightful start, of course."

"That's as maybe. But is your brother in?"

"He's sleeping. I daren't wake him."

"Indeed?"

"I trust our mooring fees are paid, Mrs Simmonds."

"Your brother is punctual, Elizabeth. Mr Simmonds and I have no complaint on that score. Never had. Not from our first meeting him. Though I did question the wisdom of having an intelligence gatherer living on our wharf. Yet he has made no trouble."

I lowered my gaze and made a slight curtsy. "Shall I pass my brother any message?"

"No," she said. "I will speak with him myself the next time I visit." She wrinkled her nose, as if deciding whether to mention some small unpleasantness. "You are a lucky girl to have a brother who honours his duty so. With the unfortunate circumstance of your parents."

"Yes, Mrs Simmonds. Thank you."

She peered at my ankle boots, the scuffed toes visible beneath the hem of my skirt, then at my hair, as if searching for something specific to criticise. Her gaze shifted to my sleeves and her frown deepened. I glanced down and was alarmed to see a corner of the Duchess's papers protruding over the back of my wrist. Quickly, I covered it with my other hand.

"We worry for you," she said at last.

"There's no need."

"Mr Simmonds mentioned his concern to me at breakfast this very day. It seemed to him, and I agreed, that your brother may not have the time or the expertise to invest in your... problem."

"My problem?"

"Acquiring a husband, Elizabeth. My goodness, girl, of what other problem should you be thinking?"

Several answers occurred to me, but I clenched my jaw and thus my mouth stayed firmly closed.

Leon had the face of a choirboy – a rosy complexion, a mop of flaxen hair and puppy fat around his cheeks. It was his eyes that ruined the suggestion of innocence. They flicked from the contract to the safe in the corner of his seedy office, to my face, to my chest then back to the contract, always calculating.

"The payment isn't properly due for two months," I said, touching the small bag I had placed on the desk between us. It contained a couple of gold coins but mostly silver, the very last of my savings.

He shook his head. "I'll see you in January, then. And bring the right money next time. This is a mile short."

"I thought perhaps we could agree an alteration," I said. "I could pay twice a year. Or monthly if you prefer."

"Why would I do that?"

"There'd be more money in it for you. And it would help us greatly. My brother's clients have been few this year."

He leaned back, tipping his chair, his knee jiggling with excess energy. "There's money in it alright. You got two months to get the hundred guineas. If you don't, I take the boat."

"But I've come early to negotiate. My brother would see that you're not out of pocket."

A grin began to form on his face. "It's a wager, girl. He bought the boat from me. He pays the instalments and he keeps it. But break the terms and he takes the forfeit. It's all in the contract."

"But I thought–"

"Losers always whine. It's business. He should have read the contract."

He fished in a jacket pocket for his pipe and pouch then busied his hands charging the bulb with tobacco. His eyes flicked from the worn desktop, to my blouse, to the grimy window glass then back to my blouse again. Through the wall I could hear the chinking of bottles from the public house next door.

I pulled the contract towards me across the scratched veneer, turning it to read. It was a single sheet, big as a newspaper, marked with a grid of fold lines. I ran my finger down its numbered clauses, searching for anything that might suggest a way out. I could think of no means to gather the hundred guineas in time, unless it be from the Duchess's commission. That now seemed a distant possibility.

There was a soft gurgling as Leon sucked at his pipe, a match held to the tobacco. "Knew you'd never pay," he said, speaking smoke.

"We still have time."

"Sure you do."

"There are still two months." I shivered, as if the long shadow of the workhouse had touched me already.

"She's a pretty boat," he said. "Now you've fixed her up nice for me."

I returned to the wording of the contract, searching the clauses on repayment and boat seizure. "If it's a wager, there must be a way for you to lose."

"Nah," he said. "No point in me drafting a contract like that."

CHAPTER 4

*Grind salts of potash with your gunpowder to affect
a muzzle flash of violet colour. Copper salts make a
turquoise flame, whilst calcium yields brick red.*

THE BULLET-CATCHER'S HANDBOOK

On the first of November, being three days after my
encounter in the Darkside Coffee House, the mild
westerly wind backed to a north easterly. The mercury
fell and the first thick fog of winter spread its tendrils
to swirl around *Bessie*'s portholes. In an effort to drive
out the chilling damp, everyone who could so afford
shovelled more coal onto the fire. Smoke rose from
chimneys all over the city. Thus the fog thickened,
becoming oily and sulphurous.

In a pea-souper everything seems to stop. Blanket-
wrapped, I huddled next to the stove, sipping cup after
cup of weak tea. Afraid that ice might be forming around
the hull, I would from time to time shift my weight from
side to side, listening for that tell-tale crackling in the
inky water. In such a state, I pondered with increasing
desperation the urgency of securing a new commission.

Against all odds I had for three years managed to eke out my living as an intelligence gatherer. Against the law also, for the ownership of businesses in the Republic is the preserve of men. It was *Bessie* that made this precarious existence possible. If I lost her, I would be forced to seek a shared room in a tenement. From such a place, it would be impossible to lead my double life. The spiral of poverty would surely suck me down.

Leon would theoretically require a court order to repossess the boat. That might take a couple of weeks from my failure to make payment. Longer even at this time of year, since all business runs slowly in winter. But more likely, I'd find myself confronted by a crowbar wielding mob, before which it would be hard to argue the finer points of law.

Under a bright sun I might have been able to banish such thoughts. But in the fog they festered.

It was the faint scuffing of shoes and a gentle movement of the boat that told me someone had climbed up onto the aft deck. Few would venture from their homes in the penumbral gloom of the fog. For a second, the ridiculous thought came to me that the Duchess of Bletchley might be outside, a purse of gold in her hand. Then a knuckle wrapped on the hatchway and my mind jumped to darker possibilities. I found myself glancing at the galley knives above the sink.

"Who is it?" I called.

"Will you let me in?"

Recognising the voice, I hurried to slide open the bolt.

"Julia." I took the young woman's hand and pulled her inside, quickly closing the hatch behind her. "You're half frozen, girl. Get by the stove."

"Don't fuss. It makes you sound like my mother."

The layers started to come off, scarf and bonnet first, revealing an eighteen year-old with blond hair and an impish smile. Her cheeks were always flushed when she visited. I believed this came not from the cold but from daring excitement. In crossing the threshold of my floating home she was stepping off the narrow path that good Republican society had set for her.

"What possessed you to leave the house?" I asked.

"It's Thursday," she said. "I always come on Thursday."

Time had drifted for me under the fog. "Has your lesson come round already? I'm surprised your parents allowed you out with the weather like this."

"They don't know exactly. But Mother gets so unreasonable when she's cooped up. I just had to escape."

Only now as Julia hung up her coat did I see that she had been carrying a small bag next to her body. From it she drew my leather-bound copy of *The Intelligence Gatherer's Guide to Legal Process*.

I opened the stove and tipped the coal scuttle, building the fire up in honour of my guest.

"Won't your mother be concerned if she discovers you're not in the house?"

"She thinks I'm in bed."

"And if she were to call you?"

Julia huffed. "I left a note on the pillow. Please let's not talk about it. I came here to get away from all that."

"I thought you came here to learn the law!"

Two years ago Julia had persuaded her parents to take me on as a tutor. I believe they agreed in order to discourage her interest in the law. They'd surely drawn a connection between my unorthodox home and the fact that my brother was a private intelligence gatherer. We were living proof that dabbling in the law and criminal detection yielded no good fruit. My youth and lack of training were clearly a bonus to them. Innocent of my secret life, they believed such insight as I possessed must come from books alone. And if my shortcomings as a teacher failed to discourage, the Spartan conditions of our floating classroom would surely do the trick.

Perhaps Julia's mother still clung to that hope. Her father had long since realised how spectacularly the plan had failed.

I set the kettle on the stove and selected teacups from a pigeonhole. My student paced, running her thumb over a line of carved parish names on the wall: *Sproxton, Garthorpe, Buckminster*.

"What have you studied since last time?" I asked.

She dropped herself onto the bench next to the galley table, opened the book at a marker and read the chapter heading. "The Interception of Communications."

"The whole chapter?"

"Twice. But I'm still puzzled. Is it legal to shoot down a pigeon or is it not?"

"Legal. If the bird is wild."

"How can you tell?"

"Any pigeon flying at night must be owned," I explained. "Night flight isn't natural. The birds that can do it have been specially bred and trained by the Avian Post."

"And in the day?"

"You would need to check for a ring on the leg."

"But you can't. Not when it's flying high in the air."

"I suppose not–"

"In which case, one should never shoot them down. Day or night!"

I watched her leaf through the pages until she came to the heading she was looking for. "Why is there a section on shooting pigeons?"

I sat myself next to her and angled the book to read. "I'd forgotten that was in here."

"It recommends buckshot," she said, accusingly.

I did not share Julia's cornerstone belief in the crisp perfection of legal process. Thus our conversations often came to this point. "It is a... practical guide," I said. "Our world is coloured in shades of grey."

Julia was frowning. "The law keeps us from such uncertainty. If you want to see society without it, look beyond the borders of the Gas-Lit Empire! Would you have us live like that?"

"You can't conjure an argument about the entire civilized world based on the few failed states that lie beyond it! Extreme cases make bad examples." I took a breath to steady my voice, the pitch of which had been rising.

The kettle began to whistle, giving me the excuse to leave the table and busy myself with pouring steaming water into the pot. "We shouldn't confuse the ideal of the law with its application. That's all I'm saying."

I looked back at her and saw that she was stealing a glance up the gangway towards the sleeping cabins. When I sat once more she leaned in close and whispered.

"Your brother wouldn't shoot a pigeon, would he?"

"What difference would it make?"

"His life seems upside down," she said. "Sleeping in the day, working at night. I thought maybe..."

"Maybe he breaks the law instead of catching others who do?"

"I didn't mean it so forcefully," she flustered.

"I should hope not!"

"But can you blame me for wondering?"

Indeed, my brother was all too fascinating for her. I once again resolved that they should never meet. "Don't worry for his morals," I said. "Any brother of mine is as honest as me."

Julia's visit had lightened my mood, in spite of our argument. But on the third day of the fog, I could no longer bear the confinement of the boat. Nor could I sit passively and watch the calendar counting down the inexorable approach of my financial ruin. Though I had received no word from the Duchess, there remained one dangling thread for me to reel in. Thus, I resolved to venture into the gloom.

I opened my wardrobe and stroked a hand across the hanging clothes. Freedom of movement is more precious to me than a waist small enough for a man to encircle with his hands. Thus I keep the combined weight of my corsetry and other undergarments well below the three and a half kilogram maximum recommended by the Rational Dress Society. But on this day of penetrating cold, I selected a fuller skirt with two petticoats beneath and was grateful for every layer, not minding the load pressing down on my hips.

The journey from the wharf into the city of North Leicester is simple enough in summer. But had I not made the same trip a hundred times before, I would have become lost. Though daytime, the scenery was so changed by the blanketing fog that I walked clear past the first omnibus stop before realising I had overshot, and was forced to retrace my steps, feeling foolish though there was no one to see.

With a long scarf wound over my hat to protect my ears, I picked my way along the same route I had trodden disguised as a man. Today there was little risk of being seen and no chance of being followed, but I still kept my flintlock gripped inside my rabbit skin muffler.

On entering Cheapside I ducked into a doorway and stood a moment, getting my bearings. The fog has a way of seeming like a living thing. Thickening here and thinning there, it takes on forms such as the tentacles of a submarine creature, reaching out of dark places then withdrawing. Sounds are dulled, strengthening the impression of being underwater.

Two shadows passed some twenty paces distant: a man in a top hat and a woman who led him by the hand, doubtless towards her lodgings. Soft in the distance a beggar called. It was the voice I had been listening for.

Though the Backs is poor, so much wealth passes through it, crossing the border between the Republic and the Kingdom, that even an old beggar might survive on the scraps. Tracing the crumbling brickwork with the fingers of my left hand, I picked my way towards the voice, hearing it call again, like a distant lighthouse.

"Spare a coin for an old girl's folly."

For all the wood alcohol she must have consumed in her life on the street, she saw me before I could make her out.

"Have mercy, miss," she said.

She stood there in the hollow of the doorway clutching a bottle just as she had done last time. I slipped in beside her.

"Did a young man speak with you six nights back?"

"I should not say."

"He is my brother."

"You're afraid for his virtue, miss?"

"For his life. There were three men after him. One wore a top hat of unusual height. The other two were muscled like bulls."

The old woman was frowning, peering at me more closely. "You and your brother are much alike," she said.

Feeling embarrassed by her close inspection, I turned and cast my eyes in the direction of the coffee house. "My brother told you he'd return," I said. "But it proved unsafe."

"I saw three men, just as you say. But a full five minutes beyond your brother. They'd no sight of him. No way had they followed."

The implication of the old woman's words did not reach me all at once, but spread through my mind like ripples after a stone has been dropped into a pond. If I had not been followed, they already knew where to find me. No one knew of the meeting save myself and the Duchess. I could not believe she had arranged it as a trap. Perhaps her letter had been opened, read and re-sealed before arriving in my hand. Yet I had seen no sign of tampering.

I was readying myself to leave, when the old woman said, "Beg pardon, miss, but you can't magic a coin as your brother did?"

So I pulled a hand from my muffler and passed it before her face to prove it empty. Then I touched it to her cheek, trapping a silver fivep'ny between my fingers and her leathery skin.

She smiled broadly as I held it up for her to see, but instead of snatching it, she took my hand and gently placed it back against her face.

"Where do you sleep?" I asked.

"Here. Or anywhere."

"In the workhouse you'd have a roof. A fire too."

"They don't let no drink in the workhouse, miss."

I took back my hand and gave her the coin, which she accepted, though I sensed my touch had been worth more to her.

"Tell your brother I did good," she said.

"I will."

She moved in closer and whispered. "I asked round Cheapside. No one knew the toff's name. But one knew his job, or said he did. Tell your brother, take care, miss. For the man who followed is an agent of the Patent Office."

CHAPTER 5

For every skill there is a master. Therefore, let the escapist tie his knots, let the lawyer draft his contracts and let the agent of the Patent Office sign warrants of death.

THE BULLET-CATCHER'S HANDBOOK

Though I work within and between the laws and had been reading *The Intelligence Gatherers' Guide to Legal Process* with Julia for two years, I could not call myself an expert.

The Gas-Lit Empire spans the globe. Every nation within it has a different set of laws and punishments. Each has its own quirks and loopholes.

In the Kingdom of England and Southern Wales the aristocrats hold wide-ranging privileges and are protected by garrisons of men-at-arms, which are private armies in all but name. The royal family can call on any of the fighting forces of the nation and, although its legislative power is gone, it has virtual immunity. Cold equality is the watchword of the Anglo-Scottish Republic, though it is an open secret that officials live well beyond their means and that the wealthy seem remarkably honest, for they are seldom found guilty of any crime. There are few who understand both systems, even among the ranks of the lawyers.

The Patent Office, the first institution of the Gas-Lit Empire, was established to stand apart from and above the law of any nation. Only that way could it be an independent guarantor of the Great Accord. For almost two hundred years its agents, aloof and mysterious as priests, had used their powers to expunge unseemly science from the world.

They had ushered in an age in which perfection predominated over innovation, or so the history books claimed. No patent laws curtailed the development of art and culture, yet these too had become quiescent, there being no shocks of war or technology to disturb the equilibrium.

I did not know when corruption had first begun to incubate. Such things were not spoken of openly. Rather, they were glimpsed in lewd cartoons and music-hall sketches. Laughter makes fear an easier travelling companion.

But I now feared that the Patent Office was looking in my direction. The discovery chilled me. Under the fog I had no protection from my darker thoughts and found myself wallowing in memories from childhood.

But on the seventh day after my escape from the Darkside Coffee House, the wind veered westerly and the fog began to clear. On the eighth day the sun broke through and colour returned to the world. Long grass bowed down by dew became a scatter of diamonds.

The inhabitants of the working boats emerged full of urgency as if afraid the weather might turn once more. The coal boatman's wife strung two clothes lines between trees on the embankment. Her daughters hung out the washing while her son pulled back a length of the tarpaulin from the hold and began shovelling coal into a smaller boat tied to the bow. The doors of the boathouse lay open and I could hear the dull hammering of someone beating out sheet metal.

Hoping that vigorous activity might help me shake off my dark mood I set about washing the porthole windows, wiping away the greasy residue of the previous week. Then, as the dew cleared, I laid my blankets over nearby bushes to air in the sunshine. Two men had rowed across the canal and were cutting a fallen elder into logs, singing in time to the strokes of their saw.

"You want to buy firewood?" one called when they stopped to catch their breath.

"I'm well set for coal," I said, although it was a lie.

At noon, a small dairy boat chugged along the cut, the boatman shouting out his prices as he approached. Seeing me wave, he let the engine idle and steered in close enough for me to hand over a few copper coins and receive a thin wedge of cheese in return.

The noise of industry had subsided now and smoke rose from stoves up and down the cut. I sat on the aft deck, softening the end of a stale loaf by dipping it in my tea.

That was when I heard my name called and turned to see Mrs Simmonds advancing along the towpath, waving an envelope above her head.

"Expensive paper," she said, when she had drawn near.

I watched her rubbing it between her ever-inquisitive fingers. "Fortune shines on us," I said.

"I shall deliver it to your brother when he wakes."

Frustration was building in me, for she stood side-on, with the envelope just out of my reach. "Has it the mark of the Kingdom Postal Service?" I asked. "He anxiously awaits a message from a client in Buckinghamshire."

Mrs Simmonds played out the charade of examining the letter as if she had not already extracted all the information there was to glean without actually steaming it open.

"Buckinghamshire indeed," she concluded. "Bletchley, to be precise."

"Then it would be best I wake him with it directly."

Perhaps caught off guard by this development, she turned towards me, bringing the envelope within my range. I shot out a hand and grabbed it.

"Oh..." she said, startled.

For a moment we stood, each holding a corner of the crisp ivory paper, Mrs Simmonds on the towpath and me, from the vantage of *Bessie*'s small aft deck, standing a few inches taller.

"My brother is sure to be grateful for your trouble. But I'd have checked in at the office myself and saved your shoes the towpath mud."

"Oh," she said again, then let go.

Making a small curtsy, I slipped away inside, closing the hatch behind me to be sure she could not follow.

My dear Mr Barnabus,

I wish to express my enduring gratitude that you generously agreed to consult with me. And gratitude also for your kind acceptance of my commission. I am this day dispatching by trusted courier 70 gold sovereigns, which I offer as one third payment for your services. On receipt of your report, I will dispatch a further third. The balance will be paid on the safe return of the one sought. Thus the combined fee and expenses will be 210 gold sovereigns.

I trust you will find this arrangement acceptable.

CHAPTER 6

*Only two kinds of men can be conned: those with vices
and those without.*

THE BULLET-CATCHER'S HANDBOOK

The Duchess had made no mention of the thugs who
had ended our meeting in such precipitant manner. Nor
the final backward glance with which she had pierced
my double identity. Yet it seemed these peculiarities
had not deterred her.

I might yet earn Leon's money in time.

Locating Harry Timpson's Laboratory of Arcane
Wonders was not going to be easy, however. Timpson
had elusive ways. He'd jal the gaff in double-quick
time, making pitch where the fancy took him, sending
barkers into the towns around to post daybills on any
fence, wall or tree big enough to take one, announcing
to the world that the famous impresario had arrived.

But just as quickly, on a whim it seemed, after as
many shows as Timpson pleased, they would scarper
the tober, disappearing in the night. An octagon of
yellowed grass and a thread of smoke from a heap of

bonfire ash would be all that was left to be wondered at by passing jossers in the morning.

There would be horse dung in the roadway, by which the direction of departure might be guessed. But Timpson had a way of doubling back to make false trails. Long and meandering was the route he took. Thus it would be years before any return, by which time such small debts as they had left unpaid might be forgotten.

Yet only the dead are beyond finding.

The central post house in North Leicester was a classical building of sandstone columns and marble floors. A place of long moustaches and longer rule books. I clipped up the steps and into the echoing lobby dressed in a coat and skirt of sober blue; a shade much beloved of good Republicans. The image of respectability would be unlikely to withstand close inspection, however. A plunge of lace below the neckline of the blouse permitted glimpses of my skin beneath.

"Can I help you?" asked the young gentleman at the reception desk, his voice hushed.

I offered him a flustered smile. "I've been expecting a letter from my father in Newcastle. I fear it may be lost."

"The fog may have delayed it."

"Is there a way of checking?" I asked, discreetly sliding a coin across the desk. "It's been three weeks."

He palmed the coin smoothly enough to make a prestidigitator smile. "Three weeks, you say? That would seem overdue."

His shoes squeaked on the polished stone as we walked to the desk of an overseer, who enquired if a receipt for the transaction existed. It did, I informed him, and produced a document of paper so thin it seemed translucent. Removing a pair of thick-lensed spectacles, he brought it close to his face and examined the numerous rubber-stamp marks and signatures. Without such documents the oiled machine of the Republic would surely grind to a halt. With them, anything was possible.

Nodding sagely, he dismissed the young man from the reception desk. I let out a secret sigh of relief. My usual forger being unavoidably detained, I had been obliged to employ the services of an unknown.

Carpets replaced polished stone as the supervisor escorted me deeper into the building. On reaching a door marked "Superintendent of Postal Services" he knocked and ushered me inside.

The superintendent himself sported a moustache which extended an inch at least on either side of his florid face. "Charmed," he said, taking my un-gloved hand and holding it as he dismissed the other man. He then took my coat and pulled out a chair for me.

I sat, leaning forward slightly, pretending not to notice the way his eyes lingered over the lace panel at the top of my blouse.

"Did the missing package... I mean to say, did the package contain anything of value?" he enquired, somewhat distracted.

"Indeed, sir. It was from my father and was therefore infinitely precious."

"But child, my meaning was to the contents. Did it contain money?"

"It contained something more valuable. The location to which he was about to move. Without it I may never find him again."

The superintendent's bushy eyebrows came together in a frown. "Indeed?"

"He travels," I explained.

"Then I don't understand how we can help."

"I thought that those who work in this post house might have seen the name of his travelling company – on a letter perhaps – and thus know a recent location."

"You mean the fellows in the sorting room?"

The expression of hope and gratitude that flooded my face when he said this must have been pleasing, for he flushed a deeper red and stroked finger and thumb across his facial hair.

"I fear you do not understand," he said. "Many thousands of letters pass through this office every day. To expect the sorters to remember one name from among them... there is little hope."

"I fancy they might remember this name," I said. "My father works for Harry Timpson's Laboratory of Arcane Wonders."

The superintendent hid his surprise well, but could not conceal his change of manner. Admitting a connection with a family of travelling showmen had made me instantly exotic, putting me outside the narrow confines of accepted custom and restraint. I had become a gypsy girl, in his eyes, and therefore full of possibility.

He reached across the table and put his hand on the back of mine, a gesture more predatory than comforting. "Shall we see what we can do?"

He did not wish me to venture further into the depths of the post house. But on my suggestion that I would rather accompany him through those tight corridors than be left waiting in his office alone, he relented.

I knew I was approaching my destination when we stepped through a doorway and the thick carpet gave way to functional floorboards. The thrum of distant machinery vibrated the air. On opening a second door the sound increased twentyfold. We had arrived in the cavernous expanse of the sorting room. I came to a sudden halt, awestruck.

The machine, a leviathan, occupied the centre of the room. In size I would compare it to a small house. Around it scurried an ant-like army of workers. Some hefted bulging sacks into a hopper. Others carried neatly bound bricks of letters from the far end of the machine.

My mouth had dropped open in a manner that must have seemed comical or perhaps endearing, for the superintendent observed my reaction with evident enjoyment.

"I had not expected..." I began, but then could think of no words to complete the sentence.

"There are four other machines of this type," he said. "One in Munich, one in New York, two others in China. But this, in the opinion of those who know, is the finest. Carlisle may be the nation's capital, yet North Leicester occupies the preeminent position for our postal service."

We had both raised our voices to be heard above the machine, which pounded, as rhythmic as a military band. Binding its strange music and paying out time second by second was the bass boom and exhalation of a giant piston, which powered a vertical flywheel. Other sounds filled in an intricate percussion between the main beats; clinking, rattling, humming and ringing. Regulators spun. Escape valves hissed, while here and there a dribble of steaming water escaped into small drain channels in the floor.

I felt the superintendent's hand on my back as he guided me down a flight of steps to the machine floor itself.

"If any letter has been sent from the Kingdom or the southern border area to the... ah... to your father's place of work, it will have passed through this hall and been sorted by this machine."

"But how can one ask a machine if it's seen an address?"

"Indeed child, no device can read. But here we employ a marvellous symbiosis of the human eye and the power and speed of steam."

His fingers began to stroke the small of my back. Finding him looking down at me from an uncomfortable proximity, I turned away to examine a small doorway in the side of the machine.

"What is this?" I asked.

Consulting his fob watch he said. "That, you will presently observe."

Something was changing in the room. Not the reverberating rhythm, but the pattern of movement of the workers. Each, I noticed, wore blue overalls and a cloth cap. None wore facial hair, which seemed curious. On our arrival there had been as many men feeding the monster with sacks of letters as there had been carrying away the neat packages. Now the feeding had stopped and all hands were busy on the other end of the production line.

"Cover your ears, child."

No sooner had I followed his instruction than a factory whistle blew close above us. The flywheel continued to spin, but the rhythmic boom and rush of steam abated. The workers dropped packages and trooped from the hall.

It seemed there would be no one remaining to question, but then the door in the side of the machine clanked open. I watched, amazed, as men began to emerge. They wore the same blue overalls as the other workers, but the tops of their faces were covered with goggled leather masks of unusual design.

On exiting, each used one hand to shield his eyes from the light of the room, and the other to steady himself on a brass hand rail. The fifth man out closed the door behind.

"These are the sorters," said the superintendent. "It will take a moment for them to orientate themselves."

I could not imagine how these men might exist within the belly of the leviathan, let alone operate it.

Perhaps sensing my question, the superintendent leaned in close and said, "They spend each shift suspended over conveyor belts, along which the letters travel at great speed. Each of their fingers rests on a different button, much like the keys of a stenograph. They press the buttons in varied combinations to send the letters on their way to different stacks."

"But how can five men read so much in so short a span?"

"It's a prized ability among the sorters," he said. "And they imbibe certain tonics to maintain their concentration."

The first man was by this time removing his goggles.

The pupils of his eyes seemed extended beyond the natural limit, taking up almost the entire iris. It was only now that he looked around and seemed to notice us.

"Stand straight, citizen," said the superintendent.

The man did indeed straighten somewhat, though it seemed his work had left its mark on his posture.

"We need to know if you have seen, in the last weeks, any messages addressed to Harry Timpson's Laboratory of Arcane Wonders."

The man blinked his eyes, in an owl-like fashion. He frowned for a moment then shook his head. The others had started to remove their goggles now. They stood squinting, pupils dilated like the first man, peering around themselves as if seeing the sorting room for the first time. My guide repeated his question. Three reacted as the first had done. But the fourth sucked his teeth in thought. "Timpson... Harry Timpson..."

Moving his hands in front of himself, he momentarily closed his eyes while his fingers twitched and danced, as though he were playing an invisible instrument.

"A week gone, or two maybe. I sent it on the belt to the Sleaford office."

"Good man!" exclaimed the superintendent. "Good man indeed."

I felt his palm come to rest on my back once more, so stepped away, making to take the hand of the sorter, who grinned at me myopically. His fingers seemed unnaturally smooth, as though the lines and whorls had been worn away.

Julia Swain now had eighteen years to my twenty, an age gap that seemed far smaller than at the beginning of our association. At first I had been her teacher only. But increasingly she took pleasure in sharing the small confidences of her sheltered life. Chief among these were her opinions of the young men her mother introduced, none of whom met with her approval. Her husband would be kind, sensitive and intelligent, she said. But also masculine in the way of an athlete or a soldier.

"No such man exists," I said. "Or ever has."

"Then I will remain single and read law at a university of the Kingdom."

In return for this growing openness, I began to relate stories of my peculiar life on the cut. I even admitted to some of my exploits as an intelligence gatherer, though these I presented as if I were merely acting as an assistant to my brother. In truth I felt torn. The fiction gave me the opportunity to tell her more than I could otherwise have done. But I did not enjoy deceiving her. And her interest in my brother had a focussed intensity that made me uncomfortable.

"Offering a bribe is breaking the law," she said after I had told her of the various methods by which I gained entry to the sorting room.

"Only if a jury says so. And no jury will be asked."

"And in using a forged receipt..."

"I never told him it wasn't forged."

"A technicality."

"The law can't see the difference between technicality and substance. You know that."

Julia's frown deepened. "But is it... moral?"

"You expect it to be?"

"Our law was made through moral striving," she said. "Republicans, Abolitionists, Luddites. High-minded men and women. They were driven by an ethical code."

"They were each driven by a different code." I said. "And there are so many to choose from – vegetarianism, eugenics, anarchy, communism, naturism, family planning..."

"Elizabeth!" Julia was blushing. "Mother would have a fit if she heard you speak of such things."

"There are reading rooms all across the Republic where men talk of such things. Why shouldn't we?"

"You can't possibly know what they talk of."

"My brother has told me. But perhaps I'd better continue the story?"

Julia nodded, so I narrated the end of the adventure, my escape from the Superintendent of Postal Services. Her eyes opened wide and round as I stood in the middle of *Bessie*'s galley, acting out the scene, fluttering an imaginary fan, as if overcome by the steamy atmosphere.

"He thought perhaps that a loosening of stays or laces might revive me," I told her. "But the sorters, gallant to a man, said fresh air would be the ticket. And he, though so senior in rank to them, couldn't disagree without seeming... how should we say? Ashamed?"

"Oh, but you shouldn't act so!" she exclaimed, holding a hand in front of her face, in an unsuccessful attempt to hide an expression that was half shock and half grin. "To make him believe..."

"If he took the belief that my virtue could be loosened and unlaced, then the shame should rest on him."

"But if you flaunted, isn't it natural for a man to assume?"

"It wasn't the cut of my blouse or the angle from which he looked down that made him think that way. It was the suggestion of gypsy blood."

"How could he think that of you?"

"You believe I'm not a gypsy?"

Suddenly she seemed to notice the cabin in which we sat. That a boat served as my home had been the given fact of our first meeting. We sometimes discussed its practicalities but never its reason. It seemed only now that she saw in my home the signs of a restless spirit. To slip three mooring ropes would be the work of seconds.

"Are you a gypsy?" she asked. But before I could speak, she had changed her mind and blurted, "Please don't answer."

"Don't you want to know?"

"At least don't tell my parents. They'd no more tolerate our visits if you were of... of gypsy blood."

"I don't know the Romany language, if that is what you mean. Yet neither could I be happy anchored to the foundations of a house. Does that make me a gypsy in your eyes?"

"I'll never ask of it again," she said. "Nor would I respect you less if you were. You're more than a teacher to me."

I took her hands and squeezed them, feeling a sudden urge to confide the secret of my double life but fearing also that the revelation would be too great. Somehow, I had come to depend on Julia Swain as she had on me.

So I brewed a fresh pot of tea and I told her of the family of ducks that came to the boat to be fed on crumbs and of the coal boat moored next to me and the kisses the old boatman blew when he thought neither I nor his wife were watching. And I told her not one more thing of consequence.

CHAPTER 7

The great illusion is the one the audience does not see,
though it may have rested before their very faces for
the duration of the show. But greater than that is the
illusion invisible to another illusionist.

THE BULLET-CATCHER'S HANDBOOK

The slavery of indentured servitude so commonly seen
in the Kingdom of England and Southern Wales has
no place in the law of the Anglo-Scottish Republic. Yet
the women of the Kingdom have more freedoms. They
are permitted to own property and manage businesses
whereas their sisters in the Republic cannot be seen to
manage more than the affairs of a household. *Equal but
different* was the slogan of the Republic's guardians on
the matter.

So it was that my brother worked for my protection
and I for his.

During the hours of darkness my brother, or rather I
dressed as him, laboured as a gatherer of intelligence. By
day he slept, or so the world believed, whilst I managed
the smooth and proper functioning of the home. And

though the home we had chosen was a boat and his profession one that most decent people might frown on, yet as siblings together we seemed somehow more respectable.

The journey I was about to undertake, however, could not be conducted in the shadows and I would not risk the great secret of my double life in unforgiving daylight. Thus I announced to Mrs Simmonds that I would be travelling to Sleaford to seek out the graves of my grandparents.

"Un-chaperoned?" she inquired, her tone suggesting I was about to travel to Lincolnshire dressed only in Turkish bloomers.

"No indeed, Mrs Simmonds," I said. "My brother has travelled ahead to secure lodgings."

Thus, the day after the Duchess's messenger delivered a cloth purse of seventy gold sovereigns into my hand, I set out on the short trip to Anstey to begin my journey. It would have been cheaper for me to travel to Sleaford by coach but time was my enemy. Strangely, I would need to unlearn the habits of thrift for a chance to save myself from poverty.

There being no ship tethered to the mooring pylons, it was the two huge hangars of Ned Ludd Air Terminus that I saw first. Each hangar is shaped like a vast cylinder, sliced in half along its length so it can lie flat on the ground. Doors to front and rear may be rolled open, allowing the entire body of a ship to float inside. And there, illuminated by great lamps, passengers come and go via a staircase and elevated platform. Airships are indeed marvels, even in an age of marvels. Travelling swiftly from city to city, they have shrunk the globe.

I climbed to the alighting platform wearing my long cloak over a burgundy jacket and skirt. Not knowing if the carriage windows would be open or closed, I had pinned my hair up under a small hat. My belongings were already in the careful hands of the air terminus's porters, men known to be trustworthy in the handling of even the most delicate package.

The route not being of great popularity, my journey into Lincolnshire was to be below the belly of a small airship. Having shown my ticket and had it punched, I hitched up my skirts and climbed the final steps.

Though the carriage could have seated thirty in comfort, there were only eleven other passengers. Eight looked to be businessmen. A young couple sitting on their own I judged to be newlyweds, patrons of one of Anstey's many wedding chapels.

I chose a seat opposite the final two passengers, an elderly lady and her maid. Then I gazed out of the window to watch the ground crew hauling away a gas hose. Porters hurried to the safe end of the alighting platform while the bosun shouted instructions to men standing around the tethering points.

A uniformed terminus guard marched the length of the ship, whistle ready in his mouth. Having satisfied himself that all were in their allotted places, he raised his flag and seemed about to give the signal when a young man hove into view, running for the carriage door. One of his hands gripped a Gladstone bag; the other held a tan-coloured hat in place on his head. A homburg, I thought.

The guard nodded him on board then blew a shrill note. The carriage doors clattered shut. Mooring ropes swung free and the airship lifted, leaving a feeling in my stomach as if we were riding a fast carriage over a humpback bridge.

The young man slotted his Gladstone into the overhead rack, then sank into a seat across the aisle from me and fanned himself with his hat.

The rotors were turning now, the lopsided beat of the engine becoming more regular as its revolutions increased and we began to move forward. Through the window, I watched ground-crewmen hauling back the great hangar doors.

The noise changed as we emerged into the thin winter sunshine. Exhaust gases no longer puffed from either side of the engine. But turning in my seat, I could see a trail of smoke billowing from a vent at the rear of the great canopy below which the carriage was held secure.

We were rising steadily. Within half a minute the air terminus seemed no more than a collection of greenhouses. I smiled to see a flock of crows passing below us. The maid opposite me got up and pulled the leather strap to raise the window glass and the breeze in the carriage died. There was a shiver in her arm as she re-seated herself.

"Have you flown before?" I asked.

"She has not," replied the elderly lady on her maid's behalf.

"Some are nervous on their first flight," I said.

The lady's back stiffened. "*We* are not afraid."

Such was the force with which she spoke the word "we" that it seemed to be a benediction designed to encompass all the occupants of the carriage. I had to restrain myself from thanking her.

"But to fly above the birds," I said. "A little fear would not seem unnatural. Were one prone to such emotion."

The lady dabbed a handkerchief to her lips, from which I took it that the conversation had come to an end.

Far below us, smoke from uncounted chimneys clung to the earth. Of the sprawling suburbs I could see only the tallest factories. This seemed strange to me as I had not considered the morning to be particularly foggy. From this height, the four great gasometers that supplied North Leicester appeared to be a cluster of barrels floating in a wide grey sea.

A shrill cough drew my attention back to the lady opposite.

"Lower instincts are ours to conquer," she said.

"I beg your pardon, ma'am?"

"I am referring to fear. We are not like the animals, Miss...?"

"Miss Barnabus," I said.

"Animals have only lower nature. We can rise above." She raised a hand to indicate increasing elevation. It was a gesture patronising and comical in equal measure.

The young man across the aisle put a hand to his mouth and feigned a cough, though not quickly enough to completely mask his grin. I took an instant liking to him.

The lady turned to him. "You are spreading rheum around the carriage, sir. There are ladies present!"

His brown eyes caught mine for a moment. I felt sure he had seen the same amusement in me that I had detected in him.

"What is your business in Sleaford?" the lady asked me.

"To seek out the graveyard where my grandparents are interred," I said.

She nodded her approval. "And where will you be staying?"

I informed her I hoped my brother had found a bed for me at an inn or hotel near the air terminus. At this she tutted.

"Your parents approve of this arrangement?"

"My parents are no longer with me."

"Then you will stay with me," she announced.

"I cannot accept," I said. "To burden another with my keep – that, my parents would never have allowed."

She frowned. "Then take my card. If trouble finds you, and at the inns near the terminus it is not unlikely, then you must come to me."

Clear of the city air, I could now make out green fields and drifts of bare trees below. The beat of the engine had picked up in speed, sounding almost as a low hum. Cloth flaps behind the propeller now shifted sideways and the carriage began to lean to the starboard side as we turned. I fancied we were drifting lower also. The tops of the trees, being closer, seemed to slip past at greater speed.

"We're descending to catch a more favourable wind," said the man across the aisle. His voice was deep and carried an American lilt.

"The wind is less favourable up here?" I asked.

"See the vents?" he said, pointing to the engine, from which smoke and steam blew once more. "When the pilot wants to carry us higher he pulls a lever and diverts the waste gasses through a heat exchanger, then out through the tailpipe at the back. That gets the canopy hotter and makes us more buoyant. But when he wants to drop to catch the wind lower down, he puts the lever back and lets the exhaust blow from the engine. That way the canopy can cool."

I watched him as he gestured forward and aft to illustrate his explanation, noticing that his facial hair had been cropped so short as to seem little more than stubble. Though unusual, I found the effect not entirely unpleasing.

The elderly woman angled herself towards him a fraction, yet refrained from turning her neck to look him square in the eye. "Young man," she said. "Have you been introduced to this lady?" Hardly waiting for him to respond, she continued, "Then please keep your observations to yourself."

"It happens we have been introduced," I said.

"Then perhaps you would see fit to inform me of the gentleman's name?"

"Farthing," said the man, rescuing me from my lie. "John Farthing."

"I'm grateful for your presence," I said to the lady. "It permits Mr Farthing to sit here and talk with me. I'd not known he was to be travelling in the same carriage."

"It still seems improper," the woman muttered, though with less steely conviction.

"I'm grateful also," said John Farthing, flashing me a smile so warm and open that it seemed improper. I told myself that it was the American way and hoped my blush did not show.

All the while, the lady's maid sat biting her lower lip, her face turned to the window. I found myself suspecting that she had perceived more than her mistress had inthe exchange.

The rudder veins twitched and shifted, bringing us lower still as we neared our destination. At last the engine became so slow that I could make out each blade of the propeller. We inched forwards, the mooring ropes dragging below, escorted by pairs of ground-crewmen.

Whereas Anstey is a place of pilgrimage for devout Republicans and a nexus of communication, Sleaford is a sleepy market town. The terminus consisted of two mooring pylons, a small stretch of grass and a wooden ticket office little bigger than a garden shed. Streets of meanly appointed houses crowded on every side.

Being close to the mooring points, I braced myself for a juddering stop. But the engine fell silent, the propellers came to rest and the ground crew guided the ropes the last few feet, bringing our journey to the gentlest possible conclusion. With a set of iron steps manoeuvred into position below us, the carriage doors opened.

Taking a deep breath of the Lincolnshire air, I felt a thrill of excitement. After weeks of helplessness, it seemed that my future might be about to pass back into my own hands.

How is it that the very port of entry into any town or city is invariably its worst introduction? So it was with Sleaford. The streets immediately outside the terminus could not have been more than seven paces from gutter to gutter. Red brick houses of a shoddy disposition crowded to either side; their roofs overhung the uneven pavements. The smoke of many winters had darkened the walls and a greasy pallor coated the small windows.

The taxi driver who hefted my cases also carried a gnarled walking stick. This he raised to scatter the professional beggars and hopeless street drinkers who approached, pale palms upturned.

"Where to, miss?" he asked, turning the valve to let steam into the pistons of his car.

"An inn," I said. "Or a hotel, if you please."

"There are many in Sleaford," he said.

"Will any of the cheaper ones pay you a fee for bringing new custom?"

"Well..." he began, somewhat abashed. "There might be one."

"That will do then. If it's reputable."

He pulled the lever to engage the flywheel and the car juddered away. Gazing out of the side window, I let my eyes scan the bills and advertisements pasted haphazardly over walls and lamp posts, searching for any sign of Harry Timpson's name.

"Thank you, miss," said the driver, out of nothing.

Having cut through a street so narrow it seemed the taxi might become wedged, we emerged on an up-market thoroughfare with pots of flowers dotted along a wide promenade. There would be no daybills in this part of town. For the time being I gave up my search.

Presently the driver turned the wheel and we pulled up outside the overhanging portico of the Modesty

Hotel. As I handed over the fare he said, "It's nothing special but the beds are clean. Ask for Alf. Tell him Joe brought you. He'll see you right."

Alf it was who carried my cases to the room. He nodded at the mention of my driver's name. Joe was his second cousin, he said, though they were more like brothers on account of having been raised by the same grandmother. He then hobbled off, returning minutes later with a tray of bread, pickled cucumber and ham, together with a glass of brownish coloured wine.

"Any time you need service just call," he said. "Day or night."

From which I took it that my tip had been over generous for these parts.

The streets where bills might be posted being unsuitable for a single woman of good reputation, I had need of my brother's assistance once more. Therefore, having closed the wooden shutters and turned up the gas lamp, I drew a keychain from around my neck and unlocked the smaller of my two cases.

The arrangement within would have been familiar to any travelling performer. A small mirror on the inside of the lid revealed my face. Sewn pockets to either side held the pots of pigment, powder and glue, false sideburns, eyebrow hair and moustache with which I would transform myself.

Two layered trays occupied the body of the case, each divided into compartments containing male clothing, neatly folded or coiled. I made my selection, laying each item on the counterpane.

Stripped to my chemise, I began to wrap myself in a plain cotton binding cloth; one time tightly around the chest, holding in and flattening my mercifully small breasts, then more loosely around my belly just above the hip, filling in the hollow of the waist. The effect was precisely the opposite of my corset. One distortion of shape was being exchanged for another. Having lived with both disguises since puberty neither binding seemed strange to me.

Anticipating no need for a quick-change getaway, I did not clothe myself as I had for my visit to the Darkside Coffee House. Rather than false trousers that merely covered my lower legs, I could wear the real thing. Thus I dressed in all the layers with which a man would be familiar, from socks and boots to starched shirt and jacket. Of my female clothes I retained only the chemise, the innermost layer. I watched the transformation in the small mirror on the inside of my case, the makeup, false hair and top hat creating a new person before my eyes.

With the case packed away and the bed made up to seem as if a woman might be lying asleep, I turned off the gas and stood by the door in darkness, listening. Outside, the town clock struck five.

A set of back stairs took me to a tradesman's entrance unseen. Then via a cobbled rear yard and a narrow jitty I picked my way back to the busy thoroughfare. Ah, the advantages that men enjoy without even knowing. I strolled towards the front of the Modesty Hotel receiving no judgement or second glances.

The lamplighter had done his rounds already. Light shone also from the windows of shops. Enough to see by, but not enough for my real face to be perceived under the disguise. Thus I could stand as if waiting for some prearranged meeting. Turning slowly, I examined the doorways and windows on the far side of the street, the places I might have chosen had I wanted to keep watch on the hotel. Finding nothing out of place, I glanced into the lobby. And there, tall before the reception desk, looking out at the street, stood John Farthing, the same man who had provided such fine entertainment on the flight. I could not see his Gladstone bag, though he still wore the homburg.

What slim chance of fate had put us in the same hotel? Perhaps my momentary conflict of emotions had shown, for he looked directly at me. I let my gaze slide past him as if idly taking in the details of the lobby. Then I checked the time on my fob watch and turned to go. Five doors along, I paused as if diverted by the display in a shop window. Under this pretence, I snatched a look back towards the hotel, confirming that John Farthing had not followed. I felt relieved, but not entirely so. No intelligence gatherer is happy with a coincidence.

Cutting away from the main street, I entered a narrow way of cafes and eateries, the tip of my cane tapping on the uneven cobbles.

"Eels and oysters, sir," called a restaurant barker. "The freshest in Sleaford."

The next establishment boasted finest Lincolnshire plum bread. After that were a tavern, from which the din of a lively crowd drifted, a goldsmith, a gentlemen's barber and the offices of a public notary. Smells of food mixed in the chill air, and though I had eaten, I felt hungry again.

At the mouth of this street there might have been space for two carriages to pass, but it narrowed and darkened as I progressed so that after fifty yards any driver might fear scratching his paintwork against the walls. The further I walked from the main thoroughfare, the more bills and advertisements I found pasted. In places they lay on top of each other several sheets deep, smoothing and obscuring the contours of the bricks beneath. I scanned advertisements for "Liver Tonic", "Fossop Lamp Mantles co.", "Marmite Spread" and "Manchester Brass Cleaner". Not finding what I sought, I strolled on, deeper into the warren.

Here lampposts were covered also, and the doors to rear yards and walkthroughs. Were the bills not scraped off periodically, it seemed the town might one day be lost under paste and cheaply printed paper.

It was not until I began to peel back the layers that I had my first sight of the great Harry Timpson. In the fifty years since he gave his name to the Travelling Laboratory of Arcane Wonders his image had become famous throughout the Republic. Though he must now be an old man, it was the same youthful picture, magnificently moustachioed, that peered out at me from a torn daybill.

The Great Harry Timpson,
~ explorer, scientist, emeritus professor ~
is proud to offer a very final viewing of his famous
Laboratory of Arcane Wonders. His last ever tour of
the Anglo-Scottish Republic presents the culmination of
his life's work, a collection the like of which has never
before been assembled. Exotic beasts and men, arcane

engines, impossible magic, controlled explosions and
a demonstration of the alchemic process whereby base
metal is transmuted into gold before your eyes.

In the white space below the text, printed in a cruder
typeface and a darker ink, somewhat smudged, I read:

The Goose Field. Off Lincoln Road. Five days only.

I guessed the bill to have been there no longer than
three weeks and no less than one. As to the stated
duration, if Harry Timpson announced five days, he
would surely scarper the tober after four.

"Read your mother's name in your palm, sir," called
a breathy voice. I turned to see the woman who had
addressed me from the other side of the road. She wore
a brightly coloured gypsy skirt and her hair was tied
back in a scarf. Though confident in my disguise, I
knew my hands would not bear scrutiny.

"I see the letter 'm' in her name," she said, stepping
closer.

Born and raised in the Circus of Mysteries, I knew
the ways of readers and palmists. "The letter 'm'?" I
asked.

"You have a keepsake from her," the woman said.

"Less than you might believe."

"There is sadness," she said. "And still fresh. How
many years? Two? Three? It is too short a span."

I made to walk away but she stepped in front of me
and leaned in. "You will not leave the pain behind,"
she whispered. "It is a great sack of stones lain across
your shoulders. Why do you carry it so far? Oh, but it

is tied to you. Lashed in place with terrible ropes and cunning knots. Is it a heavy weight?"

I found myself nodding, though I had intended to remain a blank slate, unreadable by her tricks.

"So heavy" she said. "And you so young."

"I'm sorry. I need to go."

This time she grabbed hold of my elbow, halting my move to step away. "Not is all as it seems," she said. Then, examining my face more closely, added, "Oh, but there are secrets as well as pain. You carry them also."

"Everyone has secrets."

"There will be a journey," she said. "Before you can be released of yours. A long and dangerous road to make you free."

With my gloved hand, I reached into a pocket and drew out a silver fivep'ny, which she took with quick fingers and the trace of a smile.

"Where will my journey take me?" I asked.

"North, south, east or west." She watched me as she intoned the compass directions. "Your companion will be the south wind."

With her use of this phrase, I knew for sure she was trying to read me cold. I had heard it used many times by fortune-tellers in the Circus of Mysteries. First they would search for a reaction on mention of the compass directions. If they detected nothing they would offer an ambiguous answer. To be a companion of the south wind – what did that really mean? That I would travel towards its source or travel with it on my back? By my reaction to the suggestion she would plan her next speech.

"I will travel north then? Or south?" I asked.

She did not answer but her eyes remained on mine.

Fortune-tellers were common enough in the Kingdom. But until this encounter I had not thought they would be found among the rationalists of the Republic. Perhaps she had found a home in a travelling show. I wondered if she had seen me examining Harry Timpson's picture. Other people had walked past without her accosting them.

"What about the Laboratory of Arcane Wonders?" I asked. "Which wind does it travel with?"

She took a half-step backwards. "What is your business?"

"No business that could harm Harry Timpson," I said. "Which way should I travel to meet him? North, south, east or west?"

"He moves with the whirlwind," she said, though I had clearly seen her slight nod on the word "west". She stepped back again, out of the meagre light and into the shadow of a walkway that ran between the houses on the other side of the road.

When I followed she had already gone.

CHAPTER 8

To read the future in palms and tea leaves is not to read the future at all. Rather it is to see the present with dizzying clarity.

THE BULLET-CATCHER'S HANDBOOK

The Circus of Mysteries nurtured me from infancy, taught me the ways of the road and the stage. And when I could stay with it no more, the women and men of that troupe launched me into the world, though at great risk to themselves.

Among the many lessons of my childhood was to peer into the depths of the jossers' mistrust. Those folk in whose towns and villages we pitched, who paid good money to attend our shows, could just as easily come with lighted torches to burn us in our caravans as we slept.

Thus it was our habit to send one or more of the company ahead by a day's ride to gather intelligence and gauge the mood of each town. By a code of marks in chalk on gate posts on the approach, these outriders would warn us of their findings. Such men might pose as fruit pickers or navvies, depending on the season.

Or fortune-tellers, if they had that gift.

There could be no doubt that the gypsy woman was attached to Harry Timpson's show. Her reaction to my question also told me that he was near. He would surely not return to the town so soon after leaving. Thus she could not be in the van of his company, but rather in the train.

Why he would leave people to watch a town after he had left it, I could not fathom. My question to the gypsy was valuable information, however. Harry Timpson would soon be informed that a young gentleman was trying to find him. I did not believe the fortune-teller had pierced my disguise.

In nodding when I had said the word "west" she had indicated the direction she wanted me to travel – though whether this was to lead me to his camp or to send me away from it, there was no way to tell.

Standing stock-still in the deep shadow of the yard behind the hotel, I waited and watched. Twice, servants had come and gone – a porter who'd hefted a crate of empty bottles and a chef who'd stepped outside to stretch in the cold air, the sweat steaming from his bare arms. Though I stood now alone, yet shadows shifted on the dimpled glass as people moved within. It seemed I would not have the chance to slip in through the back door, unobserved as I had left.

Stepping up the front steps of the Modesty Hotel, I felt glad of the dimness of the gas lamps in the lobby. The desk clerk made a small bow.

"May I help, sir?" he enquired.

"I'm here to meet Miss Elizabeth Barnabus, my sister."

He ran his finger along the line of door keys, finding the gap where mine should have been hanging. "I'll send a boy to call her," he said.

"I wouldn't want to wake her if she's sleeping. Please don't knock loud."

The boy said he would not, then scampered away up the stairs.

It was only now that I caught sight of John Farthing, sitting at the back of the lobby, a newspaper open on his lap. He nodded and raised his hat.

"May I use the conveniences?" I asked the clerk.

Once out of sight around the corner of the corridor, I quickened my pace, taking the back stairs two at a time. Waiting out of sight on the second floor, I heard the boy knocking on my room door, a gentle tap as promised. After a moment he gave up and headed back towards the lobby. In five strides I was out of my hiding place, had slipped through the door and turned the key behind me.

In other circumstances I might have welcomed the attentions of the attractive John Farthing. But not this day. Unlocking the smaller of my cases, and pulling the false hair from my lip and cheeks, I began the transformation in reverse, watching my female face emerge in the small mirror as I wiped away traces of adhesive and dark pigment. Moving swiftly but surely, I folded my male clothes and unwrapped the chest binding, placing each item into the small case.

Outside the door a floorboard creaked. I pulled on a dressing robe and began brushing my hair out loose and long. A gentle tapping on the door sent my heart beating double time. I locked the case and hung the key around my neck so that it lay concealed where no gentleman would search.

The knock came again, louder this time.

"Who is it?" I called.

"I need to speak with you." The voice was an urgent whisper.

"I am undressed, sir."

"Please make yourself decent. This is the hotel manager."

Lifting my small case to the wall, I covered it with an embroidered cloth snatched from the coffee table. Speaking to the door, I said, "Why do you call on me?"

"A man's been seen prowling. I need to check your room for security."

"I'm un-chaperoned."

"The maid is with me," he said.

Taking a deep breath, I unlocked the door and began opening a crack so that I could look through into the corridor.

He gave no warning. With a single abrupt movement, the door crashed full open and I was stumbling back, trying not to fall. Then he was inside and the door had closed behind him. I looked first to the face of John Farthing, then to the crossbow pistol he held in his hand, its needle-pointed bolt directed at my chest.

"I'm sorry," Farthing said, reverting to his American accent. "Cooperate and we'll have this over quickly."

I made no reply, but backed away to match his advance.

"Where is he?" Farthing asked. His eyes swept the scene, taking in the cupboard, the gap under the bed, the small dressing room – all places where a man might hide. My hands felt the cold plaster of the wall behind me. My eyes flicked from the crossbow bolt to his trigger finger, resting against the side of the weapon, to his face. My mouth tasted sour from panic.

Farthing circled, bringing himself to the window, which he checked with his free hand. "Where?" he asked again.

"I'll scream if you touch me," I said.

"Don't take me for a scoundrel, Miss Barnabus."

Though his words were edged with determination, his aim had dropped from my chest to the floor. Stepping now to the small dressing room, he snatched a glance inside.

I managed to swallow. "Sir, you astound me!"

"I'm flattered if you were surprised," he said. "But you're not astounded or I've misjudged you. You say your brother arranged your lodgings?"

"He's not here."

Opening the cupboard, he ran a hand through my hanging clothes with practiced efficiency. "Then where?"

"I take it you're a bounty hunter?"

"Wrong."

"You're most certainly a liar."

"Very well," he said. "Talk of lies then. You say you haven't seen your brother, but he was in the lobby only minutes ago."

"You're mistaken."

"I don't think so. He has your eyes." So saying, he knelt in one sudden movement, bringing himself low enough to see under the bed. Then he was up again, wearing a puzzled expression and rubbing his brow with his free hand. "Frankly, Miss Barnabus, your evasion is suspicious."

"How can I evade with that thing pointed at me? Who's paying you to do this?"

He perched himself on the corner of the bed and rested the crossbow pistol on his lap. "Being the one with the gun, it's me who asks the questions."

I took a sideways step and lowered myself into a chair, gripping the wooden arm rests.

"You're not what you seem, Miss Barnabus. You travel with an invisible brother. You profess an interest in tombs and graves. Fashionable as that may be, it doesn't fit with what I have seen of you."

"Will you at least tell me your true name?" I asked.

"I'm not the accomplished liar you showed yourself to be on the airship flight," he said. "My name is John Farthing, just as I said."

"But you're not what you seem."

"What do I seem?"

"Then – a pleasant man. A witty travelling companion."

"And now?"

"Not a hotel manager."

"I'm sorry," he said for the second time. "That was untrue. But I'd no other means of gaining entry without raising a cry."

"Now you seem a bounty hunter," I said. "A hired thug for a rich aristocrat."

My words seemed to sting him. "I'm an agent of the law," he said.

"The law of the Republic or the Kingdom?"

"Of the International Patent Office." Then, perhaps noticing the way my grip had stiffened on the arms of the chair, he added: "Please don't be afraid."

How easily fear and anger may be confused.

• • •

It had been five years since the Duke of Northampton moved against my family. His method had been bribery, his chosen vehicle, a corrupt agent of the Patent Office.

The Circus of Mysteries was charged with some fabricated infringement. It took all of my father's capital to pay the fine. The Duke then bought up our debts from various creditors – small sums individually but substantial when combined. His lawyer explained to the court that the Duke was a generous man and would accept a lifetime of my servitude in lieu of the money owed.

My father appealed, delaying the moment when I would be claimed, giving time for us to prepare and plan my escape. The saddlebags were packed and my costume laid out ready. But when word came that the Duke's men-at-arms approached along the lane towards the gaff, the troupe were out pasting daybills in the villages around and no horses were left for me to ride.

Thus I ran.

The clay soil clung to my boots as I skirted the fields. With my feet as heavy as iron, I jumped ditches and ducked through gaps in thorn hedges. I carried only the set of man's clothes I wore, a belt stuffed with coins and a bindle in which the food for my journey had been tied. The food had been planned for two days. My father could not have guessed it would need to serve me for ten.

The Duke was not to be easily cheated. Denied his prize and outraged, he ordered his men-at-arms out, not merely to track my path as we had feared, but to ride hard and cut off those roads I might have taken to the border.

When they ripped through our pitch and found me missing, they reported also that my brother was gone. Audience members from the previous night's show had seen him on stage. They would later swear to it before the magistrate. But my brother hadn't been seen since. Not by a josser nor any member of the troupe.

Thus it became known that he was the one responsible for cheating the Duke of the girl he had desired to own. In my flight I had broken no law. How may chattel commit a sin? The crime lay with my brother. He had taken from the Duke his rightful property. My brother was a thief, so to speak. Within days a good likeness of his face had been pasted on billboards throughout the border counties.

For myself, the Republic offered safety. When I finally waded the river north of Atherstone and dropped to my knees on the bank, exhausted from hunger and cold, I had moved beyond the Duke's reach. The Republic recognised no man's right to the ownership of another human being. But for my fictional brother things were different. Though the Duke, as an aristocrat, could not himself cross into the Republic, yet the men in his employment could come and go with the flourishing of a permit.

A diplomatic scandal would ensue if they kidnapped an innocent woman and rendered her across into the Kingdom. Border skirmishes had been fought over lesser crimes. But to snatch a wanted man, a criminal – this would raise no comment among the masses.

As for my father, I never saw him again. He died in the debtors' prison.

"Tell the truth and there's nothing to fear," said Farthing, still sitting on the corner of my bed.

"You think me an accomplished liar?" I asked. "Look at me. Watch me say it: since arrival in Sleaford, I've not set eyes on my brother. I've not heard him speak. He's sent me no message."

John Farthing did look. His eyes held mine steadily as I spoke. They were not pure brown, as I'd thought before, but flecked with grey. "I can't decide," he said, "if you are such an accomplished liar as to be one of the most dangerous people I've ever met, or if you're perhaps telling the simple truth. It'd be more comfortable for me to think you honest. In the airship I'd thought..." He shook his head.

"I have told the truth."

"And yet I can't help feeling there's more you haven't said."

From his face, I knew the decision had been made but not which way it had gone.

"Up," he said, gesturing with the crossbow pistol. "You'll need clothes for a night journey."

He had given no sign of noticing my travelling case of male disguises hidden beneath the embroidered cloth. Its discovery would be a disaster. Thus I used misdirection to draw his eye – a show of fluster and embarrassment as I lifted my other case onto the bed and selected a set of under garments. It would have been too obvious to fool a conjuror, but Farthing seemed taken in. He blushed as I gathered bloomers, camisole and corset. These, together with a blouse, skirt and shawl from the cupboard, I took to the small dressing room, closing the door behind me.

"I'll hear if you slide the bolt," he said.

"The world will hear if you try to force yourself on me!"

"You mistake me," he said.

"What else am I supposed to think?"

There were a few seconds of silence before he spoke again. "Please talk to me as you change."

The window of the dressing room being ajar, I peered out and cast my eye up and down the wall of the hotel. A drainpipe ran from the gutter just above me all the way to the rear yard, some thirty feet below. People used to say that children raised in the Circus of Mysteries were deprived of a proper education. But there are some things an acrobat can teach you that a Latin master never could.

"Talk!" ordered Farthing.

"Of what?"

"Of anything so that I know where you are. Tell me where you were born."

"We haven't been introduced," I said, reaching out to grip the drainpipe – cast iron, it seemed, painted over and smooth to the touch. Testing it, I felt it shift a fraction, though not too much to alarm me. Back inside and away from the window, I quickly began to change, pulling my corset around me and hooking the eyes at the front.

"Not introduced?" he said. "You remind me of your lie in the air carriage. Will I regret believing your brother didn't make it to your room? I ask again, where were you born?"

"In the Kingdom," I said, unrolling my stockings up my legs.

"Why is your voice strained?"

"You wish me to give an account of my under garments? Is this for your work, Mr Farthing, or for your pleasure?"

"I... Forgive me. Where in the Kingdom?"

"I don't know."

"A foundling?"

"A daughter of loving parents."

"Your father's profession?"

"Are you thinking of proposing marriage?"

He made a noise like a cough, and I remembered how he had used just such a sound to cover his laugh in the air carriage. After a moment he said, "You have a way of steering the conversation, Miss Barnabus. I don't know if you do it to avoid answering or merely to rile me."

"I'm not accustomed to being questioned as I dress! It flusters me."

"Your father?" he asked again.

"Ringmaster of a travelling show."

Our conversation had passed back and forth like a tennis ball but now it paused.

"I may think you more of a liar for admitting such an upbringing," he said at last.

"Ironic that you'd like me to lie so that I might seem trustworthy!"

"Why is this taking so long?" he asked, his voice coming from close to the door, as if his ear were pressed against it.

"I take it you're not a married man, Mr Farthing. Else you'd know what women must go through as we dress!"

"You're right," he said. "I'm not. And I apologise."

"For the lies or the threats?"

"They're tools of my office. But if I've gone beyond the professional... I'm sorry."

That was the third time he'd said it. Agents of the Patent Office should be made of sterner stuff. It occurred to me that were I to weep, the sound might dislodge him from his equilibrium. He would try to find calming words to speak through the door. I would run water into the basin, as if composing myself and washing the tear tracks away. Twenty seconds from my silence, he would begin to suspect. Ten seconds beyond that he would burst through the door to see me clambering down the drainpipe. I would have slipped into the night before he could run the stairs and reach the ground floor to give chase.

"Miss Barnabus?" he called. "Please speak."

The drainpipe felt too smooth for a reliable grip. And to find answers we must sometimes turn to face those who would chase us. Thus I opened the door and stood before him, fully dressed.

"Please don't present your actions as virtue, Mr Farthing. I've nothing but contempt for you and for the office you serve."

CHAPTER 9

*Which is easier to switch – the bullet into which a josser
has scratched his name or the gun that is to fire it?*

THE BULLET-CATCHER'S HANDBOOK

Two years after the end of the British Revolutionary
War, the first nations signed the Great Accord. With
the ink still wet they put their signatures to a second
document – the charter that established the jurisdiction
and powers of the International Patent Office. More
nations signed and the Second Enlightenment spread.
Soon it encompassed the globe, as did the Patent
Office itself.

When the Earl of Liverpool coined the phrase Gas-
Lit Empire, it was to ridicule the leaders then rushing
to add the names of their countries to the agreement.
This was no empire, he said, because no single
government ruled over it, nor would gas lighting ever
reach beyond the cities. Yet, he had misjudged the
mood of the age and the name quickly passed into
common usage, the irony seemingly lost on the vast
multitudes of working men and their families who

regarded the awful powers of the Patent Office as having been established for their own protection.

Perhaps it did once protect the common man. Those machines legitimised with a patent mark never put great numbers out of work. And for almost two hundred years warfare had been restricted to the level of the border skirmish. But if the founding fathers believed the power they had bestowed would not corrupt, they were naive.

Listening to the horses' hooves beating time on the road, I watched the lights of Sleaford thinning towards nothing. John Farthing sat next to me, bracing himself against the lurch and sway of our progress. The crossbow pistol he had now folded away. I might have had the slim possibility of escaping through the door. But where could I run? He had followed me to the airship in Anstey. He would know of my home on the canal cut.

The role of informative flying companion had suited him well. Witty, modest, easy to trust and unthreatening. But for the starched and disapproving presence of the elderly lady who'd sat opposite, would I have been so easily taken in by the illusion? Perhaps he had chosen exactly that persona to counterpoint her lecture on Republican morals.

What is a chameleon's colour, when all pretence is stripped away?

I had seen conmen in the Circus of Mysteries working easy marks among the jossers. But too long in that game and they forgot the person under the disguise. Then they would grow overconfident and try to play a member of the circus troupe. Invariably they were found out. Confronted, a new story would emerge – an unhappy childhood, a widowed mother, a disease of the mind, a momentary lapse of morals, deep regret, a plea for forgiveness. They would beg for one more chance. But with each new face, we saw more clearly that, far from being disguises to cover the person hidden underneath, the lies had corroded whatever they once were until nothing remained.

"I must endure your bad feelings towards me," John Farthing said, speaking into the taut silence. "But please don't think badly of the Patent Office."

"Thinking badly is the only power you've left me."

In truth I had some remaining power. Where running and hiding are impossible, one may still misdirect. Thus my real secret remained safe, for the moment at least, contained within the smaller of my two travelling cases, resting next to the wall of the hotel room, concealed under an embroidered cloth.

Becoming aware that we had slowed, I peered outside. The moonlight revealed a stone gatepost just beyond the carriage window. We were turning onto a long, straight gravel road lined with tall poplar trees.

I had no doubt now that we were heading towards one of the many mysterious properties owned by the Patent Office across the land. But as to the nature of what I would find there I could not guess. Popular belief had it that the Patent Office possessed vast resources and had nigh unlimited manpower at its disposal. How else could it keep watch for the stirrings of new and unseemly technology across the entire civilised world? Yet it was so secretive that, notwithstanding its many tentacles and vast reach, its inner workings remained entirely mysterious.

The dark shape of a large building loomed ahead. The horses slowed towards a stop.

Farthing opened the carriage door and held it for me. "Speak only the truth," he said.

"Or what?"

"Please spare me another stain on my conscience."

Stepping out onto the gravel, I saw that the building was some kind of manor house. A set of low steps ran from the drive up to a terrace along the front of the building. The grand entrance sat plumb in the centre, with two sets of bay windows symmetrically arranged to either side. Strangely, none of the windows were lit, though the sulphurous tang of coal smoke in the air suggested the presence of humanity somewhere near.

While Farthing was instructing the coach driver to stable the horses, I turned full circle, hoping to see lights in the distance or any sign of habitation. There was none. A thin mist clung to the ground, from which the black fingers of bare tree branches reached towards the sky.

It was through a servants' door at the rear that we entered, stepping from the chill damp of the night into the dry cold of a boot room that seemed to have been long unoccupied. Striking a lucifer, Farthing lit a storm lantern and held it high.

I followed close behind as he walked along a corridor. Shadows swung as we progressed. Through open doorways I glimpsed a scullery, a pantry, a kitchen. Then we emerged into a grand hallway and a sudden warmth.

Though I had not witnessed any sign of occupation when standing outside, I now saw a crack of light under the door opposite.

"Who lives here?" I asked.

"No one."

"Then what is it for?"

"For the work of the Patent Office."

"But how can...?"

"You're here to answer questions, not to ask them." So saying, he rapped a knuckle on the door.

I had never seen a room like the one into which we stepped. In scale it fitted the grandness of the house. Ornate plaster coving edged an exuberantly painted ceiling depicting Jesus watching Saint Peter haul in a net laden with fish. The gold leaf of their haloes shone in the lamplight. The religious theme and conspicuous excess dated the room to before the British Revolutionary War.

A generous fire burned in the stone fireplace opposite me. Bookcases lined the other walls. Only when I glanced up and around did I realise why the place made me feel so uneasy, for it was entirely devoid of windows.

Stepping forward I took in the seating. Six leather wing-backed armchairs arranged in a horseshoe, and a seventh chair placed at the focus of the others. It was towards this that Farthing directed me. Only when I took my place did I see the room's sole occupant – a gaunt and deeply wrinkled man with such a sunken frame that he had been hidden within the embrace of the armchair.

"Miss Elizabeth Barnabus," Farthing announced from behind me.

The fact that he had not himself taken a seat gave me no comfort.

The gaunt man smiled encouragingly. "You are brother to Mr Edwin Barnabus?" Coming from such a desiccated figure, the voice resonated with a surprising volume.

"Who are you?" I asked, hoping my own voice did not betray the dread that had started to replace my anger.

"A servant of the Patent Office," the wrinkled man replied.

"I'm Elizabeth Barnabus," I said.

"And your brother?"

"I haven't seen him since arriving in Lincolnshire."

Behind me, John Farthing cleared his throat. "He was in the lobby of her hotel. And asking to see her."

The skin of my arms and the back of my neck prickled as a sweat started to break.

"What do you know of your brother's business?" the wrinkled man asked.

"He finds information," I said. "And people."

"For whom?"

"For paying clients."

"And who is presently paying for his services?"

I hesitated, but not for more than half a second. In all likelihood this was information they already possessed. "He's in the employ of the Duchess of Bletchley."

"Indeed?"

The wrinkled man's eyes flicked to where Farthing stood. Being such a slight movement, I might have missed it altogether. But danger sharpens the senses and speeds the mind.

"How did he contact her?"

"By letter, though it was the other way around. She contacted him."

"Just that?"

"I believe perhaps they met," I said.

"And your brother took an accomplice with him to that meeting?"

"I know of none."

The wrinkled man waved his hand in the direction of a low table near one of the book-lined walls. Farthing hurried to it and retrieved a green metal box of the sort shelved in the strong rooms of banks. Returning to my side, he opened the lid and tilted it for me to see the contents. A flintlock handgun rested on the velvet lining. The wooden stock carried the emblem of a running fox inlaid in turquoise. It was unmistakable. It was one of a kind. My father had given it to me on my twelfth birthday. And it should by rights have lain snug in its hiding place strapped to the underside of *Bessie*'s iron boiler.

The room seemed to sway. I gripped the arms of the chair tighter, willing my panic away.

"Your brother's accomplice carried this gun, or one so alike they might have been twins."

I stared but did not speak.

"Interesting, yes? A crime was committed with this gun. It was thrust into the mouth of a man. He feared for his life. One of his teeth was broken. His possessions were robbed. You understand? And that man being in the employ of the Patent Office at the time brings the crime within our jurisdiction."

"I don't believe..." I began, but my mouth was so dry that I was forced to stop to allow saliva to return. "...he wouldn't do this."

"It was not your brother, but his accomplice."

"He has none."

"You claim he always works alone?"

"To my knowledge, sir."

The wrinkled man pressed his hands down on the arm rests of his chair and levered himself into a standing position. He approached with a stiff gait, as if the movement brought him pain. Reaching into the box he picked up the gun and turned it in his hand, running an arthritic finger over the turquoise design.

"An interesting weapon," he said. "Turkish perhaps? Or Persian. Old, certainly. We have an interest in non-standard weapons. Perhaps you knew this already?"

His eyes were on me as he turned the gun. There could be no adult within the borders of the Gas-Lit Empire who was unaware of the penalty for patent crime involving weapons. Or that the case would be tried by the Patent Office's own judges and the punishment carried out by their own executioners. I forced my breathing to slow.

"Our clerks have examined it – the metallurgy, the bore, the lock – nothing is quite as it should be."

"Is it illegal?" I asked, my voice a whisper.

He replaced the gun in the box. "Perhaps not," he said. "It could be argued either way. Lawyers do as they will. But there are no patent marks. The product of an unlicensed workshop, I imagine."

Farthing closed the lid. "Miss Barnabus admits a family connection to a travelling show," he said. "Such weapons are common among circus folk."

"Common is hardly the word," said the wrinkled man. "Turquoise. There is silver here. And other metals, I'm told."

"I meant non-standard weapons," Farthing said. "The travelling people have a fondness for craftsman devices. The lack of a patent mark is only a crime should the device be sold."

"It seems Miss Barnabus has no need of a lawyer then, with the astute John Farthing speaking on her behalf!"

I could not see Farthing's reaction, as he was already carrying the box back to its resting place on the table.

"Do you trust him to defend you?" the wrinkled man asked.

"Me? I thought it was a mysterious accomplice that you'd accused."

His mouth curled into a half-smile. "I do believe you may be as elusive as your brother. But then you are twins. What else would we expect?"

The air became dank as we descended into a vaulted cellar lined with empty wine shelves. From there John Farthing led me into a wide corridor with three cell doors in a line down one side.

"It's the law," he said, without conviction, as he ushered me into the furthest cell.

The door closed behind me. The bolt clanged outside. I listened to his footsteps receding, waiting until the sound had disappeared before testing the handle. This I did quietly, for I would not give him the satisfaction of hearing my inevitable failure.

Measuring three paces by four, the cell was furnished with a metal bed, on which lay a mattress some three inches thick, two folded sheets, three blankets and a towel. A small table stood against one wall. On it rested a water jug, a basin and a bar of grey soap. I found the chamber pot on the floor in the corner. Being below ground level, there were no windows.

Placing the oil lamp on the table, I tried to focus my attention on the mundane act of spreading and tucking sheets. It must have been the small hours of the morning but my mind raced from one dark future to another. When eventually I slept, it was to a dream of fleeing across ploughed fields, and though I could not see or hear my pursuers, I somehow knew them to be close behind.

On waking, I discovered a plate of bread and ham resting on the flagstones next to the door. Also a bottle of weak red wine and a pewter cup. Pushing the small recessed panel at the base of the door, I discovered a fraction of an inch of play. It would have slid all the way to the left but for some catch mechanism or bolt on the outside. Thus, I reasoned, no one had entered the room as I slept. This knowledge gave me some small comfort. However, from that time, I took to leaving the oil lamp on the floor in front of the sliding panel.

I was awake to hear the approaching footsteps when my next meal arrived. A bolt clanged. The small panel slid. I glimpsed a foot shifting and a knee coming to rest on the floor. The brittle movement suggested my gaoler was an elderly man.

Perhaps taken aback by the proximity of the lantern, he did not immediately reach through to retrieve the empty plate, but lowered himself until he could peer through. Lying dead still on the bed beyond the immediate illumination, I must have been invisible to him. There was a pause then a second plate of food scraped over the stones through the hole and the panel clanged closed. I was alone once more.

Bread and cheese this time.

After the third meal, I had lost any sense of day or night, and began to worry that my lamp might run out of oil. Unscrewing the filling cap, I reached my little finger into the well and found it more than half empty. With the wick turned down, it might last me as long again. I checked the oil often after that, its level becoming my only tangible measure of the passage of time. And as I sat, looking at the blank walls, I thought about my small travelling case.

There could be no doubt that John Farthing or one like him would be sitting in my room at the hotel, waiting, crossbow pistol at the ready, perhaps in the dark, listening in vain for the return of my non-existent brother. Eventually he would search. And when he did, my case would yield up its false hair, adhesive, skin pigments, male clothes and binding cloth. I had many dark feelings regarding agents of the Patent Office, but there was no doubt regarding their collective intelligence. In that small travelling case lay the history of my escape from the Kingdom and the secret of my double identity in the Republic, should they wish to read its contents.

What then?

Indeed, what had caused the Patent Office to take an interest in me? Not the heirloom pistol, surely. Not my status as a fugitive from the Kingdom. You may think me a fool when I admit that it was only now, with the lamp wick turned so low that the walls faded from sickly yellow to dark grey, that I perceived their interest might be more with the Duchess of Bletchley than with myself. Or, indeed, with her missing brother. But why they would seek to question me rather than approach her, I could not understand. There can be no one more conspicuous than an aristocrat of the Kingdom, and, therefore, no one easier to find.

The next time I slept it was without dreams. I woke in complete darkness, for the lamp had at last run out of oil. A noise had woken me. Being thick with sleep, it took several seconds before I understood that I was hearing booted feet approach along the corridor. The bolt clanged. The door swung open and dazzling lamplight flooded in.

I held a hand up to shield my eyes.

"Miss Barnabus," came John Farthing's voice from behind the lamp. "We must go."

He stepped back into the corridor and I could at last see his face. Frown lines creased his forehead, and I wondered whether he carried bad news. Or perhaps my unkempt appearance and the smell of the chamber pot had disgusted him.

"Where now?" I said, surprised at the dry sound of my voice. How long had it been since I last spoke?

"To the hotel," he said.

I held my hands out in front of me, wrists together. "You wish to shackle me?"

"I've treated you with respect," he said.

"You may as well lead me into that place in chains as expect me to walk into the lobby in this state."

• • •

We sat side by side as the carriage took us back to Sleaford. Farthing's only words were to the driver. He had from somewhere acquired a lady's hair brush and allowed me time with a hand glass, so that when we stepped down to the pavement in front of the hotel, it was only my crumpled clothing that drew curious glances.

Farthing walked with me to the reception desk. "Is Miss Barnabus's room still held?"

"Yes sir," the receptionist said, passing him a key, while taking in my dishevelled appearance.

Farthing placed the key in my hand. "She was taken away on urgent business these last two days," he said. "Please send a girl for her laundry. She'll need a hot meal also."

At the foot of the stairs, I turned to face John Farthing. "I'm free to go?"

"You are."

"You needn't accompany me further."

"I would like the opportunity to explain," he said.

"You're going to tell me why you held me? How many days was it? I still don't know. Once the oil in the lamp ran out I was in darkness."

He winced. "Sometimes all our liberties must be curtailed for the good of the common man."

I turned on my heel and began to climb the stairs, aware that he followed. Aware also that the receptionist watched with a disapproving frown. Perhaps he did not notice what he was doing to my reputation. Perhaps he did not care. He was still with me on the second floor, a pace behind as I unlocked the door to my room.

"Goodbye sir. I hope I never see you again."

I did not turn to speak these words, but stepped directly inside and made to shut him out. His hand stopped the door from closing.

"I need to explain," he said.

"Didn't you hear me?"

"Some things I can't say. But others I feel honour-bound to tell you."

So vividly was I aware of everything around me at that moment, every sound and movement and smell and nuance of light and shade, that it seemed the room began to spin. Perhaps this was a reaction to release from my confinement. But it seemed to me at that moment as if I stood at some sort of crossroads, where all possibilities were open and waiting for my decision.

My eyes flicked to the wall behind the door, the place I had left my travelling case so thinly disguised. The embroidered cloth that had covered it rested back in its place on the low coffee table. Of my case there was no sign.

Farthing stepped into the room. "You think we're tyrants," he said. "I know this. But believe me when I tell you that agents of the Patent Office have no motivation save the protection of the common man."

"You live in poverty?" I asked.

"We sacrifice much."

"You go hungry at night?"

"This isn't what I want to discuss."

"You're fined and forced into debt?" I asked. "Your family ruined?"

"I have no family!"

"Then you're free from pain."

"I'm trying to help you."

"But you're not listening to me!" I shouted, turning away before the tears began to spill down my cheeks.

"I wish you to pass a message to your brother, wherever he's hiding. He isn't important to us. But the man he seeks... this is different."

"Who is it?" I asked.

"The man we seek has created a dangerous and unseemly device. It's patent crime of the first order. Tell your brother that, according to the law, to withhold information from our investigation is the same as to be a conspirator in the act itself. He'll know the penalty."

CHAPTER 10

Nothing excites a crowd more than seeing a man who they have already witnessed making a mistake going on to attempt the bullet catch.

THE BULLET-CATCHER'S HANDBOOK

After Farthing had left, I stripped down and washed, scrubbing the cloth over my skin to remove every trace of the unlit house. Then I dressed in clean clothes and took a brush to my hair once more. Anger at my enforced confinement had kept other reactions at bay. But now my fury began to cool. I held my hand in front of my face and saw that I was shaking.

A gentle tapping triggered my heart to a double-time beat.

"Room service," came a voice from the other side of the door.

My hand hovered near the bolt.

"It's Alf," the voice said. "I have something for you."

I pulled back the bolt.

He stood in the corridor with a tray of food and drink. Beef and potatoes and carrots and gravy and a pot of mustard. A bottle of ale and a glass. I took the tray from him, my mouth too dry to voice thanks.

"I have your case, miss," he whispered. "Beg pardon, but I took the liberty of removing it after you were taken. Men came to search. I hope I didn't do wrong."

The next morning, I took a sheet of the Modesty Hotel's embossed notepaper and wrote:

Dear Lady,

Having pursued your brother to Sleaford, where I believe he stayed some two weeks gone, I find I am no longer able to continue with your commission. I would be grateful if you could let me know where to return the fee (minus those expenses already incurred).

Yours faithfully,

E Barnabus

PS On leaving Sleaford, I believe your brother headed west.

I wafted the paper in the air until the ink had dried, then folded it into a hotel envelope on which I wrote: "The Duchess of Bletchley, Buckinghamshire". Though I did not know the street or town, I felt confident the Kingdom Postal Service would find her easily enough.

Such is the speed of air travel and the efficiency of its integration with other modes of transport that I was able to jump down from a steamcar taxi that very evening and, with the aid of the driver, haul my cases along the short stretch of towpath to *Bessie*'s aft deck.

Dusk had turned the surface of the water black and silver. I stood watching the taxi puffing away. The smell of frying onions drifted across from a neighbouring boat. Suddenly I felt alone. How could I have believed my luck would change? Instead of earning the money I so desperately needed, I had wasted time and accumulated troubles.

There could be no doubt that John Farthing or some other agent had rummaged the boat. How else could he have produced my pistol in the unlit house? Yet, as I crouched on *Bessie*'s aft deck and ran my finger around the edge of the hatchway, I felt the stub end of a matchstick trapped just where I had left it four days ago. The searcher had been an expert and had covered his tracks.

The galley smelled of old wood and lamp oil, as it always did. Walking towards the cabins, I shifted my weight from side to side, tilting *Bessie* in the water, as if to prove to myself that only ropes held her in place. If January came and I still lacked the hundred guineas, I could perhaps haul her away up the canal and try hiding from my creditor. How long could I last before he found me? It seemed the moonlight flit would prove my only option. The Duchess was my sole client. But to pursue her brother would be to defy the Patent Office. And I would rather play dice with a creditor than with the hangman.

I opened the cold iron stove and looked inside. It remained ready, just as I had left it. I struck a lucifer, watched it flare then held it to the kindling. There would be hot water for tea within the hour.

My sleeping cabin did not seem to have been disturbed, though I felt certain it had been searched. Skirts and blouses hung in the cupboard just as I remembered them. I brushed my fingers over the pigeonholes. Shoes, boots, underwear and chemises – each item lay in its proper place. I lifted a roll of stockings and felt beneath them for the slim pile of letters which I kept as if hidden.

The sky outside had faded almost to black. I lit a lantern and moved through to the other sleeping cabin, supposedly my brother's. For the sake of appearance, I had arranged it as I supposed a man would have done. One creased shirt lay dangling over the edge of the bunk. A pair of mud-soiled shoes I had left in artful asymmetry near the door, one on its side. It was in the secret compartment below the head of the bunk that I perceived the first evidence of the searcher's hand. I knew to lift the mattress, unblocking a hole in the top of the compartment before pulling out the hidden drawer. Thus I set up no air currents and did not disturb the scrap of tissue paper I had placed there.

Yet someone had disturbed it.

The Duchess of Bletchley's letters lay uppermost in the compartment. Underneath were bills, letters from earlier clients and receipts. There was nothing here that the Patent Office did not already know. Yet the proof that they had been on my beloved boat left a feeling of queasy weakness in my stomach. I sat on the bunk and placed my face in my hands.

Two things remained for me to check. Lifting a plate in the galley floor, I looked down on the axle that had once turned *Bessie*'s paddlewheels and the small oil reservoir that had kept the drive mechanism lubricated. I gripped and twisted the cap of the small tank. It unscrewed with a metallic squeal of protest, revealing a dark but dry void below. Also the end of a length of wire, which my thin fingers were able to grip and pull, lifting a small woollen bag clear of the tank. The dull clink of coins was enough to reassure me that the agents of the Patent Office had not been tempted to steal my money in the same way that they had stolen my turquoise inlaid pistol.

Reaching around below the driving shaft, I felt for the small shelf that had served as my pistol's hiding place. My fingers closed around something. I pulled it up out of the hatch, knowing what it was, even before it came into my sight.

I sat on the floor of the cabin, staring at the turquoise inlay on the stock of my pistol, asking myself if I had perhaps misjudged the efficient John Farthing and the wrinkled man. Had the emotionless rules of their order obliged them to put back what was not theirs? More likely they had returned it with such care in order to entrap me. If they found it in my hands, I would not be able to claim innocence a second time.

Gently, ever so gently, I reached into the access hole and placed the pistol back on its hidden shelf, not daring to make a sound, fearing the door might burst open before I had the hatch fully closed again.

CHAPTER 11

To make pleasure from deception is the art of the illusionist. But the deception of a conman brings anger and shame. Beware the difference, for the line is very thin.

THE BULLET-CATCHER'S HANDBOOK

Using money from one creditor to pay off another is a mark of desperation. Failing to do so is the road to ruin. I could take the Duchess's gold and run. But she would surely send men after me, as would Leon. What chance was there of escaping the both of them? If I was forced to haul *Bessie* along the canal in a moonlight flit, it would be better to have fewer people hunting me down.

Sitting in the galley of my beloved boat, I contemplated my situation. I could already see the wooden boards that made up the floor of *Bessie*'s coal bunker. If the weather remained mild I might last another ten days. The coal boatman would help me if I asked, though I had no prospect of paying him back.

Winter is a creditor from which no one can hide.

Holding the caddy at an angle, I filled a spoon with tea leaves, then after a moment's consideration tipped half back. I would return the Duchess's purse, though perhaps a few coins lighter than it should have been. I wondered how precisely she might be able to calculate the cost of my trip to Sleaford.

So preoccupied was I with these thoughts that the slight tilt of the boat did not alert me. Only when a bony knuckle rapped on the hatch did I become aware of the unwelcome presence of Mrs Simmonds, wife of the wharf owner.

She knocked again and I cursed my inattentiveness. Usually I could prevent her from gaining access. But to get rid of her now without explicit rudeness would be impossible.

"I'll be with you directly," I called.

Whether she actually mistook my words for an invitation was not clear. However, the result was the same. The hatch opened and she stepped down into the galley, her waspish face all curiosity as she peered from fixture to fixture hungrily cataloguing the details of my existence.

"Such a delight," I said. "Do come in."

"Good morning, Elizabeth," she said, before returning her attention to the galley pigeonholes in which crockery and dry foodstuffs were stored.

I made a small curtsy. "Mrs Simmonds."

"How were your ancestors?" she asked.

It took me a few seconds to understand her meaning. "Dead, alas," I replied.

"Well, yes. That is to be expected. But how were their graves? Are they together or in separate plots? Is there a vault?" She seemed genuinely concerned – a fashionable interest in death, no mere affectation in her.

"We didn't find them," I admitted, truthfully. "May I offer you a cup of tea?"

Mrs Simmonds arranged the hoops of her skirt and with some difficulty slid onto the small bench next to the table. "Tea would be agreeable, thank you. But what a disappointment you must have had. To have travelled so far and found none of your kin."

"We're a far flung family," I said, pouring steaming water into the pot, then, as an afterthought, adding the half spoonful of tea leaves I had omitted earlier.

"A family should have a home," she said. "I'm descended from five generations of Loughborough men and women. Mr Simmonds is descended from seven. Just think of that. Seven generations! St Mary is like a home to us. Our families lie shoulder to shoulder, Elizabeth. Shoulder to shoulder the entire width of the churchyard."

It felt inappropriate to sit directly opposite the woman to whom I paid my mooring fees. Indeed, her skirt filled the space below the table and the thought of my knees pressing into it did not appeal. Thus, having placed the pot, strainer, sugar, cups and saucers, I remained standing. She seemed to find this arrangement acceptable and proceeded to stir the water in the pot.

"More leaves, my dear." She reached for the caddy. "One spoon for each person in your party and then one more for seemliness."

"Thank you," I said, watching my precious reserves of tea disappearing into the pot.

"I worry that your brother–"

"I'm sure I will find a suitable husband when the time comes," I said.

"Yes, yes. That too. But I worry you have no teacher for these skills. Your maid will run rings around you if she sees your lack of knowledge. When you manage a household of your own – a regular household, that is – you'll be in her power and no recourse."

"Thank you as ever," I said, sipping from the cup she had given me. The taste pinched my mouth. Too strong. Too bitter.

She spooned a great quantity of my sugar into her own cup and then slurped noisily, with obvious satisfaction. "To business," she said. "Your rent. It falls due–"

"In three days," I said.

"Indeed. But since Mr Simmonds and I will be away, we'll need payment today. Your good example has shamed us into action. We're travelling to Loughborough to visit our families and attend to their various memorials."

"My brother should wake later."

"We'll expect him this evening," she said, with a look of satisfaction that made me suspect I had missed something important. Then she pulled a blue and white striped envelope from her purse and handed it to me. The markings belonged to the office of the Avian Post and were unmistakable.

I thanked her, hiding my surprise. "I'll put it in his hand," I said.

"But Elizabeth, this letter is addressed to you."

I saw then that her eyes were on me, intently examining my reaction.

• • •

I sat for many minutes after she had gone, turning the envelope in my hands. I had never before received a message by Avian Post. The address must have been written by the pigeon master at the local loft. The script had a left-leaning slant.

Miss Elizabeth Barnabus
c/o The North Leicester Wharf
North Leicester

I held the sealed fold of the envelope to the light and brought it close to my eye. If Mrs Simmonds had steamed it open, I might expect some wrinkling to remain. When casually dampened and dried, paper does not return to the same pristine flatness, though the heat and pressure of an iron can sometimes do the trick.

Inserting the tip of a thin knife under the flap of the envelope I slit carefully along its length. Inside, I found a sheet of pale blue paper onto which lengths of white silk ribbon had been glued. It was on these that the Duchess had written her message:

Elizabeth: I have had recent business dealings with your
brother but he has terminated our relationship. I am
taking the liberty of writing directly to you regarding
this matter. When I sent payment to your brother, it was
in the form of coins. I trust he may have retained the bag
in which they were conveyed. If you examine the inner
seam, you will find a maker's label. You will have no
trouble in locating the maker's premises. If your brother
wishes to return the remaining coins, I would be grateful

if he could entrust them to you, to be carried to the
bag-maker's assistant in the aforementioned shop, this
coming Friday during the afternoon. Go alone.

An official notice printed at the very bottom of the
page informed me that the message could be erased with
soapy water and the ribbon sold back to the local Avian
Post loft at a rate of one penny per inch.

John Farthing's warning had caused me to put the
quest for the Duchess's brother out of my mind. But
with her message in my hand, questions started to
return. Why had she addressed it to my female persona?
The cryptic language told me that she expected it to be
opened *enroute*. Clearly, it would have been read by the
local pigeon master as he glued it to the paper. But did
she fear that it would also be read by the Patent Office?
Who did she believe was being spied on – herself, my
brother or perhaps both? And if John Farthing had read
it, what would his reaction be?

Upturning the small woollen bag, I spilled the Duchess's
remaining gold sovereigns onto the galley table and began
arranging them in piles of ten. From her initial payment
of seventy coins, sixty-one remained. Two coins would
pay *Bessie*'s mooring fees for the month. Another three
might keep me in coal and food during the same period, if
I lived frugally. But one hundred would be needed to pay
off Leon, securing my boat and my livelihood for another
year. Picking up a coin and turning it in the lamp light, I
wondered at man's strange fascination for this metal.

Night conceals but twilight conceals doubly so. With
dusk falling, I climbed from the forward hatch onto the

crutch of the boat, face bewhiskered, enjoying the ease of movement granted by male attire. Fashions for bustles, corsets and hooped skirts would surely vanish should women experience such freedom. Even the rational dress I habitually chose did not allow me to clamber the shortcut from the towpath up the steep embankment. Dressed as my brother I took pleasure in the scramble.

Having reached the shadow of the wharf keeper's cottage, I stood to watch and listen as was my habit. The resident tabby padded towards me from across the yard, pressing its brow to my outstretched hand, knowing me by scent. I could feel it purring as it leaned its body against my leg.

The evening air smelled of damp earth and decaying leaves. A factory steam whistle sounded in the distance. Some poor workers' shift had ended. To start one's labours before dawn and return home after the sun had set was not a life I wished to contemplate. My frugal existence amid the peace of the cut would seem as luxury to the uncounted masses who laboured in the mills of North and South Leicester.

Loose chippings of gravel crackled under my boots as I stepped to the door which, on my knocking, was opened by Mrs Simmonds. She beamed, taking my gloved hand and attempting to pull me into the brightly lit hallway.

"Such a pleasure," she said. "So unexpected."

"I should not," I said, letting the words resonate in my chest, keeping the pitch low. "I have a cold. You wouldn't want to catch it."

"Nonsense." She pulled again, but I slipped her grasp and dipped into my pocket for the coins.

Her husband stepped into the hallway behind her, receipt book and pencil in hand. Where his wife's sharp movements suggested a heron on the hunt for small animals, he put me in mind of a sleepy toad, an impression heightened by the magnifying lenses of his spectacles. I passed him the money, which he accepted with a slow nod.

"My dear," he said to his wife, "I believe we should respect Mr Barnabus's wish."

"But I want him to meet our guest."

"Nevertheless–"

"He would be enchanted to meet her. And her him."

Mr Simmonds slipped a sheet of carbon paper between the pages and wrote out a receipt in blocky, deliberate letters. "Thanking you kindly," he said.

His wife muttered something under her breath, then stepped back into the house. A moment later she had returned, leading her guest by the hand.

"Mr Barnabus, I have the honour of introducing you to Miss Julia Swain. Miss Swain, may I introduce Mr Edwin Barnabus."

Julia curtsied, her eyes averted from mine. In the light of the hall, I could see she was blushing. "I was just leaving," she said.

Mrs Simmonds smiled with the satisfaction of one whose plan has just come to fruition. "Then you must walk her home, Mr Barnabus. It isn't safe for a young lady to be out at this time of night."

"It wouldn't be proper," I said.

"Then I shall accompany you as chaperone."

Shoulder to shoulder, I would have stood two inches taller than Julia Swain, but the boots I wore had been made to include lifts. Thus I found myself looking down on her from an unaccustomed angle as we walked the road up the hill towards her house. Mrs Simmonds insisted we go ahead, though she kept close enough to be able to listen in on our conversation.

"It's a beautiful night," Julia said.

"Yes," I replied.

"And November on us already. Ned Ludd Day will be here before you know it. Do you prepare through the winter or leave it to the last moment?"

"I don't really... that is, I was brought up in the Kingdom."

"Then you give gifts at Christmas? To your sister perhaps?"

"Indeed."

"Surely you must have built models of the Infernal Machines or seen them smashed."

"Never."

"It's hard to imagine not doing. It's such a part of our winter. Evenings by the fire. Gluing and painting. Together as a family." She paused for a moment as if gathering her courage, then said in an artificially casual tone: "Perhaps you could come to our house on Ned Ludd Day. With your sister of course. We would eat the feast and sing the hymns together. Then you could see Father smashing the Infernal Machines for another year."

We walked on in silence for a while. Though I kept my gaze forward, I was able to see her on the periphery of my vision stealing coy glances in my direction. This was a meeting that should never have happened.

"How are you acquainted with Mr and Mrs Simmonds?" I asked, reasoning it would be easier to pose my own questions than to evade hers.

"My father is a registered inventor," she said. "He has seven patents to his name. Two of them concern the steam propulsion of boats. Mr Simmonds visits on occasion to consult."

Hearing Mrs Simmonds's footsteps closer behind us, I turned and asked, "Is your husband a frequent visitor to the Swain household?"

She flustered and tutted as she fell back to a distance of some fifteen paces.

"This was my first visit," Julia whispered. "Though I've long been intrigued to meet you, I wouldn't have had it happen in this way. Your sister is my teacher. And yet more than a teacher."

"She enjoys your classes," I said.

"Don't think too badly of Mrs Simmonds. She means well enough. She has two sons, grown and fled to Carlisle where I hear they have good jobs and families of their own. Arranging the lives of others is her small consolation."

Light shone from the front windows of Julia's house, revealing strands of thin mist which hovered over the road in front of us.

"I knew it should be in the night that I saw you if ever, Mr Barnabus."

"How so?"

"Your sister doesn't speak of you beyond saying that you sleep during the day, and I don't press her. Please don't take this badly, but there's nothing of the ordinary about you. I'd half imagined you as

Mr Stoker's vampire, though a gatherer of private intelligence is almost as exotic."

We had reached the front door and I found myself facing her. "I'll not ask you in," she said. "I don't think you'd accept. But please believe me when I say this brief meeting has been more than pleasant. For me at least."

"I'm no more than a shadow," I said, "and can have only such friendships and feelings as a shadow might. A vampire would be more substantial."

She made to take my hand, but I was already turning away.

CHAPTER 12

Illusion is story. Weave it with characters and feelings and love and loss and the audience will follow you as surely as the children of Hamlyn followed the Pied Piper.

THE BULLET-CATCHER'S HANDBOOK

At the end of the British Revolutionary War, the generals took a ruler and drew a line across the map. The border ran from the Wash in the East to Wales in the West and was so placed as to cut no city or town. But when news spread that the birthplace of Ned Ludd, father figure of the revolution, lay inside the Kingdom, Republicans took to the streets in protest. It seemed war might break out again. The generals hastily rectified their mistake by signing the Anstey Amendment, redrawing the line to include a small southward loop. But in doing so they split Leicester in two.

The impossibility of securing a border across the Backs makes Leicester unique. Only in the divided city can people cross with such ease and the differentiated cultures of Kingdom and Republic bleed through into each other. Perhaps that is what had drawn me to live there.

Notwithstanding this mixing, the clothes I could see on the far side of the border post were noticeably brighter. Skirts in the Kingdom were worn shorter also. Here and there I could glimpse ankles and flashes of colourful stockings. But fashion was merely the outer symbol of something more profound, something elusive as a half-remembered scent. It was a way of thinking, a love of mystery, a pleasure in rudeness, a preference for Anglo-Saxon words over Latin, a mixing of races. It was the sum total of a thousand small differences, each of which might be irritating or pleasing to a degree but when put together formed a quality that I yearned for and knew I could never again possess.

Two guards in blue Republic uniforms sat in the glass-fronted booth a few paces away from me, their muskets leaning next to them. Two Kingdom guards in red sat in an identical booth on the other side. The protocol of the border demanded that guard numbers always matched. Today this symmetry extended to the way their guns had been balanced in the corner of the booths and to their indifferent sleepiness.

There being so many cheaper and easier ways to pass between the Kingdom and the Republic, this crossing was left as a place of parades and symbolic exchanges of prisoners. I doubt a more porous border had existed in the history of the Second Enlightenment.

I pictured myself stepping forwards, ducking under the barrier and disappearing into the crowds on the other side before either set of guards had stirred. It would be easy. And yet others would see.

Just as the border had made Leicester boom as a city of smugglers, so too had it boomed as a place of spies.

Some worked for the government of the Kingdom, some for the Republic. A few perhaps for the Patent Office, though that could only be a guess. By far the most numerous of the intelligence gatherers of the border were private traders in information. People like myself.

As I stood, gazing into the Kingdom, I became aware of a portly man in a blue coat and top hat who stood just to the other side of the barrier adjusting his fob watch to the clock tower standard. He took a casual glance in my direction.

The hour was indeed growing late.

Humberstone Gate, being the last respectable thoroughfare in North Leicester before the Backs, was home to a vibrant mix of businesses. Many were tailors and outlets for factory-produced woven goods. There also were delicatessens, retailers of fine porcelain, estate agencies, banks, and one steamcar showroom.

Having stopped to ask directions from a newspaper boy, I stepped down a side street and immediately found the shop I was looking for. A wooden sign cut into the shape of a Gladstone hung over the door and bags of every description crowded the small window display.

A bell tinkled as I stepped inside.

The girl behind the counter flashed a smile of welcome. "May I help you?"

"Are you the bag-maker's assistant?" I asked.

"I'm sorry?"

"I was told to meet the bag-maker's assistant. This afternoon."

"What name should I give?"

"Barnabus," I said, surprised to be asked.

The girl beckoned and I found myself following past racks of bags spaced so closely that I had to sidestep to avoid knocking them from their hangers. The smell of leather and new wool prickled my nostrils. A narrow doorway at the very back of the room brought us to a short flight of stone stairs leading up towards a windowless storeroom. From there, a wooden ladder granted access through a trapdoor to the upper storey.

Lifting her head, the girl called out, "It's Barnabus."

With a clunk the trapdoor above our heads opened. The girl curtsied and scurried back to the front of the shop.

The wooden joints of the ladder creaked at my weight. Gripping tightly, I climbed, rung by protesting rung until my head emerged through the opening and I found myself peering into a bare room of floorboards and uneven plaster. Thin daylight streamed in through a large window of frosted glass. And there, looking down at me, stood the Duchess of Bletchley herself, wearing a coarsely woven travelling cloak and an expression that might have been cold determination, though I fancied it was anger.

"I brought your gold." It was all I could think to say.

She waited until I had climbed into the room before making her reply. "Most kind. Minus your expenses?"

"I've located Harry Timpson."

"You've succeeded in narrowing the search to Lincolnshire. One of the largest counties south of Carlisle. Would you call that a triumph of detection?"

I held out the bag of coins for her to take, but she made no move beyond a momentary flick of the eyes. "Living easy on my money for two weeks then announcing that you have grown tired of the assignment – this sounds like sharp practice. Not only have I entrusted you with payment in advance, I've exposed myself to danger in crossing the border. Twice! I will not accept your resignation."

"You *will* not?"

"I will not, indeed!"

I stepped away from the open trap door and began circling. The Duchess turned, keeping her stern face towards me. Her rebuke had thrown me off balance. But the authority of the aristocrats did not extend to this place. And the further she pushed, the thinner her pretence of righteousness seemed to me.

"When the thugs chased us," I said, "when they ended our first meeting, I had thought they came for my brother. But it wasn't so. They came for yours! You knew this but didn't warn me."

"We each escaped," she said.

"You brought me into their gaze. Even before our meeting, you knew this would happen. Your letters, so secretive.Your payment – the bag carrying a hidden label. You prepared all this but didn't warn me of the danger. You're not the injured party! I've been followed. My home searched. I was imprisoned by agents of the Patent Office. Kept for days in a room without windows or light!"

The Duchess of Bletchley raised a hand to her chest and held it there. At last she took the small woollen bag from me, opened it and ran a slender finger over the coins inside.

"I could have run with your gold," I said.

When the Duchess looked up to me again, her sham anger had disappeared. I felt her eyes evaluating me. "We had no time on our first meeting to haggle over a price," she said. "Is there too much danger for you, or insufficient money?

"Life is more precious than gold."

"Life and gold are synonyms," she said. "You of all people should know that. Had your father the money to repay his debts, you wouldn't have become the property of the Duke of Northampton."

"We never borrowed from that man!"

"And yet you owed."

"The Duke of Northampton..." I spat onto the wooden floorboards between us, trying to rid myself of the taste of his name. "...that man... through bribes and forgeries he ruined us."

"I've read your history," she said. "Your family's wagons, tents and effects seized by the court. I know of your flight from the Kingdom. Yet, had you the money, this ruin wouldn't have come."

My eyes were stinging. I screwed my face into a snarl, trying to stop the first tears from spilling, then turned away from her and leaned my hands against the cold plaster. "You've got your gold," I said, my voice sounding shrill. "Now go."

But instead of leaving, she stepped closer, dropping her voice to a whisper. "How much would it cost to pay the debt owed the Duke of Northampton? How much to pay the expenses of the court and win back the effects of the Circus of Mysteries?"

"It's gone."

"It could be restored."

"No."

"Nine thousand guineas would pay Northampton and clear the expenses of the court. Your life returned."

"No!"

"We're both victims, Elizabeth. But your misfortune may be reversed. Mine also, with your help."

"My father died. That can't ever be undone!"

"I'm begging you," she said, her voice cracking. "Please help."

Slowly, I turned. She stood a pace from me, her face creased with pain. I hadn't noticed insincerity in any of her expressions. Yet seeing her now, I understood that everything before had been affectation by comparison.

"Nine thousand guineas would pay for a hundred gatherers of intelligence," I said.

"Only a fool would take gold and risk their life. Yet a fool couldn't find my brother."

And there it was: the real reason this woman had selected me. Not because of my fine reputation as a gatherer of intelligence, though that had been a pleasant fiction. Not even for my childhood background in a travelling show.

How long had she expected the investigation to last before the Patent Office intervened? One week? Two perhaps? And when that happened, she knew I would drop her commission and run, as would any of the legion of intelligence men she could have approached.

Desperation was the quality that made me uniquely fit for her needs. She had gambled on the proposition that I, or my brother, would risk a death sentence in the Patent Office Court in exchange for the chance of return to our home in the Kingdom.

"Money and life are not the same," I said.

"They are for me, Elizabeth. For you also. We're of one kind. Tragedy has made fools of us both."

I watched as she stepped to the trapdoor and swung it closed, cutting us off from the world below.

"What did you see in the Darkside Coffee House?" I asked

"I saw you half revealed."

"You researched the records of my birth? My history?"

"I needed to know who I was commissioning."

"And you didn't think to blackmail me?"

"Would you have succumbed?"

I did not answer. For a moment we each seemed to be waiting for the other to blink. Then she said: "It seems I chose wisely."

"You would pay nine thousand guineas?"

"For his safe return, yes."

I shook my head. "I won't face certain death for any money."

"Nothing is certain. Please hear my story."

We sat in the corner of the room, the Duchess rigidly upright, her back against the wall, feet stretched out in front of her. I kept my legs crossed under my skirts.

"He is beautiful," she said, speaking of her brother.

"Not handsome, then?"

"He has a delicate masculinity. A sculpted face. You'll understand when you find him."

"If I find him. Are there no pictures?"

"There was one. A small portrait. Very fine. The frame alone would be worth a fortune. The Patent Officers took it – for their investigation, they said."

The injustice of her story rang true. The very people who had chased him from his home also stole the last reminder of his face. Yet I had been taken in by the Duchess's stories before and did not trust the way her story resonated with my own.

"I think you miss the picture more than you miss him," I said.

The flush of anger rose quickly in her cheeks. "Withdraw that!"

"Why? You spoke of the fine frame with more passion than you did your brother's face. Perhaps you loved him once."

"You push too far!"

"Why did you leave him, then?"

"I didn't leave him!"

"You married the Duke of Bletchley. You joined his household and left your brother."

"Those with wealth or title have no choice in marriage," she said.

"Then you don't love your husband?"

For a moment neither of us spoke. I had learned one thing in the exchange. Her outrage had been real; so too must her love be.

"Why do you treat me so?" she asked.

"To find the truth."

Tiredness seemed to overtake her. Her shoulders slumped.

"Tell me how he disappeared?" I said.

"There are workshops in the grounds – a ramshackle collection of buildings. The Duke wished to convert them into stables, as I believe they may have been in the past. Yet they were stacked with obscure artefacts. Believing there might be something of value hidden among the dust and cobwebs, the Duke employed my brother to sort and catalogue the hoard."

"Whose was the workshop?" I asked. "Originally, I mean."

"An uncle of the Duke, dead some twenty years. The man had a fascination for exotic science."

"He was an inventor?"

She shook her head. "A collector. They were bought from private sales, though none had a patent mark. My brother has a way with devices. Retorts and chemicals that would be a mystery to others, he could perceive the uses of.

"I used to sit with him as he puzzled over clockwork machines and steam devices and obscure arrangements of lenses. The Duke's uncle had a hoarder's instinct. But he was no librarian. He left no catalogue and little by way of written explanation. Three months my brother worked and not a tenth of the task completed."

As the Duchess spoke, I thought of the nine thousand guineas she had offered. Everything in me wanted to go blindly forward and take it. I wanted to retract my impertinence. I wanted to grovel and receive my old life back in return. But if her story proved untrue, all she promised would be illusion. I became aware that I had been holding my breath.

"It's almost dark," I said. "We should go soon. They'll be shutting up shop below."

She put her hand on my arm, stopping me getting to my feet. "First let me tell you of Harry Timpson. All my troubles began when he came to Buckinghamshire."

"Timpson is a Republican," I said. "He'd never take his show across the border."

"Yet so he did. His Laboratory of Arcane Science pitched its tents not half an hour distant from the hall. The Duke paid for everyone to see the show – guests, servants and all down to the least parlour maid. My brother seemed galvanised by the prospect.

"Indeed, the show proved exceptional, though my brother couldn't settle through it. He sat there fidgeting – to the embarrassment of all. At the intermission the men went off to smoke and drink. I took refreshment with the rest of the womenfolk.

"But my brother didn't return for the second half. Nor when the show was done and the carriages lined up to carry us home. When he was still missing the following morning, the Duke sent out men to search. They found Harry Timpson's big top had disappeared in the night. A week later we received word that the Laboratory of Arcane Wonders had crossed back into the Republic at a border post just east of Leicester. My brother had passed beyond my reach."

"You didn't see him again?"

"No."

The Duchess lifted herself from the floor and stood, straightening her skirts for a moment. I got to my feet and faced her squarely. Being the same height, my eyes were level with hers. Despite the difference in status, we seemed to have reached a moment of equality. Dusk had entered the room and I could see only the half of her face illuminated by the thin light that filtered through the frosted window.

"When did the agents of the Patent Office arrive?" I asked.

"The very day that Timpson crossed back into the Kingdom. There were two of them only. One was old and somewhat gaunt. The other was much younger and spoke with an American accent. They presented their papers to the Duke. I recognised the younger man. He'd been in conversation with my brother the night before he disappeared. At the time I hadn't known what he represented."

"The agents removed something from the workshops?" I asked.

She shook her head. "I watched all day as they searched."

"A small object perhaps? Something they could have concealed in a pocket?"

"To judge by their expressions, I'd say they didn't find whatever they were searching for. They placed the seal of the Patent Office on the workshops and that's been an end to it. None of us have crossed the threshold since."

She held the purse of coins out towards me on her upturned palm.

There was a scuffing noise below the trapdoor. "We'll be closing in five minutes." called the shopkeeper.

I reached out and took the purse. "We're just leaving," I said.

CHAPTER 13

Never repeat a trick, for the same eyes may not be misdirected twice. And never return to the same pitch. Even should they think they want more.

THE BULLET-CATCHER'S HANDBOOK

Three weeks had passed since Harry Timpson set out from Sleaford continuing the endless pilgrimage that is the inheritance of all travelling peoples. Enough time for his scouts to have found a pitch in a fresh town, to have wrung the population dry and then to have moved on again. If fortune smiled on me, I would find him soon enough. If not, I might be wandering the lanes of Lincolnshire until snows made travelling impossible and Leon had seized my precious boat.

The gypsy I'd met in Sleaford had indicated that I should travel west. There being no better choice, I set out in that direction, hoping to hear word of Timpson's passing in the villages around. Spending the Duchess's gold with what felt like reckless abandon, I hired Alf's cousin Joe and his steamcar taxi to transport me. He expressed his pleasure at the commission. Doubly so when I added extra coins to his fee, explaining that he would be bodyguard as well as driver.

Ten miles west of Sleaford we pulled over at a rest stop to let the engine cool. I sat in the passenger seat and watched Joe work the arm of a roadside pump. Having filled a tin bucket, he poured water into the car's capacious tank, then went back and repeated the process. As he was thus engaged, a pony and trap clopped to a halt immediately in front of us. Joe and the trap's driver stood for a moment in conversation, Joe mopping his brow with a green handkerchief whilst the other man jumped and jogged on the spot, as if wishing to loosen stiff joints after miles of travel.

Sliding out of the seat, I straightened my skirts and was about to approach the newcomer to ask if he had heard news of the Travelling Laboratory, when I noticed the gatepost nearest the pump. On its flat surface, positioned so that it would not be easily seen from the road, were three chalk lines, one horizontal, the other two crossing it vertically, the line on the right side having a small kink near its base.

I had not seen such a mark since my childhood. Yet there was no mistaking the sign of the broken-legged man – a symbol that used to be drawn by outriders of the Circus of Mysteries indicating that a good pitch lay close ahead.

From somewhere distant I seemed to hear a voice shouting my name. My father's voice. It sounded so real that for a moment I wanted to call back to him.

I had thought the broken-legged man was part of a secret language known only in the Circus of Mysteries. Yet here it was on a gatepost in the Republic, the chalk still fresh. Such marks could last three weeks in dry weather. But at this time of year, with the dew heavy each morning, they would be unreadable in half that time.

Pulling the glove from my hand, I rubbed a thumb over the rough wood of the gatepost. Chalk dust crumbled away under my touch. An absurd idea began to take shape in my mind. Perhaps the Circus of Mysteries had somehow survived and my father with it.

"Miss Barnabus?"

Joe's call pulled me back from my thoughts. Concern was written on his face. The emotions washing through me must have shown.

"Miss Barnabus?" he said again.

Making myself smile, I said: "Did the great Harry Timpson pitch his tent in Sleaford last month?"

The trap driver stepped towards me, touching a hand to the brim of his bowler hat. "So I hear," he said.

"It's a shame I missed the chance. His show is famous. But he'll be long gone by now."

"Why miss, no. That is, I don't mean to contradict. But you've most excellent luck. He came back."

"He never does that."

The man laughed and scratched the back of his head. "You'll trust your own eyes I hope. Climb this rise and you'll see his tents pitched in a field to the right of the lane."

The car remaining too hot to drive, I walked the low hill. Joe, striding beside me, brought his hefty stick down on the road with a dull thud every other pace.

"Expect you'll be wanting your money back," he said, when we saw a flash of green and white striped canvas through the trees. "There'll be expenses to take out first."

"Harry Timpson never returns so soon," I said, more to myself than to my driver.

"But that's him sure enough."

"You saw him before?"

"Aye. And worth the shilling it cost. Changed lead into gold, he did. That I'll never forget."

More of the canvas emerged as we started down the other side of the hill and the trees thinned. The big top itself had been pitched off-centre in the field. I counted fourteen wagons clustered near the rear hedge. Smaller tents and wagons stood near the gateway – the usual assortment of fortune telling booths, freak-show tents and animal exhibits. Three campfires burned in different parts of the field and I could smell the wood smoke on the air. Taken together I judged it to be twice the size of the Circus of Mysteries.

Skewbald and piebald horses had been tethered to the right side of the field and were grazing circles in the long grass. It was a sight familiar yet foreign. I felt my heart constrict in my chest, such was the pang of longing that washed through me at that moment.

"This is what you came for?" Joe asked.

"You must keep the payment in full," I said.

"I won't argue with that."

"But I'll need one extra service."

The darkness had closed in around us by the time we again approached the Laboratory of Arcane Wonders and a gibbous moon shone between broken clouds. Joe put me down from the steamcar half a mile short of my destination. Then, with a look that could have been disapproval or an expression of concern, he made a turn in the roadway and chugged off back towards the town. I listened to the departing beat of the pistons until they were quieter than the wind in the trees that crowded the road. Then I waited another minute more.

It was on foot and unencumbered by my travelling cases that I arrived at Timpson's pitch. Stepping from the lane, I carried only a canvas bag slung over my shoulder and the few small but incriminating items that I had concealed in the lining of my long coat.

It seemed that a show was in progress. Two lines of lit torches made a path from the gateway, down across the grass to the big top. A dull light shone through the canvas from within. At the very entrance to the tent a young woman stood. Even at such a distance I could see that the skirt she wore had been cut shorter at the front than the back, so as to reveal her thighs. A red top hat rested on her head and her sequined jacket glinted and sparkled in the torchlight. Other than this woman I could see but one soul – a slight figure crouched near a fire on the right-hand side of the field next to a line of tethered horses.

Within the tent a crowd cheered. It was the sound of home, yet I had not heard it in five years. I felt the skin on the backs of my arms tighten into gooseflesh.

Keeping to the shadows, I turned left and picked my way around the outside of the field, using the boundary hedge as my guide, one hand brushing its branches and the few papery leaves that still held on.

The crowd had fallen silent in the tent and a man's voice now rose and fell, the words muffled by distance. I could not tell exactly what he was saying, yet his polysyllabic exuberance was unmistakable. A ringmaster was at work, whipping up the audience into ever greater levels of expectation. Could it be Harry Timpson himself? The voice sounded too youthful and vigorous. Yet a man such as Timpson would find it hard to turn his back on the performing life. He would surely travel until infirmity stopped him. When that happened, would the show that bore his name continue or would it be broken up? The trick gimmicks and scientific devices would be one-off artefacts crafted in secret. None of them would bear a patent mark and thus none could be legally sold. For all his fame, the estate of the great showman would be nothing more than canvas, rope, horses and a handful of wagons.

The sale of the Circus of Mysteries had raised a mere eighty-three guineas once the vultures of the court had pulled out its heart. A show that had given work and home to so many, that had entertained and amazed crowds in the towns and hamlets around the Kingdom – reduced to its component parts it had proved insufficient to pay the fees of the lawyers who had destroyed it.

My path was bringing me ever closer to Harry Timpson's big top, which had been pitched towards the left side of the field. Its silhouette loomed above me. I could smell dew-dampened canvas and the acrid smoke of burning tar from the torches. The long side-ropes angled down to wooden stakes embedded in the grass near my feet.

I was starting to be able to make out individual voices in the crowd – a woman who laughed like a braying donkey, a man who called out, "More! More! We must have more!" In the background a creature roared. A lion, I thought.

Ducking under a rope, I reached out and touched the canvas wall with my fingers. Somewhere here would be a vertical line of metal eyelets where two sections of the tent would be laced together. Easy enough to untie at the bottom and slip inside. Had the night been windy I might have tried. But in such dead calm, the movement of the material would easily be seen. Putting my face close, I closed my eyes and inhaled.

Having picked my way around the back of the field past the sleeping wagons, I found myself climbing a gentle incline, heading for the lane once more. I could smell the tethered horses before I saw them. They sensed my presence too, though the member of the troupe who had been left to watch over them did not. He was hunkered down, warming his hands by a small log fire, blind to anything beyond the flickering circle of light. When I'd seen him from a distance, I'd thought him to be a man. But I now realised this impression came from ·his greatcoat, an oversized castoff gathered in at the waist by a length of string.

The mare nearest me stamped and snorted, setting up a movement along the line of animals. The lad extended his scrawny neck and peered out tortoise-like from the coat, but on seeing nothing in the darkness he returned his attention to the fire.

Inside the big top the heavy beat of a drum had started up, followed by a gypsy clarinet, mournful yet sensuous. The audience quickly joined in, stamping and clapping, urging the musicians into an ever faster tempo.

The horses were still once more. Among them were animals I had not seen on my first visit earlier in the day. I judged these beasts to belong to members of the audience, who would have paid to have them watched. The show would be approaching its climax soon. When it ended, the field would be flooded with people. There would be no hiding after that.

I readied myself, rehearsing some phrase in my mind with which to assuage the suspicions of the lad by his fire. But then, as I prepared to step out of the shadows, a broad hand clamped down on my shoulder.

"Now then, miss," came a breathy voice from just behind. "Don't be making a bolt for it. Turn slow and we'll see what we've got."

CHAPTER 14

The man who desires not certainty will have no interest in illusion.

THE BULLET-CATCHER'S HANDBOOK

A scar on the left cheek made Silvan's face asymmetric. A burn, perhaps. It stood out starkly pale, even in the firelight. More of it I guessed lay concealed under his thick sideburns. Yet he was not unhandsome.

That is how I first saw Harry Timpson's lieutenant, smiling directly at me from where he sat on the step of a bow-topped wagon, one of five men playing cards on an upturned box. The smile contained no warmth.

"Where did you say you found her?" Silvan asked of the man who gripped my shoulder.

"Sneaking round the horses."

"I would have seen her," said the lad who'd been keeping watch.

"Would have. Could have. Didn't," said Silvan.

The lad stood biting his lip, as if awaiting judgement. Silvan gestured with a jerk of the head and the boy scampered away into the dark. All the men were looking at me. Silvan drew in a breath as if about to make his pronouncement.

"I want a job, sir," I blurted, before he could begin.

Whatever the man had been about to say dissipated into a stream of air blown from between his pursed lips.

"I can clean and cook and paste up bills and feed the animals. I can–"

"Whoa there. We've no work."

"But please."

"And no bed for a well brought up girl."

"I'll sleep on the floor."

"She can sleep in my wagon," said a man with a forked beard sitting on Silvan's right.

"Choose your man and you'll have a place to sleep," said Silvan.

All the others grinned and chuckled at my discomfort, though keeping an eye on their boss. Such talk would have been unthinkable for most Republicans. Yet the world of the travelling show has always stood apart, with its own codes, dress and language. The smile dropped from Silvan's face and the others fell silent.

"The animals have their carriages," I said.

"You'd sleep in the beast wagon? The lions would like that well enough."

"In the wagon but outside the cage."

"Every town has a girl like you," Silvan said. "She sees the show and conjures a fancy for escape. She begs and weeps. But we don't take her. Else there'd be a train of angry fathers and husbands following behind us."

"I've no father and no husband. I can sew canvas and mend tents."

Silvan picked a long-necked bottle from the grass beside where he sat, put it to his lips and upended it, his eyes not leaving mine as he swallowed.

"Let her gamble for it, Silvan," said the man with the forked beard. The words sent a thrill of fear and excitement through me.

"Not the cards!" called the one who sat nearest me, who I now saw to be a dwarf, a fact his seated position and the uneven firelight had conspired to conceal.

"Please let me play," I said.

"Why would I?" asked Silvan. "And why would you?"

"To win a place in your travelling show."

"You have money?"

"I have a little, sir. Teach me your game and I'll do my best."

Silvan aimed a kick at the dwarf, sending him scrambling to his feet, vacating the pile of rope on which he had been sitting.

"Take a place at the high table." He flourished his arm, to gesture with mock courtesy. "We'll teach you."

"The game is called Wild Eights," said the dwarf who, having sacrificed his seat for me, had been assigned the role of tutor and was making no secret of his annoyance at both misfortunes.

"I haven't heard of it," I said, which was a lie.

"Don't suppose you've heard of poker, neither," said the dwarf.

"Indeed I have."

"The rules?"

"No, sir. But I know it's played in the bars of the American Republics."

"The two games are much alike," he said, spitting towards the fire but not reaching it. "You look for patterns in your cards. Two the same, three the same.But just the number, not the suit. And eight doesn't count for a pair, though it can be anything in a straight."

While pretending to give full attention to my teacher, I watched Silvan pass the bottle round the circle. Each man took a swallow except the dwarf who, being busy with his lecture on the ranking of cards, missed his turn. If he had spoken to me with better grace, I might have felt sorry for his night's growing total of indignities. Doubly so, for I knew the rules well enough already.

"Got it?" he said at last, tapping a stumpy finger on his forehead. "Has it all sunk in?"

"The game costs a penny to join," said Silvan. "He didn't tell you that."

Following Silvan's lead, I dropped a coin on the upturned box, then watched as he dealt a pile of five dog-eared cards to each player.

"Look at 'em but don't show," the dwarf hissed in my ear.

"Not even to you?"

"You want my help or not?"

I spread the cards clumsily in my hands and turned them for him to see: a three, a seven, a ten and two queens. He nodded his approval.

Silvan tossed a couple more pennies onto the box. The man with the forked beard did the same.

"You must match them to stay in the game," said the dwarf.

Everyone waited as I selected two pennies from the small collection of copper and silver resting on my skirts. Their eyes glinted in the firelight.

Next came an exchange of cards, each player choosing some number from his hand to throw face down, to be replaced from the body of the deck. When my turn came the dwarf pulled all but the pair of queens. The cards I was dealt by way of return added nothing.

Silvan threw down another two pennies. The man with the forked beard shook his head and sat back.

"Put in your money if you think your hand better than his," said the dwarf.

"By what should I know?"

"By his bid. By the number of cards he swapped. By his face, which must tell you most of any clue."

I threw my coins down then watched as each of the following players folded and dropped their cards.

"You see," said Silvan, "it comes to a simple question. Do you think your cards better than mine or worse?" So saying he flicked a silver fivep'ny onto the pile.

"You must match his bet," said the dwarf. "Or more than match it if you wish to see his cards."

"But I don't wish to spend more."

"Then you must fold your hand and say goodbye to the money on the table."

"I don't wish that either!"

At this all the men laughed except the dwarf, who seemed to bristle at the slowness of his pupil. Another indignity. "Choose," he said.

So I threw in a fivep'ny and another penny besides and watched as Silvan laid down three twos on the box. The dwarf blew air through his lips, disappointed. "He beats you."

"But queens must be worth more than twos," I said.

"Did you not listen? Three of a kind beats a pair. No matter the number or the face."

So began the draining away of my few coins. In the round that followed, my cards held no promise and I folded directly, losing only one penny. Once again, Silvan bid heavily but this time no one would face up to him and he scooped the coins without ever showing what he held.

Then the pack was placed into my hands.

"Shuffle it," said the dwarf.

I made to imitate the shuffle I had seen the others perform. But not a second had passed before the entire pack splashed onto my lap and spilled from there to the floor.

The men roared with laughter. Even the dwarf could not help but join in. I pretended to fluster as I regathered the pack, letting it slip from my hands a second time, making such comic show of my ineptitude that even Silvan broke the careful gaze he had been keeping on me.

"Satan's teeth, but you'll ruin those cards, child," said the man with the forked beard.

At last I had the pack together again. More or less.

"That'll do for the shuffle," said the dwarf, grabbing it. As he dealt for me, I noticed a small hole in his left hand between the thumb and first finger. A sword puncture, I thought.

This time my cards seemed fair, with two tens holding a promise of some reward. Thus tempted I played and lost more heavily than before. At least it was not Silvan who won the round, but the man sitting to his left.

On the sixth round, the deal passed back to Silvan. Having won nothing, the pile of coins in my lap was almost gone. I dropped a penny onto the box and picked up my cards. The dwarf leaned in close again, but this time I held my hand from him.

"I know the rules now, sir. I'll do it alone."

"I can give this advice without looking. Fold now. Give up. Go away. You've lost nothing but pride and a handful of change."

"You heard your teacher," said Silvan.

I peeked at my cards: a two, a seven, a useless eight, a jack and a king. Nothing.

After one round of bets there were only the three of us remaining. The man with the forked beard swapped three cards from the deck. I placed my whole hand down.

"Five cards please," I said, my voice sounding very small.

"Never do that!" hissed the dwarf in my ear. "Never. Never."

"I will play as I wish!"

Silvan dealt five from the deck, his eyes fixed on me, his face expressionless as I inched them from my chest and looked down to see what I had been given.

The man with the forked beard threw in a fivep'ny bit. I did the same. Then Silvan picked two silver tens from his pile of winnings and cast them onto the box.

"Too rich for me," said the man with the forked beard.

"I wish to play," I said. "Yet I've no money left."

"Bet she's got something of value," said one of the men. "What about her pretty clothes?"

"You can't do that!" said the dwarf. "She can't do that!"

"She can gamble her clothes if she wishes," growled Silvan.

Hands trembling, I unbuttoned my long coat. Slipping it from my shoulders, I untied the shawl I wore underneath. This I threw across to him. He caught it. For a moment he rubbed the material between his thumb and fingers. There was no smile now. "You should listen to your teacher," he said, then added another two silver tens to the pile.

All eyes turned back to me.

"You'd have me undress?"

"I would have you run home," he said. "But it's not mine to choose. Make your bet or fold."

I stood and gathered my coat in arms. "This is worth more than all that money."

Silvan scooped his winnings into his hands and spilled the whole lot onto the make-do table. "I place this against your coat and everything else you wear down to the innermost layer."

"It isn't the fabric that you ask, it's the sight of my flesh exposed!"

"I ask nothing."

"All here would see me. And all on my lonely walk back to Sleaford, too."

"My money is in the pot," said Silvan. "There's nothing else."

"There's a job and a place to sleep."

"Don't do this, lady," said the dwarf.

"It's hers to bet if she wants!" Silvan shouted, then glared around the fire at all the other men, who had fallen silent now. None were laughing. They looked at him half in fear.

"Bet your pretty clothes if you have no shame," he said. "And I'll bet a job for you. Expect no pity though. It's your ruin, not mine."

"Will you not back down?" I asked.

"I will not."

"Then I make the bet of all you ask, but not my camisole, which I'll keep."

Silvan dealt his cards onto the box. "A two, a three, a five, a six and finally an eight."

"It's a straight," said the dwarf, his voice bleak. "For the eight counts as wild."

"How do my cards stand against it?" I asked, laying all four aces on the box.

A second of silence passed. Then Silvan was on his feet and had marched away out of the firelight. The man with the forked beard swore and then everyone was talking at once – all but the dwarf, who seemed too shocked at first to utter a word. Then he leaned in close and whispered.

"Next time you're going to cheat, don't make it aces."

CHAPTER 15

The secret of deep deception is to tell the truth.

THE BULLET-CATCHER'S HANDBOOK

The other men had no complaint with me. Indeed, when I stood from the pile of rope on which I had been sitting and straightened my skirts, summoning the courage to follow Silvan, it was they who called me to sit again.

"Leave him be, lass," said the man with the forked beard. "We're each as honest as the next, but you'll be wanting to keep an eye on your winnings."

Blushing, I scooped the coins from the upturned box onto my shawl, gathering it into a makeshift bag.

"You'd not played Wild Eights, eh?" he said.

Much swearing and guffawing followed. Silvan's bottle was doing the round again. This time the dwarf got his turn. Of all the men, he was the one who had not smiled since my victory. Nor did he smile as he placed the bottle in my hand.

"Now you're one of us, it seems," he said.

I was being tested again. Though whether I was expected to drink or pass the bottle on, I could not tell.

I sniffed. It seemed to be some sort of rough spirit. I put it to my lips and tilted it back. Though I'd only taken a few drops, a burning sensation filled my mouth. Taking a sharp breath, I began to cough.

"What are you doing to the poor girl?" came a breathy voice from close behind me.

I turned and saw the familiar face of the gypsy fortune-teller from Sleaford. Today she wore a loose skirt of striped cotton. Three lengths of green cord hung from her wide belt, each weighted at the end with a glass bead. A tightly tied headscarf held her hair in place.

Travel west, she had said. And here she was.

"What's your name, pet?"

"Elizabeth," I said.

"And they'll not have fed you neither. Come. I'll see you're settled."

Tania was the fortune-teller's name, or so she said. The strands of hair that spilled from her headscarf at the back were jet black. But the dry crack of her voice had some years behind it. At first I had guessed forty-five, but the wrinkled skin of her neck and the deep crow's feet that spread from the corners of her eyes suggested I might be a decade out or more.

I was to sleep in her caravan along with two other unmarried women, both performers of some kind. This arrangement should not have been a surprise to me. It is what I would have done in Silvan's shoes, forced to accept a stranger into the community of the travelling show. To find someone's secrets, there could be no place better than in the wagon of the fortune-teller, exposed to all her reading arts.

"Silvan ought to've brought you here straight-ways," she said.

Under her instruction, I had hefted a pile of blankets from the belly box under the wagon. These we were rolling out on the floor next to the stove. "We'd have put you up without fuss."

"I don't want to be trouble," I said.

"Always room for one more. I'm on the bottom bunk of the cot. The girls sleep top to toe above."

"Silvan didn't want me," I said.

"Don't you listen to him."

Using a fold of her skirt as if it were an oven glove she opened the black, iron stove and fed in sticks until the fire crackled and flame began to lick out of the opening. The door closed with a snug clunk.

"They get work enough out of us," Tania said. "No harm in comfort, eh? All of them was new once. Even the boss."

As the stove heated, so the kettle began to rumble. The lamplight caught the steam as she poured boiling water into a blue china pot. Tania busied herself, taking down linen that had been left airing on a line strung across the width of the wagon, feeling each item with her fingers before folding it away into a drawer under the bed.

Next she poured and passed me a glass of black tea. Holding it made the skin of my cold hands prickle. I sipped and felt my heartbeat speed with its syrupy sweetness.

"That'll warm you through," she said. "Those men! Only think of number one. They'll sit cosy in a greatcoat an' let you freeze in summer muslin. Then tell how pretty and pale your skin is."

So saying, she slipped off her own coat and I saw that panels of paisley-patterned cloth had been sewn to her blouse, making it seem more like a waistcoat.

A metal bowl rested on the bench next to the stove. Out of this she tore a handful of sourdough, which she began to pat from one hand to the other. A gust of wind shifted the wagon gently on its springs.

Five years it had been since I left my home in the Circus of Mysteries, and though I had fashioned my home in the Republic to match the life I had lost, yet it was an imitation only. But here, watching Tania work the dough, smelling the yeast and the wood smoke, hearing the stamp and snort of a horse outside, here I found myself thrown back to the world of my childhood.

Back and forth the dough patted, thinning into a disk as she shifted it from one hand to the other. She hummed quietly to herself as she worked. There didn't seem to be a tune to it but I found the rhythm filling my attention.

Then she threw the dough into a hot pan. Grains of loose flour spilled onto the stove top, sending up threads of smoke, blackening then glowing for a moment before disappearing altogether.

"You've seen this life before," Tania said, without turning.

Lies take effort to sustain so I made no response.

"Silvan said you've no father and no husband," she said.

"That's what I told him."

She dipped a hand into the pan and flipped the bread, revealing the honey brown of the side that had already cooked. "It is true?"

"Must I talk of it now?"

"No child. Eat first."

In truth, my plans had not gone beyond finding work in the Laboratory of Arcane Wonders. That had seemed challenge enough in prospect – and had proved even more risky in execution. Having won my place, I could get to know the people and the ways of the show. If the Duchess's brother was still here, he would not be able to hide himself. In speech and action he would be revealed as an aristocrat.

The fortune-teller dipped into the pan once more and lifted the flat bread, which had now filled the wagon with the acrid smell of cooking yeast. Thinking back, I realised I had not eaten since breakfast. The day had been so full of preparations that I had not noticed my hunger until now.

"It's hot," Tania said, tossing the loaf to me.

The action came back to me un-thought, the shifting of the loaf from hand to hand, changing the fingers in contact with the surface each time so that no heat built up. Deftly, I ripped a piece from the edge, releasing a curl of steam. The bread was flecked with green inside and I could smell sweet marjoram. Coarse flour, rough salt and a few hedgerow herbs. Poor man's food some would say. Oh, but it tasted fine to me. Salty and yielding inside, yet crisp and brittle on the crust. I ripped another piece while Tania rummaged in a tightly packed cupboard, producing an almost empty wine bottle.

"Finish it," she said.

The loaf had cooled enough to hold in one hand now. I put the bottle to my lips and filled my mouth with the dark flavours of last summer's fruit.

Tania sat back, silent. From somewhere she had found a needle and length of saffron thread, and seemed to be fully focussed on the act of sewing a length of emerald green cord onto a plain cloth belt. But every now and then she raised her eyes and smiled at me.

The wine and food and the warmth of the caravan had loosened the tight knot I had worked myself into during the card game. Too much perhaps. For now I began to perceive what my actions must have already revealed to the perceptive fortune-teller. Even the manner in which I sat, legs crossed comfortably under the full skirts, would be information to her. My ease in holding the hot pan bread, my comfort at drinking from the bottle, the whole meal relished as a delicacy long missed.

My eating slowed as I approached the end. What story might this woman desire to be true? Certainly nothing bland would serve. A juicy bone of scandal would be the ticket. Something to throw to Silvan that would prove her worth. But what lie might I sustain?

Stopping sewing, she watched me drain the last of the bottle. "Better my dear?"

"Much."

"Travellers' food."

"It's been five years since I've eaten in a wagon like this."

"It burns your heart to miss it so."

"Yes," I said, knowing there was no point in denying what the woman had already perceived. Yet knowing also that she performed the same magic she had woven for me in my male guise in the back alley in Sleaford – thrumming my emotions rather than my thoughts, making them resonate. Had she already divined that I might twist the facts but had no power to deny my feelings? Might she work a different trick on a different person?

"To be forced from that life. To be exiled from the road. Ah, we are never whole again."

I tried to cover the sudden rush of emotion by standing and smoothing down my skirt.

"Tell me of it dear," she said, as I knelt again.

"It hurts too much," I said.

"Were the lanes of the North or of the Kingdom your home?" She reached out and rested her hand on mine. "You're a child of the Kingdom."

"Yes."

"So far from home."

"Yes."

"And cast out against your will."

I placed my face in my hands. A melodramatic affectation perhaps, though it served to delay the inquisition for a minute more. Tania was but a few shrewd guesses away from divining my identity, or close to it. She would tell Silvan, who would whisper it around that he had money in exchange for information about me. It would not be long before news came back that I was sister to a private intelligence man. And from then, how long would it be before I woke in the night to find his hand pressed down on my mouth and my throat opened with a razor?

A laugh outside the wagon broke into my thoughts. Footsteps approached and voices. I dropped my hands into my lap. Tania's eyes were on me still, though I could see she listened as I did.

"Just one kiss," a man cajoled.

"What must you take me for?" This was a woman. A young voice coloured with a smile.

"I take you for a lady," a second man said. Local by his accent. "A fine lady. And beautiful."

"Would a real lady put her soft lips to yours?" teased the woman.

"A gentleman would pay a king's ransom for such a gift."

"You are that gentleman?"

"I am! I am!"

The wagon shifted on its springs with the weight of someone climbing onto the step outside.

"And the king's ransom?"

"It shall be yours! In the morning, fair maid."

"You want your kiss on account then?"

The fortune-teller stepped past me and opened the door.

"Gentlemen," she said, "So gallant to escort Lara to her berth."

Tania's frame blocked any view of the pantomime outside, but the cold night air stole past her. I took a deep breath, feeling my senses sharpen. The cloying emotion was suddenly gone and I knew what I must do.

Moving quickly and silently, I took off my bonnet, lay down and wrapped myself in the blankets. No time to undress properly. Beneath the covers my fingers worked undoing the buttons of my coat.

"We are gallant," one of the men outside was saying.

"We are gentlemen," said the other, the slur of his words telling the story of his evening.

"Thank you Mr Jim," said Lara. "Thank you Lord Billy."

"Goodnight gentlemen," said the fortune-teller.

The wagon shifted as the two women moved inside and the door closed once more. But I was already curled up in an imitation of sleep, safe from further questioning. Until the morning.

CHAPTER 16

For the sickness of exile the only cure is return. But the sickness of the travelling showman, which is in reality the sickness of the wanderer, will admit no cure.

THE BULLET-CATCHER'S HANDBOOK

Lara slept on the upper bunk. In the morning when I woke, I found a second woman, Ellie, feeding split logs into the stove. The two were so alike that I guessed them to be sisters. The fortune-teller was nowhere to be seen. I had little doubt she had stolen out early to whisper her findings in Silvan's ear.

Happily, Lara and Ellie asked no questions. Rather, they bathed me in smiles and seemed to have made the decision that I needed looking after. Lara shaved slices of smoked pork into a pan and soon the wagon was filled with the smell of it. I watched as she added barley and water, cooking up a savoury porridge. While she did this, Ellie was busy clearing out half a shelf of the wagon's one cupboard for me to store my bag and clothes. "It's all safe here," she said. "The jossers won't come in."

"Nor the men of the troupe," added Lara. "They don't dare cross Tania."

Ellie nodded. "Don't pay too much mind to what the men say. They'll talk like they were giants and you a lamb to be gobbled up, but you're one of us now. Don't let 'em take no liberties and they'll catch on soon enough. Watch out for Yan the Dutchman, mind."

"Can't keep his hands to himself," Lara explained.

"Yan?"

"Beard split like a fork." She gestured below her chin to illustrate.

"I saw him last night," I said.

"But what he can do with the lions is a marvel," said Ellie. "They're like kittens to him.

"There was a big man at the card game. A giant almost."

"That's Sal the Knife. I did a turn as his target. He's big but he's got a delicate touch. Threw them so close I could feel the wind of it on my cheek when they thudded into the board. But never a graze. Not from Sal."

"He won some money in the card game," I said.

"Everyone's talking about the game," said Lara. "You skinned Silvan something wicked. Fabulo says it's cause he taught you good."

"Fabulo – is he the dwarf?"

"The same. He's strutting the gaff like king cockerel this morning. Like it was him won it."

"He was prickly as a thistle last night," I said.

"Dwarfs is like that," said Lara, knowingly.

I watched as she wiped out three bowls with a cloth

and tipped the pan, pouring a third of the savoury porridge into each. No one spoke through breakfast. The only sounds were our spoons touching the china bowls as we ate and the occasional crackle of burning wood in the stove. I had tasted nothing like it since my childhood. Perhaps it was the hunger, but it felt as if angels were singing on my tongue.

"How many days before we move?" I asked, putting my empty bowl to one side.

"He'll know when it's time," said Ellie.

"Silvan?"

"It's Silvan will tell us, but Timpson's the rum col. Timpson decides."

"I've not seen him yet."

"Nor will you. Keeps to his wagon."

"Is he very old, then?"

"Don't you go thinking age has blunted him," said Ellie. "He always wins out. He's got the nous *and* he's lucky too."

"But there's no second guessing him," added Lara. "First we're bound for Nottingham, then he says 'whoa' and we've turned on a penny and we're back over the border into Lincolnshire again."

"We never turn back," said Ellie. "Just never."

Lara nodded. "Yet here we are."

Both my young wagon mates were pretty, their natural good looks enhanced by the kind of flush that fresh air and exercise bestow, a complexion seldom seen in the grinding mill of the city. I held back from asking about their work. The question seemed somehow improper. It was one of them that I had seen standing at the

entrance to the big top the night before, wearing a
skirt cut high at the front. I could not tell which. Each
probably did several jobs. Everyone doubles up in a
travelling show.

Fabulo the dwarf stood waiting outside, a black
cigarette in his hand. Lara and Ellie curtsied to him. I
could not tell whether the gesture was mockery or if
his status really required such signs of respect. Either
way, Fabulo snarled. "She's to come with me," he
said, then turned and marched towards the top of
the field.

Nothing in his attitude suggested the triumphant
strutting that Lara had mentioned. He pulled hard on
the cigarette as if hurrying to finish it, blowing acrid
smoke into the cold morning air. At last he squeezed
the glowing tip between finger and thumb and cast the
stub away.

"You won't pull the same trick twice," he said.

"Trick?"

"And you can't play innocent, neither. Where was it?
A bar? A whore house? Where did you learn your cards?"

"I never played."

"You're not a fool," he said. "So don't talk to me like
I'm one. You cheated. And Silvan, he knows it too."

"Then why didn't he challenge me?"

"And say what? The cards you laid were not the
ones he'd dealt? To call you cheat would be to admit
the same himself."

Our progress across the dewy grass had been
slowing. Now it stopped. A grin spread over Fabulo's
face. "Ah, but you didn't see his cheating! Sure, that
would lighten Silvan's mood, if he found out."

"How would he know my cards?" I asked.

"No bullet-catcher will tell you the secret of his act."

"I saw nothing wrong in his dealing," I said. "Nor in the shuffle."

"There was nothing to see."

"Nor was the deck marked."

The dwarf scratched idly at the hole in his hand as he appraised me. There must be something obvious that I had missed. I had studied the cards, searching for the usual pattern of tiny ink dots by which a deck may be rigged. The only marks had been the infinitesimal scuffs and scratches of natural wear. How long would it have taken him to memorise such minute and random patterns? Understanding must have shown on my face, for Fabio laughed.

"You read them too?" I asked.

"No man can have such luck as Silvan," he said. "I watched three months before seeing how he did it. Worked three months more to learn it myself."

So saying, he set off again, and I perceived that we were heading for the nearest of two beast wagons in a cluster of sideshow tents. One of its wooden side panels had been unhooked and folded down, revealing the thick iron bars of cages. Two great lions sat on straw within.

"Time for you to earn your keep," said Fabulo.

The lions occupied cages to either end of the wagon. The space between was empty, though it could also have served as a cage. By a ladder we climbed to the roof, where Fabulo showed me the levers and catches that raised and lowered vertical rods to operate the doors between each section. With a clunk and a screech of metal the door of one cage swung.

The dwarf pulled back a small metal cover revealing a spy hole, through which I saw one of the beasts get lazily to its feet and move across into the newly opened middle section. I then pulled the lever back and the gate swung closed behind it.

"You catch on quick," said Fabulo. "You can shift the rods from below if your grip's strong enough. There's broom and shovel in the belly box, and bales of clean straw by the horses."

"Thank you," I said.

"Save it. The smell stays on you. Worse than dog shit."

I clambered down the ladder and into the empty cage.

"I don't know why you're here," he said. "But you've stirred Silvan up, and that's no good for no one." He stared at me. For a second I held his gaze, then feeling a blush starting to rise in my cheeks, I turned away and began sweeping the soiled straw towards the edge of the cage. "Stay clear of the bars," said Fabulo. "They're meat eaters."

The show I'd heard the previous night had been the first for three days. The men sat around playing cards. The women kept snug in the wagons. No one liked the waiting. Not that they dared ask Silvan why, counter to all previous practice, the Laboratory of Arcane Wonders lingered in one spot when the roads were still good and the locals out of ready cash.

"The weather's going to turn," muttered Sal the giant. Picking up a hatchet, a cleaving knife and a machete, he started throwing them in great arcs above his head, timing their spin so that he could catch each by the handle. Nimble work for a man of his size.

"It'll rain. Or worse, snow. We'll be stuck here all winter."

Fabulo scowled at him. "Shut your mouth."

The head of the hatchet buried itself in the turf. Sal swore under his breath, stepping back to let the other blades follow it. He rounded on the dwarf. "You're thinking the same!"

"Thinking is different." Fabulo flicked a warning glance to where I sat on a straw bale, surrounded by canvas, needle in hand.

After cleaning the beast wagons, I had been given another job. And then another. The card game having failed to get rid of me, it seemed that Silvan was now trying to wear me down with work.

Sal pulled his blades from the ground, wiping each on the grass, then on the sleeve of his dirt-encrusted coat. "She knows it. We all do."

"Saying it doesn't help no one."

We watched Fabulo marching away in the direction of the big top.

"Want me to leave too?" I asked.

"Yes!" said Sal. "You've had your adventure. Now run home."

"Silvan said there's a girl like me in every town."

"They come and then they go," he said, putting more emphasis on the word "go".

"When's the last one he gave a job to?"

"Think you're special, is that it?"

"I bet he's not let anyone in for a year or more, man or woman. That does make me special."

Stowing his blades in a canvas bag, he dipped his hand inside his coat and drew out a leather purse. "I'll put a silver tenpence on that bet."

We shook on it. His huge, rough-skinned hand gripping so tightly I felt my knuckle bones moving against each other. "Easy money," he growled. "Fabulo can be the judge of it."

It was my first time inside the big top and I looked around, devouring the detail. The benches were not tiered as I had expected, but ran in concentric horseshoes, leaving three aisles to the centre, as well as an ample walkway around the outside. A canvas wall partitioned off a section of the tent opposite the entrance. Behind would be a space for performers and equipment to wait.

None of the torches were lit but enough sunlight seeped through the sooty canvas for me to see Fabulo clearly enough. Though a dwarf and with arms and legs seeming too spindly to support the barrel of his chest, he was making progress around the ring through a series of perfectly executed cartwheels.

"Dwarf!" shouted Sal.

Fabulo righted himself. He seemed ill-pleased to have been discovered in the middle of his practice. If Sal noticed this he did not show any embarrassment. Striding forward he said, "Tell her she's not the only one given a job this last year."

"It is a bet," I explained.

"Thinks she's special," said Sal. "And owes me a tenpence. Or will when you tell her."

Fabulo spat on the sawdust. "We don't talk to outsiders!"

"You said she was one of us now."

"Not like that. Not yet."

"But the bet?"

"Your bet is off!"

The brittle restlessness of the troupe eased when Silvan announced that another show was to be staged that night. Most of the nearby villages had been sucked dry already. Therefore, riders set out to spread the word further afield, their bags full of daybills, brushes and pots of paste.

A SPECIAL REDUCED RATE
OFFERED AS A GIFT BY THE GREAT HARRY TIMPSON
TO THE PEOPLE OF THIS VILLAGE
FOR ONE NIGHT ONLY

When I approached Silvan and offered to ride out and help with the bill pasting, the man simply shook his head. He hadn't addressed a word to me since the card game, all instructions having been conveyed via Fabulo. Having refused my suggestion he turned his back on me and stalked away towards the wagon in which he spent much of his time – the place I suspected Harry Timpson himself must reside.

Painted green and red to match the other vehicles, it nevertheless stood out because of its greater length and width. Unlike the bow tops and kite wagons around it, this one had vertical sides. I'd seen Ellie carrying food to it and returning with empty plates and cups. Smoke rose day and night from its black chimney pipe. It had no windows.

Five minutes after Silvan had marched away, Tania the fortune-teller appeared at my side.

"How are you settling, child?"

"Well, thank you."

She took my wrist and drew it to her, turning it to expose my palm, the lines of which she traced with a finger. "It is time," she said, then set off, leading me behind her.

"Where are we going?"

"To find the truth."

With a shock, I realised that it was towards the large wagon we were heading. Not thinking what I was doing, I began to resist, but her grip tightened and she tugged me almost off my feet.

"Afraid of the truth?" she asked.

"No."

"I'll know when you lie."

Then she was climbing the steps and knocking on the wagon door. Before I knew what was happening, I found myself pulled into the sudden dark and incense-thick air of the interior. I blinked rapidly, then opened my eyes as wide as they would go, trying to pierce the gloom.

The low sun outside had bathed the field in dazzling light. Here the only illumination came from a curiously shaped oil lamp hanging from the roof, its feeble flame sheathed in dark red glass. To the right, a workbench ran the length of the wagon. A cloth had been thrown over it, a landscape of hummocks and valleys, hinting at the objects that must be concealed beneath. To the left, Silvan and Fabulo sat on tall stools. The dwarf's feet dangled.

"You've been asking questions," said Silvan.

"Yes, sir."

"What questions?"

"Anything to help me know my new home."

"What did you discover?"

"Ordinary things."

"But these are not ordinary times. Where did you learn to play Wild Eights?"

"I'd never played."

"Lying won't help you," he said.

"She speaks truth," said the fortune-teller, who was standing next to me, still gripping my wrist.

My eyes were growing accustomed to the dim red light now. Enough for me to read Fabulo's incredulity.

"Tania tells me you've been a traveller in the Kingdom," said Silvan.

"Yes, sir."

"Now running away from Sleaford?"

"Yes, sir."

"That's a lie," said the fortune-teller.

"Lies won't save you," Silvan said, pulling a long, slender knife from a sheath strapped to his leg. It came free with a metallic whisper, just audible in the silence.

My mouth was suddenly dry. "I live in North Leicester," I said.

Silvan looked to the fortune-teller, who nodded.

Then from the shadows at the back a new voice spoke. Though quiet, it possessed a resonant quality that seemed to fill the wagon. "Come closer," it said.

Tania pulled me forward, past Fabulo and Silvan, until I stood directly under the lamp and could make out a cot at the head of the wagon. On it reclined the great impresario himself.

With a small, precise movement, he beckoned me further forward. For no reason I could explain, my heart pumped harder at this than it had at the sight of Silvan's knife. When I stood but a pace from him he held up his hand for me to stop. In the famous illustration he wore a moustache of unusual breadth and thickness. The man before me was clean shaven, but there could be no mistaking him. The Roman nose and high forehead made Harry Timpson instantly recognisable. I found myself staring at the strange opalescence of his eyes. Flecks of light caught in them, making the irises appear to glow. Nothing in the daybill illustration had prepared me for that.

He examined my face, then the details of my clothes, down to the hem of my skirt.

"Why does a traveller of the Kingdom live in a Republican city?" he asked.

I opened my mouth then closed it again. A clock ticked somewhere under the cloth on the workbench. I could hear the blood rushing in my ears.

"Answer him," hissed Tania.

Two futures lay ahead, depending on what I said.

"Get rid of her," said Silvan.

Tania pulled my arm back towards the door.

"I'm an exile!" The word blurted through my lips as if unbidden. "I was born in the Circus of Mysteries."

Timpson inclined his body forward. "Barnabus died in debtors' prison, I hear."

I nodded.

"I met him once. He didn't seem a man who'd take risks with money."

"The Duke of Northampton bought up our family debts. He bribed an official. We were fined and there was no money left to pay.

"A crooked magistrate," Timpson mused. "That I can understand."

"He wasn't a magistrate, sir. He was an agent of the Patent Office."

"Liar," growled Fabulo behind me.

"Truth," said the fortune-teller.

Timpson shook his head. "To bribe an agent of the Patent Office... Barnabus wasn't rich. Why would the Duke take such risks to corner a poor man? What did Barnabus possess that he so desired?"

"He wanted our pretty Elizabeth," said the fortune-teller, close beside me.

"You're Barnabus's daughter? By the Devil himself!" Timpson started laughing. "She worked you like a josser, Silvan."

"I didn't lie," I said, "I'd never played Wild Eights before."

"You didn't need to. I'd wager old man Barnabus had you palming aces before you were weaned."

"Why's she here?" growled Silvan.

I twisted my hand away from the fortune-teller's grip. "I live on the canal cut, sir. I once thought that would be enough. My father used to say that for the sickness of the exile the only cure is return. But the–"

"But the sickness of the rootless will admit of no remedy," Timpson said, completing the quote. He held my gaze for a long time after that. The clock of my fate had been fully wound. Its cogs were now in motion.

CHAPTER 17

Lying is an art form. It becomes sin only if the deception is discovered.

THE BULLET-CATCHER'S HANDBOOK

Though I had won my place in the Laboratory of Arcane Wonders, Lara and Ellie were the only ones to have truly accepted me. Sal now avoided my company, having been scolded by Fabulo for telling me too much. Yan, the Dutchman with the forked beard, remained polite, though he never let down his guard. Silvan continued to be aggressive and I saw little of Tania, for she spent most of her time collecting wild food from the hedgerows.

I had been gathering such intelligence as I could amid these suspicions and hostility. The troupe numbered thirty-eight souls. Each I had now matched to a sleeping wagon. Nowhere could I find a sign of the Duchess's brother. But for Sal letting slip that I was not the only newcomer in the last year, I might have begun to doubt.

One of the five men from the card game had caught my attention, though I had yet to hear him speak. Hammocks of skin hung below his eyes, suggesting a lack of sleep, perhaps over many years. I took to watching him as he picked his way around the field – a gaunt figure, even when wrapped in a winter cloak. I sensed he watched me also. Not knowing his name, I began to think of him as the Sleepless Man.

The night after my interrogation, having at last completed my allotted tasks, I crouched in the shadow behind a stack of baled hay, keeping watch on Timpson's wagon. And there I saw the Sleepless Man again. He strolled, artificially relaxed I thought, then stopped to tie his laces, giving the impression of one who took time easily. But I saw him glance around, just as I might have done if checking for shadows out of place.

I did not make the mistake of ducking into cover when he looked in my direction, but held my breath, bracing to remain as still as the saddle that rested on the bale next to me. Only when he stepped over to the shadow of Timpson's wagon did I notice that Silvan had been standing there, as still as myself.

Of their conversation I could have heard nothing, even had I been able to approach. The Sleepless Man bent in close, his ear next to Silvan's mouth. From time to time he nodded. I saw the purse only because I had expected it. It passed from Silvan as they shook hands and was deposited beneath the Sleepless Man's cloak before he had taken three strides away.

That the Sleepless Man was an intelligence gatherer seemed clear enough. But the nature of the payment remained a mystery. I backed away, only turning to run when certain I was out of view. Blind in the shadow of the big top, I stumbled twice, but righted myself. Skirting the field the long way around gave me three times the distance to run. But I reached the horses before him, creeping the last fifty yards bent low, so as to make no silhouette above the hedge.

The horses heard me, or smelled me perhaps. Their ears twitched. One pawed the ground. Another snorted. Yet the lad who sat with them kept watch also on a bottle of cider and had no such keen senses. I observed the Sleepless Man as he approached.

"I'll be taking the grey," he said, his voice breathy, like wind through dead grass. He advanced on the finest beast, patting its flank.

"Can't have him," said the boy.

"I'm on the rum col's business."

"Then take this one." The boy made to untether a smaller mount.

"Going to tell Silvan to wait five days for news, not four? Brave lad."

The boy's hand froze on the rope. The grey pawed the ground, picking up the tension. The Sleepless Man untied it and began leading it away. "Wise choice," he said.

The horse passed within two paces of where I crouched. I watched him saddle the beast, then mount and ride out into the lane.

Five days would see a man to Leicester and back with time between to investigate. But on a fine beast such as the grey, the journey might be done in four. How long would he have to search the cut before he found my wharf? And how many people would he need to question before he learned that Elizabeth Barnabus was sister to a private gatherer of intelligence?

CHAPTER 18

*Practise every gesture, move, expression and word until
the significant appears trivial and the trivial appears
significant.*

THE BULLET-CATCHER'S HANDBOOK

Save for the Sleepless Man, I had now spoken with
every person in Harry Timpson's troupe. I knew the
names of most and was starting to understand their
places in the machine of the travelling show. The boy
who looked after the horses. The labourers who fetched
fresh hay and food supplies and who would doubtless
carry the bulk of the strain at pitching time. I now knew
that Lara sold kisses in a tent in the sideshow. I knew
that the Dutchman with the forked beard could put his
hands into the mouth of the older lion, but would not
dare put them into the mouth of the younger one. And
I knew that Ellie used her smile to distract jossers when
she took their money playing Find the Lady, for I had
caught her practising in the wagon.

Sal threw and juggled knives and swallowed swords.
Fire also featured in his act. I had seen him wet a length

of fabric with clear liquid from his flask. Touched to a candle, the fabric burned with an oily yellow flame. Plunging his hand into the fire, he would gather the material into a ball, which he squeezed, extinguishing it instantly. This he did again and again until the contents of the flask were used up.

Fabulo's place in the show was easy enough to explain. Any freakish thing would attract a crowd. There was also a bearded woman, and a lad with seven fingers on his left hand. That Fabulo could perform cartwheels would clearly be a bonus. But there was something more about him, for even though I had seen him as the butt of many jokes from others in the troupe, there was also a certain respect. This impression had deepened when I found him in Timpson's wagon with Silvan on the occasion of my interrogation.

But in all the exotic mix, I had found no one who carried the accent and manners of a Kingdom aristocrat. Reasoning that if the Duchess's brother were still with the show he must be hiding, I had started to track the food supplies. However well hidden, the man must eat.

The first jossers arrived before dusk. They mingled on the lane, none of them wanting to be the first to step onto the field, as if it had temporarily become part of a different land, foreign and exotic. Dangerous also perhaps, but infinitely enticing. What in all Lincolnshire could compare to the lights and colours promised within?

And the girls, of course. Lara and Ellie were now dressed as I had seen one of them that first night, skirts flared up scandalously short at the front, revealing red and black striped stockings. Their upper garments too were designed to catch the eye. In cut and in the full cross-lacing at front and back they more resembled corsets than respectable outerwear. Thus attired, they strolled across the field, passing close to the lane in the pretence of carrying some message to the lad who minded the horses.

I can only imagine the anticipation among that crowd of young men, now numbering more than thirty. With the dark drawing in, my two beautiful wagon mates approached the lane once more. This time they carried lamps and tapers. One by one they lit the lines of torches embedded in the turf, creating an illuminated causeway from the gate to the big top.

At such a distance, I could not hear the words they spoke to the local lads. But whatever was said, it served to break the invisible barrier. The crowd poured onto the field, following Lara and Ellie all the way to the mouth of the big top, where they formed a rowdy queue, each taking his turn to pay and step inside.

The stream of new arrivals now included women, family groups, children and old people. Most came on foot, but some rode or even arrived in carriages.

Slipping in with the line of jossers, I stepped casually to the entrance. Inside, I could see the horseshoe of benches beginning to fill. The low, expectant hum of voices made the skin on the back of my neck prickle. It had been five years since I'd heard that sound. My life had been so changed since then as to have become a new life entirely.

"Go mind the horses," said Silvan.

He had stepped in front of me, arms folded, and was now barring my way.

"May I not watch the show?"

"The horses," he said again.

People behind me in the queue were pushing to pass. I could feel Silvan's eyes on me. There was no compromise in him. I stepped aside, feeling the sudden and unexpected exclusion so keenly that I had to hurry away. I did not want my pain to be seen.

A man with bruised pride may block your path for spite and no logic will have him change. Silvan had good cause to hold a grudge. He knew I had cheated him at cards. But I took him to be a man driven more by cold logic than revenge.

Men like Silvan survive through caution. Since my arrival he had tried to keep me busy in places where I could be watched yet see little. He would be waiting for news from the Sleepless Man to back up or contradict the story I had given. Since I already knew the intelligence he would receive – that I was sister to a spy – I knew also that I must be gone before the Sleepless Man returned.

Silvan had stopped me riding out with the others to paste daybills. This I could understand. He would fear I might use such a trip to pass secrets to an accomplice. He had put me in the wagon of the fortune-teller. Another well-reasoned choice. But now, to keep me from the show itself, this seemed strange.

Whilst so many of the troupe performed within the tent, what mischief might I make outside it? Better, surely, to keep me in the audience, or have me help the performers to costume up backstage. Unless something in the show was being kept from me.

I sat on a box on the other side of the fire from the lad who watched the horses. He stole glances at me from time to time, when he thought I was looking the other way. Shyness seemed to be preventing him from speaking.

"How long have you been with Timpson's men?" I asked.

"Hmm." He shook his head and shrugged.

"Your mother and father are showmen also?"

"No."

"You ran away, then, to join the circus."

Instead of answering, he got up and scuffed away into the shadows, returning a moment later dragging a log behind him. This he placed on the ground, one end on the bed of glowing embers. I saw now from the stubs of other logs around the fire that each must have started as long as this one and been pushed inwards inch by inch as the flames consumed them. In the Circus of Mysteries we had cut our logs to length. Seeing the simplicity of this arrangement, I wondered why we had made such trouble for ourselves.

"You could go and watch the show," I suggested.

"Seen it."

"I'm sorry, but no one has told me your name."

"I'm Tinker," he said. For a moment his eyes met mine, then he was looking down again with focussed attention on a small hole in the knee of his canvas trousers.

"Tinker is a good name. How old are you?"

He shrugged.

"Do you know your birthday?"

He shook his head.

"You must have a birthday. Else when would people give you presents?"

A muffled drum started to beat out a slow march in the distance. We both turned to look in the direction of the big top. The clapping of the audience had joined in, keeping time as the drummer increased the pace, building until it formed a continuous wall of noise and the audience began to cheer. Suddenly the drum stopped. A flash of intense light shone momentarily through the canvas followed by the percussive boom of a gunpowder charge. The show had begun.

I let half an hour pass before making my move. The sounds of the show had built and subsided three times. Three different acts, the crescendo of each somewhat louder than the last.

From facing the fire, my cheeks felt hot and my back cold. I stood stiffly, as if unused to such rough living. "I need to freshen myself," I said.

Tinker squirmed in embarrassment and seemed incapable of objecting when I walked off. The field felt eerily still. The beast wagons lay empty, the cage doors open. Even with the Sleepless Man absent and the troupe busy, I chose a cautious detour, picking my way along the hedge that bounded the field, keeping to the deep shadow until I stood not ten paces from Tania's wagon. Here I waited and watched until I was certain I was alone.

With my things lying before me on the blanket roll, I unsheathed a small knife and cut through a run of tacked stitches in the lining of the coat. Opening a gap just wide enough to slip my slim fingers through, I extracted three flat, wooden pots, two of pigment and one of adhesive.

Working quickly now, trying to ignore the heavy pumping of my heart, I began to transform my face, first giving it a more weather beaten pallor, then darkening my chin and upper lip.

Feeling inside the lining once more, I extracted the hair which, when applied over those darkened areas, so changed the shape and appearance of my face. Releasing two fastenings inside the back of the coat, I pulled out the tucks of cloth that had held it in a tailored, feminine line. Thus altered it hung straight from my shoulders. The false trouser legs had been concealed in the coat sleeves. My black purse I twisted inside out and then around, releasing the sprung wire that popped it into the shape of a top hat.

The final change, the most profound and vital, was not one of dress or makeup, but of the mind. Thus when I emerged from the wagon, it was to jump two footed from the steps onto the grass, and set off towards the big top in a rolling stride.

CHAPTER 19

*The hand is seldom quicker than the eye. Therefore,
strive to make it quicker than the mind.*

THE BULLET-CATCHER'S HANDBOOK

It was as a young gentleman of Lincolnshire that
I stepped through the entrance of the big top and
dropped a silver fivep'ny into Lara's outstretched hand.
Such was the flirtatiousness of her smile that I knew
my disguise held good. She put a finger to her lips, then
flourished an arm, ushering me towards the empty
benches at the rear.

The smell hit me first – body odour and horses and
the sweet-sulphurous mix of tobacco and gunpowder
smoke, a cloud of which hung under the green and
white stripes of the canvas top. Many of the jossers in
the middle row were on their feet. With flat shoes, the
only way for me to get a clear view was to stand on the
rear-most bench.

There, at the very centre, the very focus of every
eye, stood Silvan, feet planted like a gladiator, arms
spread, whip in one hand, a sword in the other. The

extraordinary height of his top hat might have seemed ridiculous. But in this setting it suited him as a crown suits a king. He turned as he spoke, his gaze shining out like a lighthouse. For a moment, I felt him look directly at me and had to resist the impulse to step down out of view.

"...nor from the dark artisans of the great Congo forest. Ladies and gentlemen, honoured guests, the conspicuous, the miraculous wonder you are about to witness, was smuggled by the great Harry Timpson from the ice-capped roof of the world itself, from the arcane workshops of the great monastery of Lassa in the far extremities of the orient.

"Pursued by warrior priests, he scaled a mountainous glacier to carry the secrets of this machine to you. Such was the cold of that place that frostbite took three of his toes. He endured this danger; he endured this pain and loss of limb, to reveal to the world that a mechanism of brass and iron can be possessed of intellect. I present, the incredible Thinking Loom of Lassa."

The drum rolled and from behind the partition emerged Sal, carrying a carved box, perhaps two foot along each side. The wood had been inlaid with an intricate latticework of polished metal that reflected the torchlight. As he placed it in the centre of the ring, every member of the audience seemed to be leaning forward. Sal lifted the top of the box, which swung open on a hinge, revealing a mass of cogs and springs so fine and dense that it was impossible to see into its depths.

Fully open, the lid lay horizontal, revealing a chessboard on what had been the underside. Onto this, Sal placed counters, arranged as for a game of drafts.

I will confess that I can pierce the secrets of a magic show nine times out of ten. If not the trick itself, then the general manner in which it has been performed – whether by sleight of hand or card force or illusion or simple logic. But as I watched Sal wind up the machine and volunteers come forward to challenge it to the game, I could see no trickery.

Wagers were placed. Several in the audience put money on the volunteers to win. Some backed the machine. Small bets of a few coins only. But enough to have the crowd whipped up into a fury of excitement as the game commenced.

The volunteers debated their moves, sliding the white counters with their own hands. Sal never touched the machine. Its choices were signalled by ivory buttons that rose from squares on the board, showing which of the black pieces were to be moved and to where. These instructions were also executed by the volunteers.

The machine won. The crowd erupted into cheers and boos, depending on which way they had placed their bets. As the wagers were being settled, Sal picked up the box from the floor. Had he lifted it at another time, I would not have watched his movement so carefully. But the outburst of sound and noise and emotion was too perfect a misdirection. So it was that I saw the strain in Sal's arms, the tremor of his muscles as he pretended to lift the Thinking Loom with ease. And I saw also that the box was larger than I had at first assumed, carried by one who was almost a giant.

There would not have been space inside the Thinking Loom for a full grown adult to hide. Space enough for a child though. Or a dwarf.

Next came the Dutchman with the lions, a display that led directly into the acrobatics, the climax of which involved Sal lying on his back and juggling three knives and a cleaver in the air above his body. Through this cascade of sharp metal the acrobats dived in continuous stream, until Fabulo ran on from backstage and tried to join them, falling over in the attempt, prompting hilarity and whoops of derision from the audience.

At last the dwarf had his way, tripping the next acrobat in line to jump and taking his place. He launched into a cartwheel and vaulted the prone giant, at which moment the audience were plunged into a silence of dread, for the cleaver spun down in its glittering arc and thudded directly into Fabulo's chest, where it stuck.

The dwarf dropped heavily on his back and lay spread-eagled. The other three knives thudded into the earth around Sal's head. A woman on the front row of benches screamed. But Sal, already getting to his feet, raised his hands to silence the audience. With great solemnity, he picked Fabulo from the ground and stood him on his feet. Somehow the tiny, rigid body balanced as Sal stepped back. The audience held its collective breath. Then, with no warning, Fabulo's eyes snapped open and he set off, making a line of cartwheels around the edge of the ring, the cleaver still projecting from his chest.

The applause was explosive. When Sal and Fabulo took their bow, the dwarf unbuttoned his shirt and removed the thing that had protected him. Until then, I had felt confident in my understanding of the trick. But when he held it up I saw that his armour consisted of a piece of wood cut to the shape of a heart, in total no bigger than a clenched fist. The remainder of his chest appeared unprotected.

With the show an hour old already there had been no sight of the man whose name it bore. I had resigned myself to disappointment, believing that Timpson's performing days must have passed. But then the drum roll began again, the audience clapped in time, and Silvan planted his feet in the centre of the ring.

"Ladies and gentlemen. For your education and entertainment we have presented some trifling amusements and lesser wonders. But now is the moment you have longed for. It is my honour and pride to introduce the man who you have come to see, whose fame now spans the world, who has seen with his own eyes the wonders of both poles and of the far orient. The man who has dedicated his life to gathering the mystic secrets of arcane sciences. Honoured with a doctorate from the great Peking University of China and a second from the University of Tromso in the icy northlands. And now come to you on his very final tour of the Anglo-Scottish Republic to reveal and demonstrate the ultimate and most hidden science of alchemy. I ask you not to applaud, but to pay your respect through silence in welcome to the great Harry Timpson."

There is no silence so intense as that generated by a crowd in which each member is holding his breath, and is tensed into stillness for fear of the whisper of the fabric of his clothes. Just such a silence pressed in on my ears as I strained to see over the heads of those in front of me. All were on their feet.

Harry Timpson shuffled slowly from the wings, supporting himself with the aid of two walking sticks, each step seeming an effort and made with pain. He wore a dark jacket and trousers and a top hat of modest height. When I had seen him in the wagon I had marvelled at the strange opalescence of his eyes. But now in the clear light of the circus ring, his eyes were concealed beneath a set of brass goggles, the glass of which reflected the torches like two black mirrors, each perfectly round.

Standing in the centre of the ring, he turned slowly, as if searching the audience for a certain face. Only when he had made the full circle, and it seemed the audience might burst for waiting, he began to speak. The resonant quality of his voice that I had first heard in the wagon now filled the expanse of the big top.

"The earth and the heavens and everything that resides between are animated by two contending qualities – that of inertia and that of change. Left to itself a pendulum will continue to swing, a fire will continue to burn and every elemental substance will retain its unique essence."

As Timpson spoke, Sal stepped up to him and set a lit torch to the impresario's jacket, which instantly sprung into generous flame. The great showman held his arms out to each side so that he resembled a fiery cross. A gasp breathed around the audience, above which Timpson's voice rang out more powerfully than before.

"It is the destiny of man to intervene, to bend nature to our will, to conquer and change. Thus, a pendulum may be stopped and a fire may be extinguished." So saying, he ran his hands over the material and, where they went, the flames died instantly so that between two heartbeats he stood unharmed and it seemed safe, though a thick smoke rose from his clothing to join the cloud that hung in the roof of the tent.

"Thus also," he said, "may base metal may be transformed into gold. But alchemy is not like these other changes. For in this we mutate the essence of things, which is in truth to eat of the fruit of the tree of knowledge, for which crime Adam was expelled from Paradise.

"The achievement and perfection of the alchemic process has been the goal and motivation of my life and work. It was for this that I have travelled the world, accumulating such trifling wonders and arcane knowledge as you have seen tonight, and more beyond that it is not seemly to display."

Timpson raised one of his sticks and, from behind the canvas partition, Sal and the Dutchman emerged, carrying a brazier of glowing coals, their hands protected by leather gloves. Having placed it on the ground next to Timpson, they started working the bellows that I now saw to be attached to each side.

The fire quickly began to roar. The coals turned from dull red to orange and then to white. Next came the dwarf, Fabulo, with a small brick of grey metal, which he carried around the edge of the ring, holding it out for members of the audience to touch and examine. "It's lead sure enough," whispered one, who stood close to me.

Timpson poked one of his sticks into the heart of the fire, scraping away a layer of coals, revealing the top of a crucible, the lid of which he dislodged. Audience members were being escorted to inspect the brazier now, one of them carrying the small lead brick. Sal used a pair of tongs to take it from the volunteer's hand and drop it into the crucible. All this happened in plain sight with no possibility of deception.

The ring emptied again. Fabulo was left working the bellows while Timpson addressed the audience.

"The transmutation of lead into gold cannot be accomplished through the power of heat alone. The organic and galvanic forces are required also. This..." He drew a vial of white powder from within his jacket. "...this is the extract of a lichen taken from the fiery crater of Mount Erebus on the Antarctic continent."

Unstoppering the vial he shook it high over the brazier, sprinkling out a little of the powder. For a moment it seemed that nothing had happened, then the coals began to crackle, glowing green and blue.

"The mixture now stands in flux, poised between two elemental states."

Whilst Timpson had been speaking, Sal and the Dutchman had beenhauling a second piece of equipment into position next to the brazier. A shining globe sat atop the contraption, seeming marvellously reflective, though below it were arranged but the cogs, shafts and belts of an ordinary machine. Sal began to turn a handle, setting up a low, keening sound. With him working on one side, the dwarf Fabulo pumping the bellows on the other and the fire between them now sending up green sparks, I realised that my mouth was hanging open. Closing it, I glanced around the audience and saw many similarly entranced by the unearthly scene before us. While we had been staring centre stage, Ellie had gone around extinguishing torches, plunging the rest of the space into near darkness.

A bullwhip crack snapped my attention back to the middle of the ring. The audience gasped. There, lit by the eerie glow from the brazier, I saw a new wonder. With another percussive release, a shard of lightning jumped from the globe of Sal's machine into the centre of the fire.

"Faster, my friends!" Timpson commanded.

Sal speeded up his turning of the handle and the keening sound rose to a higher pitch. Fabulo, his brow slick with sweat and reflecting the weird light, pumped faster also, sending up a plume of sparks from the coals.

Crack! Another lightning shard jumped into the fire. Timpson took a second vial of powder and shook it over the machines. The blue-green glow flared brighter, then changed to red and then to yellow. Bathed in this new light, the three men seemed themselves to be transforming into gold.

Crack! The lightning machine discharged again. A fresh cloud of sparks flared up towards the dark canopy above us.

"Now!" Timpson commanded.

Fabulo jumped from the bellows and hauled a casting block from below the brazier. Sal took a pair of tongs and lifted the crucible, the view of which had not been obscured through this whole demonstration. Everyone in the audience craned forwards as he tipped a stream of white hot metal into the block. Timpson produced a large flask of water, which he poured over the glowing metal, sending up a great rush of steam.

Lara and Ellie were ushering more volunteers into the centre of the ring. My decision was made within a fraction of a second. The ring remained dark. There would be a crowd. Ellie and Lara would not notice. I jumped down from my place on the bench, stepped forward and slipped in among the other audience members being escorted to inspect the steaming metal bar.

But the torches around the ring were being re-lit. When I finally approached the newly forged gold bar on the ground, I found myself within a circle of bright light.

"Touch it," said Ellie.

A man on the other side of me bent down and pressed his thumbnail into the metal, leaving a slight dint. "It's gold sure enough," he said. "And hot still!"

The audience started to applaud. The crucible lay on its side on the ground next to the gold bar. Gripping my coat, I lowered myself carefully, praying that no one push me. To fall would be to risk revealing my secret. Though my calves were covered by the false trouser legs, my skirt could only be hitched up so high.

Crouching, I reached my hand towards the bar as the others had done, but then shifted sideways and brought it close to the crucible. No water had been poured on that vessel, yet it was cold.

I could not tell if Timpson had seen my tell-tale move or the delicate fingers of my ungloved hand, for his dark goggles made it impossible to know in which direction he looked. Quickly standing, I joined the other audience members returning to their places. I now knew where the trick of his alchemy must lie.

That crucible was not the one that had been in the fire. Why would he go to the trouble of swapping it unless it held the secret of the trick? There would be a hole in the bottom, through which the melting lead must have run. And hollow walls, containing real gold, poured out through a small hole in the crucible's lip. Back in Timpson's windowless wagon the gold bar would doubtless be chopped small and fed back into that secret space within the crucible, ready for the next show.

I skirted the canvas wall behind the benches and was out into the clear night air before the commotion of the volunteers returning to their seats had ended. Behind me, Silvan's voice boomed out over the excited crowd.

"Ladies and gentlemen. As the final proof of our alchemic process, we will now divide the bar and offer half ounce pieces for one pound each. These you may keep in memory of this great occasion, or may sell at your leisure for their real market value, which is clearly double that amount."

His words stopped me mid-step, for they had turned my logic upside-down. If the alchemy were merely a trick, there was no way for Harry Timpson to sell the gold at such great loss.

CHAPTER 20

The alchemist, like the magician's ingénieur, works behind a veil. The name of neither isknown nor are their discoveries published abroad. Yet the product of their imagination may change the balance of the world.

THE BULLET-CATCHER'S HANDBOOK

Tinker wasn't the sort of boy to ask where I had been. But Silvan would be sure to question him.

"I'm sorry I got you into trouble," I said.

He risked a glance at me from under the mop of his hair.

"The day I first arrived," I said. "The boss dressed you down on account of not keeping watch."

"I should've seen you," he said

"It was your bad luck. I'm light-footed so you were never going to hear. No one would've. But I didn't want to bring you trouble. Here..." I tossed an apple, which he caught two-handed. The skin was wrinkled, but the flesh would still be sweet.

"For me?"

"For you."

"Where'd you get it?"

I looked left and right, as if checking that no one was within earshot. "There's a farm down the road with a shed out back and barrels of apples in straw. That's what I was doing all this time."

"For me?"

"Yes," I lied.

"You did it for me?"

"To say sorry. But you mustn't tell. I don't want to be thrown in gaol for thieving."

The lad seemed thin and hungry, so I expected him to take a bite. Instead he lovingly sniffed the skin then stuffed the apple into the folds of his over-sized coat. "No one never got me a present before."

They say it is bad luck to speak lies to an innocent. If so I was damned for sure and felt the full weight of my guilty conscience for manipulating Tinker so. The apple had come with me from Sleaford. I'd devised the story to keep him from telling Silvan about my wanderings.

A drum and trumpet under the big top were keeping up a marching beat. No act would follow Harry Timpson's display of alchemy. I imagined the troupe and the animals parading around the ring while Sal or Fabulo snipped up the gold and sold it off to eager jossers.

It was that final twist that still perplexed me. A gimmick crucible could surely create the illusion that I had seen. But no sleight of hand could make it possible for Timpson to sell gold for half its market price.

Tinker had been staring fixedly into the embers of the fire. "I'm glad you came," he said. It felt like a confession.

"Thank you."

"I ran away," he said. "Dada beat me so I ran."

"I'm sorry."

"Wasn't you what beat me."

"I mean, I'm sorry you had to run. I had to run once."

"From your dada?"

"From a cruel man who wanted to own me. He was an aristocrat and I ran from his men-at-arms. Over the fields and across the border to get away."

I looked up from the fire and was surprised to see Tinker staring at me directly, his brow creased with concentration.

"You come across the border?"

"Five years ago. Have you been to the Kingdom?"

"It's where I'm from."

"When did you join the troupe?"

Tinker bit his lip. Suddenly he was looking anywhere except into my eyes. "Mustn't speak."

"Tinker?"

"He told me not to say."

"You don't need always to do what Silvan says."

"Not Silvan."

"Harry Timpson then?"

The boy shook his head.

"Tinker, look at me. Who are you afraid of?"

"Not afraid..." he began.

But one of the horses snorted and whatever Tinker was about to say, he swallowed. I put a finger to my lips by way of warning. We both waited. A twig snapped in the dark and a moment later Silvan was stepping into the small glow of the fire. Tinker shrunk back into his coat.

"How was the show?" I asked.

"The jossers leave happy," Silvan said. "And with lighter purses than they brought. But I've interrupted. Boy?"

"Boss?"

"What were you speaking of?"

Tinker squirmed.

"He was saying I shouldn't ask so many questions. I was born with the sin of curiosity."

"I want to hear it from the boy."

Tinker nodded vigorously. "Like the lady said."

"So she's a lady now? I think not. For she cheats and lies. Did you know that boy? Cheating and lying are the habits of no lady."

"What lies have I told?"

"You don't deny cheating at cards?" Silvan asked.

"I've cheated in no fair game."

The music in the big top reached its crescendo and abruptly ended. The buzz of excited voices became suddenly louder as the audience began to emerge.

"I will find you out," Silvan said. "Boy, get the horses ready for their owners."

Tinker jumped to his feet. Silvan stared me down for a second before wheeling and marching away.

I had thought that Timpson might sell only a trifling weight of gold. Thus his financial loss could be covered by the box office. To spend in that way would spread his fame. It might be worth it. But mingling with the jossers as they drifted away, I found many eager to show off their spoils. Each clutched a piece clipped from the newly forged bar. Each piece weighing half an ounce or more.

I stood watching the crowds departing down the lane until their distant voices were swallowed by the sound of the wind moving through the bare trees. An unfamiliar doubt nagged at the back of my mind. What would it mean for the world if the trick were not a trick at all?

CHAPTER 21

Do not allow rules to become a stockade around your imagination. Magic must be beyond any law.

THE BULLET-CATCHER'S HANDBOOK

It was Sunday morning. Fabulo and three of the minor performers had ridden off to attend mass in Sleaford, a practice tolerated in the Republic. I'd have placed money on Silvan and Timpson being Rationalists. Others in the troupe would probably be Christians for weddings and funerals but good Republicans on Ned Ludd day.

By contrast, the Circus of Wonders had been home to a cartload of contrasting beliefs. Christians, Moslems and Jews mixed in with a pinch of witchcraft and a sprig of druidry. Cold rationalism might hold sway in the Republic, as it did in France. But in the Kingdom people boasted of their beliefs and would not discount the superstitions of others. It was not uncommon to see several contrasting religious symbols hanging from the same neck. Better to be safe than sorry.

The winter sun had risen and driven away the mist. In another hour the canvas might dry out. It seemed a perfect day to strike camp. The show had milked the surrounding hamlets dry. The troupe ate and drank, consuming money every day, making none. I could not understand why Timpson clung to this pitch. The turf around the gate had already turned to mud.

I wanted to question Tinker, to follow up on our interrupted conversation from the previous night. But Silvan had done a good job of keeping the boy busy on errands and out of my reach.

My morning chores being finished, I sat watching Tania, the fortune-teller. She walked the line of the hedge with a deliberate step, as if she were encircling us with a spell for protection – though what she might fear I could not guess.

I was the one in danger. For five days I had bunked in Tania's wagon. Going to sleep each night, I had gripped my knife under the blankets. And each morning I had woken with a start, fearing Silvan might be standing over me.

In the distance Tania stooped, plucking something from among the weeds and with a deft movement secreting it in the purse that hung from her belt. She had hardly broken step and was moving on again with the same, slow progress. It seemed she was not laying a charm, but gathering herbs. Either way, there was something of the pagan about her. Tania and Timpson were strange allies.

With a show supposedly built around science, the Republic was the true home of the Laboratory of Arcane Wonders. The more I learned of the temperament of Harry Timpson and his lieutenant, the stranger it seemed that they had ever chosen to cross the border into the Kingdom.

I did not attempt to move quietly as I followed the dewy footmarks Tania had left in the long grass. Thus I knew she had heard my approach long before the moment I drew level.

"You surprised me!" she said. "Creeping up like that."

"May I keep you company a while?"

We walked on, side by side. The angle of her head had changed, I noted. No longer was it cast down to the base of the hedgerow. Instead she gazed ahead and her focussed attention was replaced by something more aloof. So consumed had I been with the task of avoiding the fortune-teller lest she extract more information from me, I had not until that morning considered the possibility of information flowing the other way.

"You'd gone from the wagon before I woke," I said. "How do you move so quietly?"

She lifted her skirts a few inches and I saw that she walked barefoot. "Shock you, do I?"

"No."

"I think you lie," she said.

"A little shocked, perhaps. Are you picking herbs?"

"Something to sweeten the broth."

"And for other things? Spells perhaps?"

"What's your desire?" she asked.

"Perhaps I should wish for a man to fall in love with me."

She stopped and faced me. "What do you know of men?"

I ignored the question. "In the circus where I was born there were some who said they could mix up herbs into spells – to make hair grow back or give you luck in cards."

"Or to make a man love you. You tried these spells?"

"Once. To banish spots from my face."

We had slowed to a stop and were facing each other. She reached out and touched the smooth skin of my cheek with the back of her fingers. "It worked," she said.

"They went naturally."

"You're comfortable thinking that," she said. "But how do you know?"

"What does Harry Timpson think of your magic?"

She snorted. "If it's his heart you're after, pretend your own is made of clockwork. Or gold."

"Indeed I'm not!"

"Then who's the man you wish to lure?"

"None. No one."

Her fingers still rested on my cheek. Her eyes were pools of still water. Everything seemed to have stopped. "Liar," she whispered.

"I asked for curiosity. That's all."

"If I could magic your lover here, would you ask me to do it?"

I stepped back, breaking the contact. I opened my mouth to protest that she had me wrong. But a clatter of hooves in the lane broke into my awareness. Someone was shouting in the distance. A rider entered the field at a gallop, jumping down before the horse had fully stopped.

Suddenly the whole camp was in motion. Silvan ran across the field, leading a horse towards the wagons.

Sal had made his way into the lane, hauling a great tree branch behind him. Tania lifted her skirts and sprang off. I found myself following, not knowing why.

Tinker scurried past and I grabbed his arm before he could get away.

"What's happening?"

"They coming! They coming!"

"Who?"

"Gotta hide. Quick!"

We were running together. I still had his arm in my grip. "Who? Who is coming?"

Silvan had somehow managed to harness the horse to a wagon already. He jumped up onto the beast's back and kicked in his heels. The wagon lurched forwards, heading for the top of the field. Tinker dived under the nearest beast wagon. Knowing how filthy it was down there, I held back from following. But when the boy beckoned wildly I got down on my knees in the mud and followed, dropping flat to the ground next to him, panting for breath.

"Bad men coming," Tinker hissed.

Silvan had turned his wagon onto the lane already and was whipping the horse forward into a trot. Sal, who had headed off in the other direction, now dropped the great tree branch he had been dragging, and though I could not see where it had landed, the intention was clear enough.

The running and shouting having started to die down, I now heard a new sound, quiet at first but growing rapidly louder. Iron wheel rims and horseshoes clattering against stones. A team of four white horses came into view around the bend, pulling a substantial black coach. On seeing Sal, the coachman pulled back on the reins and grabbed for the brake lever.

I could not hear Sal's slow replies, but the coach driver's words were clearly audible.

"Get that thing out of the road... I don't care... Now! Do it now!"

Sal made a show of failing to shift the branch he had a moment before been hauling. The doors opened and the carriage swayed on its springs as four thickset fellows clambered out – rough types all of them. At first, extra hands only added to the confusion, with Sal pulling as they pushed or pushing as they pulled, until one drew a knife from his belt and the giant backed away, hands raised.

By the time the coach had reached the gate, Silvan was long gone. From my hiding place in the mud, I scanned the field, trying to make out which wagon he had taken such pains to remove. Not Timpson's own. Nor any of the sleeping wagons, all of which remained in place. Feeling Tinker flinch, I turned to see what had frightened him.

Two gentlemen in top hats had clambered from the coach and were instructing the four men who had done battle with Sal and the tree branch. One of the thickset men hurried back up the field to stand guard by the gate. Another set off in a loping run, following the perimeter hedge. The other two headed for the wagons, hollering and hammering on doors.

"Harry Timpson! Present yourself!"

"Everyone out!"

Fabulo emerged from behind the horses.

"Where's Timpson?" one of the thickset men demanded.

But instead of answering, Fabulo strode towards the coach, next to which the two men in top hats stood waiting.

"You missed the show," called the dwarf as he approached them.

I could not make out the answer but saw Fabulo folding his arms and planting his feet. "You have no right," he said, his voice loud enough to carry to all the other members of the troupe in their hiding places.

Meanwhile, an argument had broken out at the gate where Silvan was trying to enter the field on foot. One of the top hats waved a signal for the man standing guard to step aside.

Next to me, Tinker had covered his muddy face. I put my hand on his shoulder and gave it an encouraging squeeze.

Silvan had taken up position next to Fabulo, matching the dwarf's folded arm stance. The two gentlemen were arguing with them. I saw Silvan shaking his head emphatically. Tinker leaned in closer to me.

"You're not doing that!" announced Fabulo.

When it happened, it was so quick that to blink would have been to miss it. The man in the top hat who had been facing us pulled a sword from inside his cane and flicked the point down towards Fabulo. The dwarf jumped back, stung, clutching his upper chest. He twisted as he fell to the ground.

Silvan leapt forwards, knife drawn, but the man with the sword stood over the prostrate Fabulo and could have finished him in one movement. Silvan dropped his knife, which landed point first in the turf and was then kicked away.

Tinker was crying silently. I could feel the shudder of his sobs.

The man with the sword put his foot on Fabulo's chest. "Tell them!" he shouted.

Spitting fury, Silvan turned and called. "Everyone come out." And then, after a moment of silence: "Come out now!"

People began to emerge from their hiding places in ones and twos, gathering behind Silvan. The swordsman lifted his boot, allowing Fabulo to roll free. Blood had spread across the dwarf's white shirt, staining a circle the size of a saucer. Yet he moved freely enough and I suspected it was his pride that had taken the worst of the hit.

The other top hat – the one without the sword – had arranged the members of the troupe into a rough line, and seemed to be questioning each in turn. There had been a paper in his hand and though he was now mostly hidden from my view, I guessed he was compiling some kind of register.

"Any more?" asked the one with the sword. "You bring down trouble on yourself if we find you later."

"Come," I whispered to Tinker.

He shook his head, his eyes screwed tightly closed.

But the man with the sword had not finished. "And you'll bring down trouble on your friends also."

"Come," I said again, leading the boy by the wrist out from under the wagon, taking up a position behind the end of the line with Sal's giant frame in front of us. I had yet to see the face of the man compiling the list, but now I was close enough to hear him speak.

"Name?" he demanded.

"Ellie Samuelson."

"Your work?"

"Usherette and cashier."

"Name?"

"Lara Samuelson."

"Work?"

"Same as Ellie."

Tinker had turned to stare at me. He must have been able to feel the sudden tension in my grip as I listened to the voice. I glanced behind me, looking for a way to run. But one of the thickset men stood near the rear hedge.

"Name."

"Vincent Salieri."

"Your job?"

"Entertainer."

"You're all entertainers."

"I throw knives." These words Sal hissed through his teeth.

"And you behind?"

The man's arm reached between Sal and Lara, making them stand apart so that he could see us. His deep voice and American accent had been unmistakable. But it was only now that I was able to see John Farthing's face.

CHAPTER 22

You may devise a switch, a gimmick tamping rod, a cunning barrel breach or any other plan. But also devise the means to double check before the gun is pointed at your head.

THE BULLET-CATCHER'S HANDBOOK

John Farthing opened his mouth and then closed it again. He glanced over his shoulder to where the other agent was instructing the men, sending them off to search the wagons.

"You boy," he said, pointing at Tinker with his pencil. "Name?"

"Sam," said Tinker.

"Family name?"

"Smith."

"Sam Smith," said Farthing, adding the name to the paper in his hand. "What's your job?"

"Boy," said Tinker.

Farthing echoed the word as he wrote it.

I braced myself. Silvan would shortly have all the excuses he needed to come at me, knife drawn, something he had clearly wanted to do since I arrived. My best hope was that Farthing would arrest me and that I would be bundled away in his carriage. As for those members of the troupe whose trust I had gradually won, I could not bear the thought of the betrayal they would feel on learning that I was a spy, or at least the sister to one.

"And finally..." said Farthing, turning to me. "Name?"

"Elizabeth."

"Family name?"

"Barnabus." Anger sounded in the pitch of my voice. That he should toy with me in this way.

Braced for his sarcastic response, I watched as he wrote on the sheet of paper. Yet when he had finished and straightened himself once more, he held the sheet turned in my direction and I saw that where my name should have been, at the bottom of the list, he had written instead "Elizabeth Brown". Having held it still for just long enough for me to take in the words, he stepped back to his colleague.

Tinker snuffled as he wiped his nose on the sleeve of his coat. Sal turned and placed his huge hand on my shoulder. The gesture was at once protective and accepting. It seemed the shared ordeal had ushered me across an invisible barrier. I stood now on his side, part of the troupe. Part of a family set square against any prejudice or injustice the world might throw against us.

"We've had this before," he whispered. "We get through."

At last they permitted Tania to go and forage for herbs with which to dress Fabulo's wound. The Patent

Office men were still searching the wagons, hauling out boxes of belongings, emptying bags of clothes onto the wet grass, treading clean linen underfoot.

The dwarf's wound proved long but not deep. Tania pressed sphagnum moss onto his skin, together with a twist of some pale leaves I did not recognise. Having bound it in place with a strip of cloth around the barrel of Fabulo's chest, she pronounced herself satisfied.

"A clean cut," she said. "It won't fester."

Of all the blades Sal must have thrown at the dwarf during their act, the first scar would come from the sword of a Patent Office agent. Lara and Ellie fussed over him, bringing a flagon of red wine to ease the discomfort. He grumbled and frowned, but I suspected he might not be so unpleased with the way his part in the affair had resolved.

The Patent Office man went into Tania's wagon and began throwing my belongings out onto the mud along with everyone else's. I watched as he stood on the steps delving into the pockets of my coat. But he did not probe the lining with his fingers, so its secrets remained undiscovered and I began to breathe again.

The final wagon to be searched was Timpson's, wherein I assumed the old impresario to be waiting. John Farthing led the men inside, closing the door behind them. The wagon shifted on its springs as they moved within. No clothes or equipment were ejected. And when they emerged some thirty minutes later, I saw them shake their heads in disappointment.

"We'll start at the bottom of the list and work our way back up," said Farthing, pointing in my direction. "Bring the woman and the boy."

So it was that I found myself sitting in the gloom of the large carriage, its blinds closed. Tinker clung to my arm, more frightened than I had seen him before.

"Don't be scared," I said, though that was exactly the emotion pumping through my veins. "They won't hurt you."

"They'll take me back," he sobbed.

"They're after bigger fish than you, Tinker."

"But..."

"Hush now."

I had no timepiece, so could not say how long they had already kept us stewing there. With each minute that passed my confusion changed more into anxiety. Sure enough, Farthing had recorded my name as Brown, not Barnabus. He had held the paper so that I could see it, though whether that had been deliberate or merely chance, I could not say.

Explanations tumbled in my mind, each more extravagant than the last. He wished to hide my identity from the other agent. He wished to accuse me of giving a false name and on that pretext arrest me. He wished to dispose of me and leave no paper record. I would be murdered without witness, my body disposed of in an unmarked grave.

Tinker's presence in the carriage was another question. Whereas I had given my true name and a false one had been written, the boy seemed to have given a false name which had been recorded faithfully. Perhaps they expected us to give each other away.

"Tinker," I whispered. "I may need to tell these men some... things. To get us out of here."

"What things?"

"That doesn't matter. But Silvan mustn't know what I say. Nor Fabulo. Not even Mr Timpson himself."

"Don't understand."

"I will say anything to keep us safe."

"They'll take me." He blurted the words.

"No."

"They'll take me back!"

"Back where, Tinker?"

"Bletchley."

The boy's words hit me like a slap across the face. In that moment, all the elements of my confusion seemed to crystallize. I gripped Tinker's shoulders and knelt in front of him so our faces were only inches apart. "You know the Duke and Duchess of Bletchley? Is this what you couldn't tell me the other night?"

He squirmed, trying to look anywhere but into my eyes. "Mustn't say!"

"Who are you trying to protect?"

He started shaking his head from side to side.

"If you're trying to help the Duchess's brother, then tell me now."

"Can't."

"I want to help him. That's my purpose. My one mission. But I can't help unless you first tell me what you know."

When the glass marble is pushed down into a bottle of soda water, the liquid within will sometimes erupt with great force. So it was with this taciturn boy. It seemed that all the words he had held back from saying in the week I had known him were ready to gush out.

"Timpson tried to take the machine," he said. "They fought terrible. So he ran. Took the machine with him. Made me promise not to tell."

"A machine? Does it belong to the Duchess's brother? Is it a gun? A weapon of some kind? Speak quickly."

"It's a box like this..." He gestured, holding his hands apart in front of him to the width of perhaps a foot and a half.

"But what does it do?"

"It draws light in the air. Easy as drawing a line in the dust with a stick."

There were voices outside the carriage now, Farthing and the other agent, growing louder as they approached. So intent was Tinker on telling the story that I doubt he heard.

"It drew a great line in the sky. That's when they saw it and came for him and we ran to Timpson for help and to hide. But when Timpson and him have their fight, he offs without me."

The carriage lurched on its springs. I leapt back into my place. The door swung open, revealing the two agents who stood silhouetted against the low winter sunlight. Tinker shrank back into his oversized coat and his mouth shut tighter than an oyster.

CHAPTER 23

Consuming fascination and fastidious revulsion are but the same emotion travelling under different guise. By their aid will the benches of your theatre be filled. And by their whim will the mob drive you from your pitch under a rain of firebrands and rotting fruit.

THE BULLET-CATCHER'S HANDBOOK

The two agents sat on the opposite side of the large carriage from us, both still wearing their hats. Farthing's arms were crossed, his expression unreadable. The other man was examining the list of names and occupations. His swordstick leaned against the seat next to him.

"Sam is short for Samuel?" he asked, not looking up from the paper.

I gave Tinker's arm a squeeze. In all the upset, I feared he might have forgotten the name he'd chosen for himself.

"Just Sam," said Tinker.

"When did you join this..." he hesitated, as if searching for the correct designation, "...this circus?"

"Summer."

"And where are your parents?"

"Ain't got none."

"Your guardian, then?"

The boy shook his head.

"Then you should be in an orphanage. What town do you come from?"

"This is his home," I said.

"The purpose of an orphanage is to raise orphans. The purpose of a circus..." He faltered, as if voicing his thought might render the idea yet more distasteful. "I hardly need to elaborate on the implications for his moral education if he remains exposed to all of this... this burlesque cabaret."

"All this what?" I asked, indignation making me sound more waspish than was seemly, or indeed safe.

"Thievery and dwarves," he said, as if the words belonged together. As if they made his argument unanswerable.

Indignation rose in my throat like bile. When all people acted within the bounds of approved moderation, would the Patent Office then be satisfied? Would the human character one day require a patent mark and all those that fell beyond their narrow approval be stored away in warehouse prisons like so many unseemly machines?

"I would rather be born a dwarf than cut a man with a sword for no just reason!"

"Don't take that tone. I am an agent of the Patent Office!"

"I'll look after the boy," I said. "Put me down on your list as his guardian if you will."

"We're behind schedule," said John Farthing. "Orphans aren't our business today."

Both agents were staring at me now. Farthing with what could have been irritation, the other man with evident anger. I felt a blush rising in my cheeks. Looking down, I saw the mud that caked my blouse. Fouled straw from beneath the beast wagon had become caught in the fabric of my skirt. My impulsive words seemed suddenly ridiculous.

"From this offer of guardianship, I gather you regard yourself to be of good character," said Farthing's companion. His gaze returned to the list of names. "Elizabeth Brown. Your age is?"

"Twenty."

"Your home?"

"Here. This circus."

"Your real home, please?"

"This is my real home," I said.

I braced myself for Farthing's contradiction, but he remained silent. His mouth had thinned to a pale line and he seemed to be avoiding my gaze. Either he was playing a different game from his colleague, or this was a charade which they had devised together. Surely they could not believe that a game of "hard man soft man" would win my trust and that I would simply confess my secrets when Farthing next had me on my own.

"How long have you been here?"

"I was born in the circus, if that is what you mean."

From within the folds of his cloak, the agent produced what I took to be a silver and gold cigarette case. But when he snapped it open, I saw it to be the hinged frame for two miniature portraits. Each picture showed the same young man. In one he stood face forward. The other showed his profile.

"Have you seen this man?"

For a moment I stared, amazed by the object held before me. A scroll of inlaid lapis lazuli curled around the outside of the frame. Here and there diamonds caught the light. But it was the pictures of the young man that rendered me unable to speak. So fine was the brush work that it seemed more like a real person than a painting. And what a face – the chin finely sculpted yet strong, the cheekbones high, the eyes like sapphires. He was clean shaven, contrary to the prevailing fashion.

The Republic's austere guardians had power and money, no doubt. But they would never display it so conspicuously. Only an aristocrat of the Kingdom would have both the means and the appetite to flaunt their wealth with such a trinket. A lifetime of labour from a working man might not earn sufficient money to pay for such a thing. It was surely the picture of the Duchess's brother, of which she had spoken.

I knew that the Patent Office could seize property. But in taking an object of great value from a person of influence, they had demonstrated their power with shocking clarity.

The agent lowered the picture. "Well?"

I could sense Tinker's anxiety through the tightening of his grip on my arm.

"It's a pretty picture," I said. "Who did you take it from?"

"It's not your place to ask questions."

"I should like to meet him," I said. "He's a handsome man."

"We're wasting our time." The agent folded the case closed with a sharp click. "You boy," he said. "Come with me."

No sooner had the carriage door closed than John Farthing was on the edge of his seat and whispering at me. "Don't you understand? I can't protect you."

"Why would you want to?"

"Keep your voice down!" he hissed. "You're on the watch list. You'll be taken if your identity's discovered. Tell me what you know and I'll try to keep your name hidden."

"I know you're searching for the man in the picture," I said. "He must've been here, else why would you be? And coming in force tells me that he must be in possession of some device you think unseemly."

"Don't play games. Where's he gone? And where's the device?"

I folded my arms and pressed my lips together, mirroring his position of a few moments before. I should have been scared. But for some reason the only emotion I could feel was fury. This man who had pretended to be so charming on our first meeting – how could he think he would fool me again against all the evidence? Perhaps I was angry with myself for having been so completely taken in.

Seconds passed as we stared each other down. It was Farthing who broke.

"Was the warning I gave not sufficient?" he said. "I know it's for your brother that you do these things. But the Patent Office is blind to sentiment. It can't afford to see the person – only the action. I might think of you in a positive light. But the law can't know the difference between your neck and the neck of an anarchist."

"How do you think of me then?"

"That's not the point."

"Maybe I am an anarchist."

"If you knew the forces at work in the world, you'd not joke so."

"Don't mistake this for humour!"

"There are people who'd have the Gas-Lit Empire come crashing down. If they could."

"I'm flattered you think me so dangerous."

"I don't!" He bunched his fists, as though he was the one who had the right to feel anger. "I'm trying to protect you," he said.

"Are you indeed? I'm presented with two agents, bad and good. It's the oldest trick of interrogation! You suppose me so dim-witted?"

"By all the codes of office, I should deliver you for prosecution."

"Then tell me why you haven't."

"A feeling."

"Feelings are permitted?"

He sat back and looked down at the floor of the carriage, his expression strained. "Now you make a joke of me. But there's something about you. I can't rid myself of the hope that you might be redeemed–"

"Redeemed!"

"–and that the Patent Office might benefit more by your freedom than your punishment."

"The Patent Office! You can't know how much I hate it."

"Why must you take all my attempts at generosity and throw them back in my face? I'd see you set free. But you push me. You provoke. As if you want me to be a tyrant. And the last thought on your mind as you're led to the gallows will be self-righteous conceit believing all your prejudices proved true!"

I un-gritted my teeth to speak. "I need no more proof of tyranny."

"Our only desire is the wellbeing of the common man."

"I am not a man."

"Of that," he said, "I'm well aware."

CHAPTER 24

Without story, your illusion is but trickery and hoax. With story it is transmuted into magic. That is the greatest trick of all.

THE BULLET-CATCHER'S HANDBOOK

Two hours after the men of the Patent Office had departed, Silvan drove the missing wagon back onto the field. He did not pull in the reins, but brought the horse to a halt with a word. Then he beckoned me over. I followed him around to the back of the wagon, the door of which was opened from within by Harry Timpson, his eyes hidden by the smoked glass of his goggles. He reached out a hand. "Help me," he said.

With Silvan holding his right arm and me on his left, we guided him down the steps and across the rough grass to his usual wagon. When we were inside, Timpson lowered himself onto his cot and dismissed Silvan with a wave. The door closed and I found myself alone with the great impresario.

"Why did you leave?" I asked.

"The Patent Office and I have a long history," he said. "I don't wish to unnecessarily put myself or my collection of devices in their gaze."

"Then the devices are illegal?"

"Do you know what that means – illegal? The Patent Office has built great libraries of books, the only purpose of which is to attempt to divide the seemly from the unseemly, the legal from the illegal. Two centuries of precedent. The wisdom of generations of lawyers and judges. They drew a line, but the harder they laboured to sharpen it, the wider it became. It's now a chasm into which the entire Gas-Lit Empire might fall and be lost forever. The question is not whether my machines are illegal, it's whether our glorious Patent Office is positively disposed to my case. As it happens, they are not."

My eyes had started to become accustomed to the gloom in Timpson's windowless wagon, which I now saw to be in a state of disarray. Boxes lay overturned on the work bench. Clothes had been strewn in a haphazard fashion over the floor. Even the cot mattress lay askew.

"Did they find what they were looking for?" I asked.

Timpson unbuckled and removed his goggles, revealing the milky opalescence of his irises. "The Patent Office moves in mysterious ways. I doubt even their agents understand the objective that the leviathan is bent on achieving."

"The wellbeing of the common man," I said, the slogan feeling even more jaded than usual.

Timpson pointed to a flask that lay on its side under the work bench. Once I had fetched it, he unscrewed the cap and took a long draught, swilling it around his mouth before swallowing. He coughed then, sending his shrunken frame into a series of paroxysms. When I tried to offer help he held up his hand to ward me off. At last he accepted a handkerchief from a pile on the floor, with which he dabbed under his eyes and around his mouth.

A minute passed before he had the breath and composure to speak again. "I've spent my life searching for the elixir," he said. "That substance which, when perfected, will transmute base metal into gold. You've seen my show?"

"I wasn't permitted, sir."

"And that would stop you? I recognise a kindred spirit, Elizabeth Barnabus. You're like your old man. Do you want to know why I've kept my troupe here for so long? It's dangerous, as you've witnessed. Staying still we're too easily found. And we've already emptied the purses of the locals. No more money's going to flow in."

"Then make some gold," I said.

Bending forward he selected three playing cards from a spilled deck on the floor – the queen of spades and a pair of twos. Having shown me each in turn, he placed them face down on the cot next to him, the queen in the middle. He then slid them around, middle to edge, edge to middle, back and forth, slowly enough to follow. Though old, his fingers were still dextrous.

"Now," he said. "Where's the queen?"

Knowing what to look for, I had seen the trick. But not wishing to reveal my knowledge, I placed my finger on the centre card, the one that should have been the queen but for his sleight of hand.

He turned the card over, revealing the queen of spades, which absolutely should not have been there, for he had switched it. I had seen him do it.

"You honour me," Timpson said.

"How so?"

"In the *Bullet-Catcher's Handbook* it's written that the great illusion is the one the audience doesn't see. But greater than that is one that makes a fool of another illusionist."

"But I chose correct."

"Then why the widening of your eyes as you saw the card? Did you think it was only Tania who could read minds from faces?"

"I did see a sleight," I admitted. "Or thought I did."

"Good. We shall have the truth from each other. And you've seen also the secret of my alchemy?"

"I thought I had. The crucible is the gimmick. Gold is hidden in its walls. The lead runs out through a hole in the base. But then I saw you sell the gold for half its value. Do you take the loss for fame alone?"

Timpson smiled. "You honour me again. But that secret must remain with me."

He paused to take another sip from the flask. This time he did not cough. "How old am I do you suppose?"

"My father met you. That must have been before I was born."

"Long before," Timpson said. "I was a grey hair even then. And him just starting out. He wanted a place in my troupe, did you know that?"

"He never said."

"I turned him down. He would have been ashamed to admit it."

"He wasn't good enough?"

"Too good. A man like that needs a troupeof his own. He'd never have stayed."

Timpson fell silent. The act of talking seemed to have tired him. I waited, thinking about my father, trying to imagine him as a precocious young conjuror of my own age perhaps. If I had been born male, everything would have happened differently. The Duke of Northampton would never have moved against my family. My father would still be alive and I would be the apprentice ringmaster in the Circus of Mysteries as it meandered through the lanes of the Kingdom.

Timpson screwed the top on the flask he had been sipping from. "I once believed that the elixir, when found, would lead to the prolongation of human life," he said. "Perhaps indefinitely. But every year that passes brings the truth home to me more forcefully. Death is not our enemy. It is decrepitude that we must fight."

"You're fortunate," I said.

"How so?"

"My father never achieved your age."

"But he died in full vigour. To manage the pain I must take laudanum. But that fogs my mind and puts my goals beyond reach. I choose to leave the opiates on the shelf and rely on weaker tonics. I'll not live much longer. But I'd have immortality for my name at least. And that, the elixir may still offer."

"Then you do give your gold away for fame."

"I seek the end of illusion. The elixir is close to me now. I'll pay any price to possess it. Do you understand that? Any price. The pieces are in place. I wait for the other side to make its move. I've kept the troupe here in this field so that those who've been following may find us. And I believe you, Miss Barnabus, to be one of those people. Thus I've suffered you to remain while I discover whether you're a pawn or a queen. Perhaps you're an agent of the Patent Office."

"Never that!"

His opal eyes held me for a moment. "You'll be confined until such time as your role is proved. Then we'll decide what to do with you."

I backed away, treading clothing underfoot. He reached for the smoked glass goggles, placing them over his eyes as I opened the door. I turned, ready to sprint for the lane. But Silvan was waiting for me, one hand resting on the hilt of his knife. Sal stood beside him, a full foot taller, the small bundle of my clothes and possessions clutched to his chest and an expression of infinite sadness on his face.

When bargaining with Silvan to join the troupe, I had suggested the beast wagon as a place to sleep. I could not have guessed that within a week I would find myself locked there in the cage opposite the two lions.

I was given a bale of fresh straw, half a loaf of dark bread, a hunk of salty ham and a wine bottle filled with water. Then the gate was closed and the wooden flats to either side were raised, hiding me from casual view. No sooner had they left than I was busy with the work of escape. Reaching my arm through the bars I stretched out towards the vertical rod that would, if raised, unlock the gate. My fingers groped air, inches short of their goal.

Having tried until my shoulder was sore, I gave up

and settled down for the night, wrapping all my clothes around me and burying myself in straw. There I lay, listening to the breathing of the lions in their cage and trying to fall asleep. But each time I drifted off, the cold crept into my body, waking me again. I clenched and relaxed my hands and scrunched my toes in my boots until blood and feeling returned. In my few moments of sleep, dreams came rushing in – Fabulo swearing at me, Silvan gripping a knife, Timpson removing his goggles to reveal holes where his eyes should have been.

When grey lines marked out the cracks between boards and side panels, I knew that dawn had started to spread from the east.

The ham they had given me seemed all salt and the bread was already going stale. But the cold had built a hunger in me and I devoured my meal as would any wild beast. Then I sat with my back to the end boards looking down the length of the wagon. From my confinement, I stared beyond the bars to the narrow space between the cages, then through more bars to the cage where the lions lay together.

I was to have swept the beast wagons clean the day before. But the visitation of the Patent Office had upturned our routine. The soiled straw stank of ammonia despite the cold.

A long crack ran between the side panels on the right-hand side of the wagon. Peering through it I could see the field. At first everything seemed painted in shades of grey. But as the light grew I began to make out colours – the reds and blues of the nearest wagon, the green stripes of the big top.

• • •

I must have drifted into another light sleep, because I was suddenly aware of my head falling forwards. I jerked it back upright. From within my dream I had heard a sound. I blinked rapidly, trying to sharpen my focus. Both lions were standing. One paced up and down the pitifully small cage.

The noise came again. A gentle scratching against the side of the wagon nearest the hedge. Suddenly a wooden panel began to swing down. There was a deep, rumbling growl from one of the lions and light streamed in. Before I could make out clearly what had happened, a figure had sprung into the space between the cages and the side panel was closing once more.

"Tinker!"

"Keep hush, miss. I'm not to be here." He reached into his long coat and pulled out a wrinkled apple, which he passed through the bars and placed in my hand. "Yours," he whispered.

Examining it, I realised it was the same apple I had given to him the night we were supposed to be keeping watch on the horses. "You should have eaten it."

"No one gave me a present before."

I tried to pass it back to him but he shook his head. "Eat." And such was the intensity of his instruction that I took a bite. The flesh was soft, the juice sweet.

"What am I to do, Tinker?"

"You're to stay locked and hidden. No one's to talk to you."

"But here you are."

"They'd whip me if they found me."

"Here..." I passed the apple back to him through the bars. "If we're both in trouble we should both eat."

This time he accepted it. After a moment's hesitation, he took a small bite from the other side of the apple. It wasn't a mingling of blood exactly, but there was something in this small intimacy of sharing that suggested a binding ritual.

In the other cage, the lions lay down once more. From somewhere out in the field came the sound of chopping wood.

"I was born in a travelling show," I said. "When my mother knew it was time, she told my father and he ordered all the wagons to stop. I came into this world at the side of a lane between a field and a copse of trees. I know it was the middle of the night, but I don't know where exactly."

"I was born in the stable," said Tinker.

Each time this boy had confided in me, it had been through his own volition, not my probing. So I held my tongue and let the moment stretch until it pressed against us. I took the apple back through the bars and bit again.

"They had a big house," said Tinker. "Big..." He stretched his arms wide to add emphasis. "Hundred rooms. More than that. Servants like an army."

"The Duke of Bletchley?"

He nodded.

"The Duke sent your mother to the stable? That's not nice."

"Nah, the stable was grand. And he fed us good."

"And the Duchess's brother?"

Tinkers face lit up into a smile. "Mr Orville. He's kind, like you. He sees Dada beat me, so he gets me out from the stable and has me run jobs for him in the workshop with all the machines. Fetch tools. Bring food. Gets me to turn the handles and make the wheels spin."

"Is that why you're afraid of going back – because your dada beat you?"

Tinker pressed his mouth tight closed, the pain of memories written across his face.

"I know someone who dearly loves Mr Orville," I said. "She wants to find him again. From the things you say about him, I can understand why he earned that love. He's kind and clever too. A man who can understand the ways of machines and devices. That's a marvellous thing. Did he understand them all?"

"No," said Tinker, cautiously. "Too many for that. And no saying what goes with what. Not even Zoran knows all of 'em."

"Zoran?" The name seemed familiar to me, though I could not place it.

Tinker nodded, enthusiasm beginning to animate him once more. It seemed that so long as we stayed on happy memories, he would continue to talk.

"Was Mr Zoran also kind?"

"He said not to call 'im mister. Just Zoran. He's old. Skin wrinkled like that apple. Hands didn't work proper. Like the bones went all the wrong places. And he's got fingers missing." Tinker illustrated by holding up his own right hand with the two middle fingers bent down. "Couldn't hold tools no more. But Mr Orville does that for him. One talks, the other does. They opens it up and looks inside. And they talks and pokes at it and talks more. Can't figure 'em all though. Never. Coz there's hundreds. And the papers don't say all the secrets. Never write your secrets down, that's what Zoran says."

I passed the apple back through the bars and placed it in his hand. He raised it reverently and took another bite, keeping clear of the side from which I had been eating.

My being locked behind bars seemed to be making it easier for him to tell his story. Perhaps he perceived it to have levelled my status with his. Or perhaps in my misfortune he saw something of his own history. Even now, I knew he would not elaborate the story of his father's brutality. And I guessed that would make the circumstances of their departure from Buckinghamshire a forbidden subject also.

"Can you tell me of the machine, Tinker? How did it draw light in the air?"

He resolutely shook his head, but the anxiety did not return to his face.

"Did Mr Orville instruct you to keep it secret?"

"Yes."

"Then I'll ask nothing more about it. Indeed, I don't wish to know, unless by knowing I can better help Mr Orville find the one who loves him. Did Zoran understand the machine?"

"No." The boy took another bite of the apple, content, it seemed, for me to pursue this line of questions.

"Yet, they made it draw light in the air?"

"Yup."

"Was that not its function – to draw?"

"Mr Orville didn't know for sure. Nor Zoran."

"Zoran...?" I sounded the name slowly, letting it roll over my tongue. It felt so familiar. "Zoran. Not Mr Zoran." The memory came back to me all in a rush. My father telling me stories of other magic shows he had seen in his childhood, other illusionists. There had been a bullet catching act. The Great Zoran.

What better helper could Mr Orville have employed to understand the arcane machines in the Duke's workshop? Cryptic devices and hidden mechanisms are the very crux of the bullet-catcher's art. Suddenly the pieces of the puzzle had started to interlock.

"Did they need help in understanding the machine?"

"Yes."

"Did Zoran send a message to someone, telling of the machine and asking for that help?"

Tinker nodded.

"Harry Timpson pitched the big top near the Duke's estate. But it was no surprise to Mr Orville. They'd invited him."

I did not need to wait for Tinker's confirmation. With each new thought the truth became more obvious. What could have persuaded Timpson to take the Laboratory of Arcane Wonders south across the border into the Kingdom for the first and final time? Only his life's goal.

"Tinker? Does the machine make gold?"

Tinker placed his finger across his lips, signalling that I should speak no more. It was the only indication he gave of the truth of my words. But it was enough.

With the Patent Office hard on his heels, Mr Orville had fled, taking the machine with him. First to the Laboratory of Arcane Wonders. What a sanctuary that must have seemed. And how eagerly must Harry Timpson have welcomed him. Then quickly they crossed back across the border, moving on every few days, hard to follow even should the Patent Office realise where he had run to.

And the loyal boy, Tinker, had come with them.

Did Mr Orville willingly share his knowledge of the machine? What other choice could he have? Until he learned to harness its power, it was just a box that drew light in the air. How would they work? I pictured Orville and Timpson experimenting together in the dark confines of the windowless wagon. It seemed impossible that light could change lead into gold. But whatever they had discovered together had convinced Timpson he was close to his heart's desire. His name would be immortal.

When did Orville see that glint in the great impresario's opalescent eyes and understand that Harry Timpson would share top billing with no other man? And then the fight. Orville saying some final goodbye to the loyal boy who had followed him, then running in the night, encumbered by his alchemic device.

Tinker passed the apple back through the bars and placed it in my hand. I took another small bite. Sweet juice flowed around my tongue as I chewed. "Where did he go?"

"Mustn't say."

"If I'm to help, I need to know."

So hard did Tinker press his lips together that they seemed to disappear.

"Please," I said.

Now he placed both hands over his mouth and shook his head.

Somewhere in the distance a horse's hooves slowed from a canter to a stop. Sal's voice called out a greeting. I peered through the crack in the side panels and felt my heart constrict within my chest. The tall grey mare stood near the big top, steam rising from her into the cold morning air. And holding the reins was the Sleepless Man.

CHAPTER 25

*To perform the impossible is to show that you have
mastered trickery. But to perform the improbable is to
leave a suspicion of genius.*

THE BULLET-CATCHER'S HANDBOOK

On seeing the Sleepless Man, Tinker's face flared into
an expression of alarm. He dropped the side panel next
to the hedge and slipped out, closing it silently behind
him. In a second he had disappeared from the narrow
crack of my vision.

The Sleepless Man hurried across the field in the
direction of Timpson's wagon, leaning into his stride
as one bent on a single purpose. Silvan met him
halfway. The two men put their heads close. Others
were watching at a distance, tension written into each
frozen posture.

Silvan called to Sal, pointing in my direction. The
giant shook his head in distress, but set out towards me
nonetheless. Both lions were on their feet and pacing.
The wagon seemed to resonate to their rumbling
growls. For a moment, Sal's frame blocked out my view

of the field. Then the side panels were swinging down. He gripped and lifted the iron rod, unlocking the cage. The gate swung open with a metallic clang.

"Bring your bag," he said.

"Where are you taking me?"

He shook his head. "I trusted you."

I could think of no possible reply.

My first destination was the wagon Timpson had hidden in during the visitation of the Patent Office. Though I had previously paid it no attention, I saw now that thick staves of wood reinforced the door and that its lock was more substantial than any other I had seen in the travelling show. The key appeared large, even in Sal's huge hand.

He pushed me inside. "Wait here," he said, not a trace of irony in his voice as he closed the door. I heard the lock click behind me.

Unlike Timpson's wagon, this one allowed in light through a small window high on the right-hand side. Netting hung across the glass. And inside that were two metal bars, each as thick as my thumb. I had assumed that Timpson would keep his valuables close. In a secret compartment of his over-sized wagon. It seemed that I had been wrong.

There were no chairs or furnishings here. Wood and metal boxes lined the walls, some piled three deep. I stepped along the narrow central aisle, brushing my fingertips over padlocks, metal banding, leather straps, handles and wooden panels worn down in places like the stone steps of an ancient house. Smells of camphor and wood polish pervaded.

Chinks of light in the floor revealed six small holes, each the size of a penny. I had seen similar things before – anchor points for a belly box suspended between the axles of a wagon. On hands and knees, I placed my eye close to one of the holes and found myself looking at the grass directly below. If a box had once been suspended there, it had since been removed. Feeling through the hole with a finger, I discovered the floor planking had been laid two layers thick.

Standing again, I turned my attention to the boxes, a few of which were without locks. Opening the largest of these, I found the furnace and bellows from the alchemic display, packed securely with straw. The tongs stood vertically in a corner of the box. Of the crucible there was no sign.

It was once said of a famous bullet-catcher, who had been convicted of a capital crime, that in the moments before his execution he pondered the mechanism of the guillotine, not to find a means of escape, but rather to devise a grand illusion. Could a man be so detached with his head resting on the block?

Feeling now death's sharp scythe close behind my own neck, the bullet-catcher's story seemed less fanciful. In the arrangement of props, I found myself taking some small degree of satisfaction. Had the crucible not held the secret of the trick, it would have been packed in the unlocked box with the other things.

This brief respite from fear ended with the sound of hoof-falls, the jangle of a harness and the shifting of the wagon on its springs. I fell backwards as we began to move. Scrambling to my feet, I gripped the window bars to steady myself and pulled the netting aside. Sal and Fabulo stood watching as we bumped our way over the uneven field and onto the lane.

The facts of my predicament suggested no good outcome. But it was Sal's expression of sorrow that drove the knifepoint of dread fully into my chest. Always the man for the dirty job, it would be Silvan at the reins. By the time my body was found, the troupe would be long gone.

Thoughts come swiftly when death is close. I could use the tongs to break the window glass. In the quiet of the lane, the sound might attract attention. I could shift the bottom layer of boxes a few inches and hide between them and the wagon side. I could search for a weapon and defend myself. But rushing after each new idea came a dozen fatal flaws. The lane was quiet because no one was there. No one to hear. Hiding behind a box in a securely locked wagon would deceive no one. And even should I find a blade, what chance would I have against Silvan in a knife fight?

Though it seemed hopeless, I hefted the metal tongs above my shoulder and brought them crashing against the window. The glass shattered outwards. In three more strikes, I had knocked out most of the remaining shards. If Silvan had heard the noise, he had chosen to ignore it. The window would have been wide enough for me to climb through but for the bars. A contortionist might still manage it. Or a child.

I opened boxes and crates quickly after that, bracing myself against the rocking of the wagon as it trundled along the pot-holed lane. In one I found fake knives, made from wood but coated in some silvery paint. In another, a great quantity of chain and rope. A third contained metalworking tools, pincers and files, too small and delicate to make any impression on the window bars. I tried them on the padlocked boxes, but could do nothing more than scratch the metal.

The wagon swung left, throwing me to the floor again. The light through the window lessened. Trees crowded close outside.

Onwards we rolled. Slower now. Every few moments a wheel would drop into another pothole, sending me tumbling. I could not believe he intended to take me much further.

The crate of chain and rope was somehow nagging at my thoughts. Gripping the lid, I opened it once more. Part of an escape act, it seemed. Lifting out an end of chain, I let the links shift over my fingers.

The idea was not yet fully formed, but my hands were moving anyway, guiding the end of the chain down to the floor, and into one of the six bolt holes, expecting it to stick, surprised when it slid easily through. At first I fed it from the crate, arm-length at a time. It clinked softly as it went, but as the weight that had already passed through the hole increased, it started to drag behind the wagon, and I found the links twitching and jumping treacherously as they passed over my fingers.

As the strength of the pull increased, so too did the noise. Loud enough, I feared, for Silvan to hear it over the clatter of wheel rims against the stony track. To release the pressure and quieten the rattling, I hauled out great armfuls of chain from the crate and laid them on the floor. Such was the weight already trailing behind us that should it snag, the wagon would surely come to a juddering stop.

Then, quite suddenly it seemed, the pile of chain was gone, the last links flicking through like the tail of a snake escaping into a crack in the ground. I looked back into the crate, which was half empty. Only rope remained, which I now removed.

In a second I had dropped my bag into the crate and clambered in after it. Reaching under my blouse, I unhooked my corset. With the restriction released, I crouched low and started folding myself into the smallest possible space, preparing to pull the rope on top of me and close the lid after that.

But the illusion was too perfect. The escape impossible.

Out I jumped, pulling myself up to the window, one hand gripping a bar, bringing my other hand down sharply on the jagged fringe of glass. I felt no pain. Only the welling of blood between my fingers. Wetting both hands, I reached through the window and smeared two prints outside, as if I had climbed through and hauled myself onto the roof.

Then I was back into the box, hidden under the rope, with the lid closed, feeling more calm than I had a right to. Feeling also the slow throb growing in my bloody hand.

CHAPTER 26

As a bullet can be removed through a barrel breach, so can one be added. Therefore, never trust anything or anyone, or even your own self when a gun is pointing at your head.

THE BULLET-CATCHER'S HANDBOOK

In the sudden dark and enclosure of my hiding place, three discomforts crowded in on me – the dizzying smell of camphor, the steadily increasing pain in my palm where the window glass had cut and the fact that every lurch of the wagon now sent the angles of my tightly folded body into hard contact with the walls of the crate.

I had embarked on my course of action without any clear view of an ending. Like a hunted animal, I had bolted into the nearest hiding place. Fear had driven me, not reason. But in the stillness after the chase, my mind continued to run.

The broken window.My bloody handprints.The locked door. The bars. The chain lying on the track behind us, waiting to be discovered should Silvan turn the wagon around and head back towards the pitch.

We lurched into another left turn. The back of my neck pressed hard on the wood panel behind. Three deep ruts bounced me against the floor. Then the wagon rolled to a stop. For a moment, the silence was abrupt and intense. Then the wagon swayed again as the driver jumped down, his boot falls just audible from where I lay.

A second silence followed, lengthening, becoming unbearable. I was acutely aware of the rapid and heavy beating of my heart. I tried to breathe deeply to calm myself, but with my knees pressed up to my chest it was impossible.

The lock clicked. The door opened. I felt the movement of the wagon as he climbed up. I could feel his footsteps through the wooden floor. A drop of sweat ran across my forehead. Silence again. My heart was beating with such frantic energy it seemed the crate must be vibrating in response.

Boxes were being shifted. He was searching. Slowly at first, but with increasing violence. The lid of the crate pulled away and light flooded in, filtering between the mass of ropes above me. A shadow passed over the box. Then with a crash that left my ears ringing, the lid slammed back down. His footsteps moved away. The wagon lurched as he jumped from it.

All this time I had believed the man to be Silvan. But now I knew it for sure. He cried out in anger and frustration, using such curses as I cannot repeat.

The swearing stopped as abruptly as it had started.

"Boy!" he shouted.

There was an answer, too distant to make out.

"Has she been found?"

This time the answer was closer. "Don't know, sir." Tinker's voice.

"Why did you follow me?"

"Wanted to see."

"Hell and damnation! Unhitch the horse. Quick now! She broke the window back on the lane. Can't have got far."

"No, sir," said Tinker.

"Stay here!"

I was out of the crate before the hoof falls had faded, jumping from the wagon in time to see Silvan spurring the horse away down the track. On seeing me, Tinker opened and closed his mouth like a beached fish. In half a minute Silvan would find the chain. It would take him perhaps fifteen seconds to understand its meaning. Then he'd be back up the lane at a gallop. I might have one minute before he came within sight of the place I was standing.

Why was there never time?

I grabbed Tinker's shoulders and looked straight into his eyes. "Tell him I jumped you from behind."

"But..."

"Tell him I ran into the woods. That way." I pointed to the right of the track.

"Yes, miss."

I pushed the boy back, lowering him to the ground. At first he struggled, then submitted as I rolled him in the mud. "I'm sorry," I said, pressing his head, so his cheek scraped across the stones. "First he won't believe you. But keep saying it."

"He'll catch you," said Tinker.

"Maybe so," I said, dropping to the ground next to the rear wheel.

From the holes in the floor, I'd known a belly box must have hung between the axles. Now, looking from the outside, I saw that the place it would have been was hidden from view by planks running the length of each side of the wagon. I rolled underneath and looked up. Sure enough, the six anchor points above me were arranged symmetrically within a discoloured rectangle – the missing box's shadow.

I could hear the returning hoofbeats. Damn but Silvan was quick. I wedged my fingers in a crack in one of the side planks. Placing first one foot and then the other against the opposite plank, I lifted myself into position, tightly braced, muscles trembling from the strain.

Silvan's horse thundered to a stop. I felt the thud of his feet landing. He stood not a pace from my head.

"She's gone that way," called Tinker.

"What happened?"

"She hit me," said the boy.

"Cretin child!"

There was a smack of flesh on flesh and Tinker stumbled back, landing heavily next to the wheel.

"Run – back to the gaff. The track through the woods. Tell the boys to ride out. Cut her off." As he spoke, Silvan was harnessing the horse to the wagon once more.

My muscles screamed at me, telling me to drop, sending lances of pain through my arms and legs. Then the wagon was moving, making a turn in the track. Tinker scrambled to get out of the way.

"Run, boy!" Silvan shouted.

My arms gave way and I dropped, but the noise of my fall was covered by the rumble of the iron wheel rims which were picking up speed. As the wagon lurched away along the track, I caught a glimpse of Silvan standing, reins in one hand, whip in the other.

Tinker scrambled to his feet.

"Go," I hissed. "And don't look back at me."

I waited until the sound of the boy crashing away through the undergrowth had faded to nothing, then emptied the contents of my bag onto the track and began to change my appearance. On a good day, I could have completed the transformation within a minute. This was not a good day. The lining of my jacket would not open cleanly and I found myself ripping the cloth rather than the stitches. I dropped the small pot of glue, contaminating it with grit and mud.

At last I held my hands out in front of me and saw that they shook. The harder I tried to steady them the stronger the tremor became. And worse, when I came to apply pigment to darken my complexion where hair would be applied, I found my cheeks wet with tears.

I began to gasp with sobs, my shoulders heaving. Yet I could feel no sadness. It was as if I was looking in on the grief of another person. Someone standing a great distance away.

"Hysteria." I spoke the word aloud, as if the naming it might help me to gain power over my condition. "Ignore it for now."

And somehow, that is what I did.

Thus, ten minutes later, the tears on my face having dried, but my eyes still feeling puffy and sore, I set off with the gait and guise of a young man. Knowing I would meet my pursuers anyhow, I chose to head back towards the Laboratory of Arcane Wonders. When our paths crossed, I hoped they would be in such hot pursuit as to speed past without a word.

As if from a distance, I observed myself striding along the centre of the track, swinging my arms, my chin raised a fraction of a degree, imitating that careless attitude which comes so easily to men. Yet I knew the disguise would not work. Not today. The sunlight shone too brightly on my face for it to withstand close inspection. Clothes which would have blended in during a nocturnal excursion in the city felt conspicuously out of place in the countryside. And my eyes, fresh from weeping, were sure to be red.

Silvan had left the chain where it lay. I walked next to it, surprised by its length, passing the end just before the track emptied onto a wider lane. I turned right, recognising a familiar copse of trees in the sculpture of the landscape ahead, knowing the field that had been my home for the last week must be close.

It was on hearing the approaching gallop of hoof falls that my strange disassociated state collapsed like a telescope. In one breath I had crashed back into myself. No longer did the dangers seem distant. The overwhelming urge to run washed through me. I must flee into the woods or back along the track the way I had come.

But it would not do. Straightening myself, I stepped to the side of the lane, making space for the approaching rider to pass. It was the Dutchman, his forked beard pressed back by the wind as he spurred his horse towards me. I forced my head up and looked him square in the face. On seeing me he slowed. The horse had not yet worked up a sweat. I raised a hand to my hat brim. He mirrored the gesture then kicked in his heels and the beast leapt forward once more, passing me in a heartbeat.

I took a deep breath to steady my nerves. The horse may not have been sweating, but I was. A drop ran from my forehead into the corner of my eye, the salt of it stinging.

Another sound was approaching – running footsteps. Lighter than a man's. I had already guessed it to be Tinker before he came into view. On seeing me, his run became a walk, his expression cautious. He began to frown as the distance between us closed. I did not slow as we passed, but he stopped, turned and fell into step beside me.

"Good day," I said, in my deepest, most masculine voice.

"Miss Elizabeth," he said, "I know it's you."

CHAPTER 27

*To separate the trick from the illusion is the very centre
of the bullet-catcher's art.*

THE BULLET-CATCHER'S HANDBOOK

Within the span of a month, two people had discovered
the secret of my double identity. First it was the Duchess
of Bletchley and now this boy – a horse minder in a
travelling show. But whereas the Duchess had caught
sight of me changing, Tinker had seen through
the disguise.

He walked with me. And when we came upon
other members of the troupe out searching, he told
them he had been paid a penny to guide this young
gentleman to the Lincoln Road. They swallowed the
story and hurried on past without a second look. It
happened twice. Each time, I felt a pang. In the few
days I had lived among them, I'd come to feel as if
I belonged. Now none of them would own me as
a friend.

When at last we reached the junction where Joe had
dropped me off, I began to breathe more easily. Tinker

watched as I reversed the transformation, shaking out my dark hair, turning the long coat inside out, removing whiskers from my face and wiping away the makeup. The top hat, he found especially fascinating, making me change it into a bag and then letting it spring back several times. Had his hands been cleaner, I would have allowed him to try it for himself.

"I won't tell," he said, unasked.

"Thank you."

"Can keep a secret."

"I know. You're a good boy, Tinker."

He squirmed in his shoes for a moment, then asked, "Why d'you want to find Mr Orville?"

"I'm searching on behalf of one who loves him. She's afraid for his life."

"Does Mr Orville love her back?"

"I..." The question had not occurred to me before. "I imagine he does."

"Then why don't he find her?"

"He's running with the machine. Running from the Patent Office."

Tinker scratched a line in the mud with the toe of his shoe, a deep frown on his young forehead. "He didn't know 'bout you, when he told me not to tell."

"No," I said.

"I suppose..."

He wavered, on the brink it seemed, ready to fall one way or the other.

"If you don't tell me where Mr Orville has gone, I'll have failed. There're no more clues to be had. I can't ever go back to Harry Timpson. He wouldn't let me escape a second time. But if you do tell me – and if I manage to find him – it'll be him that chooses the path. If he wants to run once more, I won't stop him."

"Promise?"

"I promise."

Tinker nodded solemnly. "Mr Orville crossed south," he said.

I stood frozen. "South..."

"Yes miss. London town."

At that moment I knew my quest was over. The one place I could not go was the only place where my freedom could be regained. It was an impossible paradox. For this, I had played dice with the hangmen of the Patent Office. For the dream of returning home, I'd frittered away days which could have been spent earning money for my payment on *Bessie*.

The only sensation I could feel was a yawning hollow somewhere deep within me.

"Where in London?" I asked, my voice flat.

He shrugged. "Ever been there,miss?"

"When I was a child."

"Will you take me there?"

"I can't," I said. "And even if I could, we'd never find Mr Orville among all those millions."

"Don't know where he's gone," said Tinker. "But I do know why. Said he needs to make the box work. So he's getting help from a Jew."

Tinker's words were the cruellest twist, for they made perfect sense to me. Orville must have run to Spitalfields, home to a colony of Jewish scientists and doctors. I now had all the information I needed to find him. But it could never be.

• • •

Tinker didn't want to leave me, but I sent him back with a penny clutched in his hand as proof he'd been helping a young man find his way. Then I waited, ready to jump behind the low wall at the edge of the lane should anyone approach. But no one did.

The spot proved so remote that no traffic passed in all the time I waited. It was so quiet that, when dusk eventually fell, I could hear the sound of the approaching steamcar long before it came into view. I'd had no fear that Joe would renege on the deal we'd made, to drive past that spot every evening at dusk for ten days, his heavy stick by his side in case of trouble.

I stepped out from the shadow as he drew close and was up into the back with the door closed behind me before the car had properly stopped.

"Glad to see you, miss," he said.

He spun the wheel, setting the steamcar around in a tight circle and off back the way he had come. I heard a clank and noticed for the first time a large, black blunderbuss propped next to him, which had shifted as we turned, coming to rest against the door.

"Best be prepared," he said, seeing the direction of my gaze. "Can't be too careful with circus types about."

"They're not all a bad sort," I said.

"Tell that to the constables! Been more houses burgled and more since that lot turned up than ever was before."

"Burglary?"

"A plague of it."

"And did the burglars steal jewellery?"

"With a passion, miss."

And there it was, like all illusions, trivially simple once I knew where to look. How could Timpson pretend to create gold and then afford to sell it at half its market value? Because he was merely selling back to the local population what his men had recently stolen from them. In spite of the bleak future that lay ahead of me, I found myself laughing.

CHAPTER 28

Some see only what they hope to see. Others see only what they fear. Few see that which is before their eyes.

THE BULLET-CATCHER'S HANDBOOK

Julia Swain ran the last fifty yards of the towpath and engulfed me in a fierce hug. At first she could not speak. I tried to hold her at arm's length to read her face, but she pulled me to her again, the hoops of her skirt being pushed out behind.

"Did they find you," she gasped.

"They? Who?"

"A man came looking. He... he said he was from a solicitor. A will being read... Your uncle's... And you to gain. Father only wished to help..."

I pulled away again and looked into her eyes. "You must breathe. In slowly. Out slowly. Just so."

"Father told him too much. Where you were. Your brother's work. Everything. When I told Father that you have no uncle... Oh Elizabeth, is there damage done? I fear we've been tricked. My father..."

Tears were brimming in her eyes.

"Your father is trusting. It's a virtue. And his goodness has come down to you. So please don't fret. The man who came would've spoken to many. And had the same story from others before he believed any of it."

"But what of your dear brother? I've not rested since."

"My brother is safe as I am."

"I must run to the house with your news."

"Indeed, they can wait a few minutes longer."

I had cleared the mess already, the shattered pieces of the cabin door lock, the scattered cutlery and books. I had refolded and stored away my clothes. Where the Patent Office agents had replaced everything they moved, the Sleepless Man seemed to have taken pleasure in the chaos he left in his wake as he searched my home. Yet after the ordeals of my previous week, the destruction seemed of little consequence.

I chose not to tell my student the full extent of the damage. She led a sheltered life, with a maid to cook and shop for her. I doubted she knew the cost of the Russian tea we drank together or the difficulty of obtaining it in the Republic. With what painstaking care I'd swept the scattered leaves up from the floor where the Sleepless Man had emptied them, gathering all I could salvage onto a sheet of paper before tipping it back into the caddy. Being squeamish about such things, Julia would not have understood.

The kettle boiled quickly, being already hot. Soon we were seated knee to knee at the small table. Low sunlight shone through the porthole, catching the threads of steam that rose as I poured. I breathed in the smoky aroma from the tea.

Julia's cheeks had been pale and blotchy when I met her on the towpath. Her rosy complexion was returning slowly. I regarded her over the brim of my cup. Her knowledge of crime had shifted unexpectedly from the theoretical to the practical. It was a difficult transition.

"Who was he?" she asked.

"I don't know his name, but he works for Harry Timpson."

"The showman?"

"The very same. That's where I've been all these days, working as a hired hand in the Laboratory of Arcane Wonders."

Julia's mouth dropped open. I usually took pleasure in shocking her, but this revelation was deadly serious.

"I told you before that I help my brother in his work. But my role is more than that. Were it possible for a woman to admit such a thing, then I'd say that I am myself a private intelligence gatherer. And even if I had no brother, this would be my work."

Still she did not speak.

"In holding this back, I wanted to protect you. But it seems my work has reached you anyway."

"But..."

"I hope you won't take it too badly."

"But this... I mean to say... this is most extraordinary. Most marvellous. Can you tell me more of your... investigation?" she voiced the word tentatively, as if trying it out.

"There's little more for me to do, save contact my employer and explain that the person she seeks has passed beyond my reach. I can hope she'll pay me another purse of gold for my trouble. Though she's not obliged to. Heaven knows, she has enough riches to not miss a few more coins."

"The one you seek, he's died?"

"He's crossed through a different veil. He took the road south to London."

"Then surely you must follow."

"I've told you before that I'm wanted in the Kingdom."

"No one would know you'd crossed."

I examined the pupil who had become my friend. I would have thought she spoke from naivety, but there was something in her eyes that suggested the danger had of itself excited her. I did not wish to dampen her innocent enthusiasm, yet some words of reality needed to be spoken.

"I was a child when I ran from the Kingdom, chased by men-at-arms."

"I know," she said. "Five years ago."

"Had they caught me, I would've been bound and delivered like a parcel to the man who owns the contract of my service."

"But if you crossed south today, he couldn't know it. Oh, Elizabeth, don't you see? My father must travel to London himself to plead a case before the Patent Office Court. I'd thought to travel with him. We could go together, you and I. No one would notice one more in the party. Not in those teeming streets."

She still did not understand. "What motivation could a man have, do you suppose, to bribe an agent of the Patent Office, causing my family to be fined? Also, he bought up our small debts and called them in. Thus we were bankrupt. All this he did to force my indentured servitude. Me, a fourteen year-old girl. They said I was pretty, in a puckish sort of way. What service do you think he had in mind for me?"

Understanding broke in her expression. "It was a silly fancy. I'm sorry. I was thinking selfishly."

"Yet here I am. Safe and whole," I said. "You must go with your father to London. It's a great opportunity. You'll see the International Patent Office Court. You can listen to the lawyers arguing the case."

The reaction of Julia's parents on seeing me safe was more muted but I could detect relief in their faces, particularly Mr Swain.

The story I related to them was less complete in detail. The Sleepless Man had an interest in a case my brother was pursuing in Lincolnshire. The investigation had not been imperilled and neither had we. I avoided all mention of my work in the Laboratory of Arcane Wonders.

When I pushed the conversation towards Mr Swain's forthcoming southward journey, everyone seemed to relax. Julia announced that she had decided to accompany him after all. There were smiles all around the drawing room.

"It will be an education," said Mr Swain.

"You will meet many people," said Mrs Swain.

"You'll bring me a present," said I.

"I'd hoped you might travel with us," said Mr Swain. "Your local knowledge would be invaluable."

"And your charming company," added his wife.

"She'd love to have come," said Julia, quickly. "But it's proved impossible."

"Wear something..." I struggled to find a word that would not seem critical of their Republican fashion sense. "Wear something brighter in colour. You'll seem less foreign that way."

Mrs Swain frowned. "We're moderate folk, Elizabeth. Modest. Bright colours don't sit comfortably with us. But perhaps if you come tomorrow, you could help my daughter choose from among her wardrobe?"

The discussion of clothes had clearly made Mr Swain uneasy. He got to his feet. "My workshop calls. Would you excuse me please?"

"Before you go, could I ask a favour?" I said.

"Anything."

"Do you have some buckets I could borrow?"

His eyebrows arched in surprise. "How many do you need?"

"How many do you have?"

CHAPTER 29

That which you perform on the stage is merely illusion.
That which occurs in the mind of your audience is pure
magic. It is the magic they will remember.

THE BULLET-CATCHER'S HANDBOOK

In the two years I had been tutoring Julia, I'd never been invited to her bedroom. Nor, for that matter, had I shown her *Bessie*'s small sleeping cabins. Yet here we were, climbing the neatly carpeted stairs of her house, the black iron stair rods shining as if freshly polished. Mrs Swain seemed to have had the maid work double time in preparation for my visit. I could smell beeswax polish from the banister rail.

"It hasn't been decorated since... well, since I was a girl," said Julia, as she stepped through the door into her room. I looked around and found myself giggling.

"Elizabeth?"

"I'm sorry. Really. It's lovely."

"Is it the dolls?" she asked.

"They're a delight. It was their... their number that surprised me."

China faces looked in on us from every side. Three on the bed. Five on the dressing table, sitting with their backs to the mirror. Six occupied the highest shelf of a dark bookcase and two rested on each side of the hearth, as if they did not wish to be far from the cheery coal fire.

"They were presents on my birthday."

"Quite a birthday!"

"Many birthdays. One doll per year." She seemed affronted.

I counted them. Eighteen. Every face wore an expression individual to itself. The hair on each was different in colour and style. Long and flowing, piled high or turban wrapped. "Do they have names?" I asked.

"They do," she said, cautiously. "But you're here to help me choose my wardrobe for the journey."

"Please tell. I must know!"

"Glenys, Ruth, Valerie, Aimee, Michelle, Sue." She moved her finger around pointing the dolls out as she spoke their names. "Tony, David, Matthew..."

"Boy dolls?" I asked.

"I went through a phase. Alison, Fleur, Anne, Victoria, Judith, Antonia, Kathryn, Mary and Liz or... Elizabeth."

"Oh," I said.

"Please don't mind. I named her the year before I met you."

I picked up my namesake, from her place near the fire. The porcelain of her face felt warm.

"Well, they are very sweet. But I don't think I could sleep with so many eyes watching over me. How will it be when you find yourself a husband? What man would suffer such a parade of lace and crinoline?"

"If he loves me, he'll not complain."

"Indeed," I said. "Three of them are boys. He should not complain."

"And if I love him, I might be persuaded to put them away." She took the doll from my hands. "Most of them."

Though Julia displayed all the modest propriety of a well-brought up Republican girl, yet exploring the deeper recesses of her wardrobe revealed clothes that better reflected the independent streak that made her such refreshing company. Sliding a row of dark dresses to one side, I discovered two skirts I had never seen her wear, one a summery green, the other decorated in hooped stripes of red, yellow and blue. Though I had not been in the Kingdom for five years and could not be sure what was in fashion, surely these would be less conspicuous than the dour charcoal and Prussian blue outfits so common among polite society in the Republic.

But when I laid my selection on the bed, Julia seemed less than pleased.

"Don't tease me," she warned.

"They may seem bright here, but..."

"But these are dressing-up clothes from when I was a girl. A lady wouldn't wear such things. People would stare."

"They'll stare sure enough in London if you dress from head to foot in bombazine like some widow in mourning."

The stripes being a step too far for Julia, we compromised on the summery green skirt. Among her blouses and coats I found a few suitable choices. I laid the most colourful on the bed. These Julia removed. Eventually we negotiated a compromise.

"But I won't be seen in them whilst still in the Republic," she said.

"Then people will stare when you arrive in the Kingdom."

"We're booked into an inn at Market Harborough. I'll change there."

She layered more modest clothes on top of my choices, concealing the brightest colours at the bottom of her case as if they were some kind of contraband she wished to hide from the customs officials.

Most of the life in her wardrobe I discovered among her underwear. It was clear that she had a taste for highly coloured silk pantaloons and bright wool stockings that I would never have guessed from her outer appearance. But when I started rummaging she pulled me away.

"I have no need of your help on that shelf," she said. "I trust no Royalist will see what I wear beneath!"

I allowed myself to be shepherded to the bed, where I sat with my back to the headboard like an oversized doll. Julia continued with her packing.

"I've never flown before," she said.

"You'll sit in a long carriage," I told her. "Much like an omnibus, but one level only."

"I've seen pictures."

"In which case, you'll know most of what there is to tell. When the feeling of strangeness has passed, one journey is much like another."

"Are you afraid to be in the air?" she asked.

"Everyone's afraid a little. Flight is unnatural."

"And what manner of men have you met on your flights?"

"Is it the men or the flying that interests you?"

She blushed. "I was thinking for you."

"Boring men. Men of business."

"Is it considered polite to speak with the other passengers?"

"It happens," I said. "A lady travelling with her maid spoke to me on the journey to Sleaford. And the man sitting across the aisle."

"How old did you take him to be?"

I called John Farthing to mind as I had seen him that first time, his clothing more relaxed, a homburg instead of a top hat. I remembered our small conspiracy, which had deceived the lady but not the maid. I hated myself for having been taken in.

"Perhaps he was twenty-eight," I said.

"A good age," said Julia.

"A good age for what?"

"Don't tease, Elizabeth. He sounds handsome, would you say?"

"How do you come by that conclusion?"

"By the look on your face as you remembered him."

"You're mistaken!" I said, my words sounding harsher than Julia's question had deserved.

Being perhaps the most honest people in England, Julia and Mr Swain hired a carriage to the border post on Gallowtree Gate, where they disembarked and carried their cases across into the Kingdom, paying a fee for emigration on one side and another for immigration on the other. They then hired a second coach and headed south towards the inn at Market Harborough. Bedford Air Terminus would be their destination the following day, acknowledged as the cheapest place from which to fly to the capital.

They had refused my offer to see them to the border, for which I was secretly glad. Difficult though it was for me to think of the journey I was not taking, it would have been infinitely worse had I said goodbye at the gate itself, looking across into a promised land that I would never reach.

Had the wind been strong and the boat tugging at its mooring ropes I might have remained asleep. But the night was dead calm. I woke in the darkness to find myself sitting up in my bunk, clutching my nightgown to my chest. Slowly the porthole resolved itself as a grey circle against the black of the cabin wall. I listened, hearing no sound but knowing from the slight tilt of the boat that I was not alone.

I groped for the pistol on the floor next to the bunk, then stepped lightly out into the gangway, placing my bare feet one after the other, mindful to avoid Mr Swain's buckets, which I had laid strategically the day before.

A shadow passed over the galley's starboard porthole. With a gentle creak the glass began to swing inwards. An arm reached through. Using both my hands, so the click would be muffled, I pulled back the hammer, cocking my pistol.

The intruder's head was inside now and he was squirming his shoulders through after it. The boat tilted further. Others must be out there on the deck.

When I loaded the gun the night before, it had been with as much black powder as I dared use, followed by a handful of pellets and plenty of wadding. The flash would blind them in this dark. The shot would spray a wide scatter of pain and confusion, but not death.

Spare powder lay where I had left it on the table. But to reload would take twenty seconds in full daylight. In the dark, one fumble and I might spill the bullets.

Suddenly the intruder dropped through. He did not seem as strongly built as I had feared. The gun could wait. I snatched a galley knife and was on him in one long stride, grabbing his coat and bringing the blade around to his chest. He did not cry out. Nor did he try to leap away. I'd expected to feel his muscles tensing. Instead they went limp.

"Miss," he hissed.

It was Tinker.

His words spilled out in a whispered rush. "They've found where Mr Orville's gone. Don't know how. I'm to open the boat so they can kill you. Then they go for him."

I pressed my mouth close to his ear. "Open the door and run."

"But..."

I pushed him towards the hatch. He looked back at me, though he could have seen little in the dark. The boat shifted again – men readying themselves to slip inside. They would have knives for this job. Silent and nimble.

"Go," I hissed. "And get clear of the hatch."

Tinker fumbled for the door bolt. I heard it slide back. Then a rectangle of grey opened. I saw Tinker's silhouette pass up onto the deck and away, then a man's body blotted out the hatchway. I raised my gun, closed my eyes and pulled the trigger.

The noise was indescribable. It felt more like pain than sound. The flash was searing, even through my eyelids. The purple after-image faded and I started to make out a dark shape flailing in the open hatchway. The sound of the man's screaming was distant and unreal. Other shapes were out there. Hands reached down and started to haul him back. In two strides I was at the hatch. I slammed it after his departing feet, slotting the bolt back in place.

Then I was at the table, feeling for the powder.

My hearing was coming back. There were voices outside. The boat shifted, tilting towards the horizontal once more. They wouldn't try the hatch again. I tapped another generous measure of black powder down the barrel, groped for wadding and shot – a single bullet this time – all tamped in place with the rod.

Suddenly I could see my hands. A flickering light had fallen on them, shining through the porthole from a fire out on the towpath. It was this that I had feared. I jumped back into the shadow. Torches were being lit. I counted three of them.

Then a brick crashed through the galley porthole, broken glass shattering onto the floor. Other crashes sounded in the sleeping cabins. A torch lunged forward. I could just see the arm that held it. It reached through the ruined porthole and flailed around, holding the flame to the cotton drapes, which caught quickly. Fire started to lick up the wall. My hand shaking, I tapped a measure of powder into the pan and cocked the hammer. Just as I was about to pull the trigger, I saw my attacker's face. It was Sal. I rushed forwards and pushed the gun barrel into his chest. He dropped the torch and lurched back. Dropping my aim, I fired into his leg.

This time I forgot to close my eyes and saw the muzzle flash. But the gun was outside the window and the shot not as loud. There was no deafness to deaden Sal's scream of pain.

The sleeve of my nightgown had caught fire. I leapt back, plunging my arm into the nearest bucket, dousing it in cold water. The same bucket I threw at the burning curtains.

The floor was wet. I slipped as I ran to my brother's sleeping cabin. A torch guttered harmlessly in the middle of the floor. But in my own cabin the flames had caught in the bedclothes. Two buckets doused it, but smoke had made the air noxious. I coughed and retched, each inhalation bringing more foulness into my lungs. Eyes streaming, I pressed two handfuls of my soaked nightgown over my nose and mouth.

Outside were shouts and running feet, distant but closing fast. I heard the barking of a large hound.

"Thieves! Thieves!" called one voice.

"Murderers!" called another.

The hue and cry had started. Other canal folk moored further along the cut were coming to my aid. I groped my way to the rear hatch, unbolted it and crawled out onto the crutch, gasping for clean air. My bare feet slipped on the wet deck.

The old man from the coal boat was first to my side, followed a step behind by his eldest son. The boy saw me and instantly averted his eyes. The old man threw a coat over my shoulders. I looked down at myself. The soaking had rendered my nightgown transparent.

Mr Simmonds arrived next, clutching an old and dangerous looking musket.

I wrapped the coat around me and tried to stand, but slipped again.

"Where is he?" my landlord shouted. "The thief, show me where!"

I gestured vaguely into the night.

The coal man's wife hurried up, a candle lantern in her hand. She looked me up and down, then turned to her son and her husband. "Bandages. Be quick! The girl is shot."

I looked down and saw that the deck was not wet with water but with blood, which seeped from cuts in the soles of my feet.

"It was glass," I said. "Broken glass. I must have..."

"But we heard shots."

"That was..." I stopped myself before the truth came out. "That was my brother."

"Is he safe?"

"He gave chase," I said.

A murmur of approval went around the small crowd who had gathered on the towpath.

"Good for him," said the coal boatman. "And good for you also, Elizabeth."

"Don't you Elizabeth her!" scolded his wife. "Get the bandages!"

At which he hurried off.

"How do you feel?" she asked

"I don't know." I thought about the broken glass and the smoke and the water damage to my few possessions. More than likely there would be holes in the galley wall from the lead shot. "Angry," I said at last. "Angry and resolved."

CHAPTER 30

A good trick may make you rich. But a risky trick will make you famous. If it goes wrong.

The Bullet-Catcher's Handbook

When I fled at the age of fourteen, the Duke of Northampton's men-at-arms in hot pursuit, I thought I was running towards freedom. Wading the river, hungry and half frozen to death, I crossed into the Republic and out of his reach.

But an exile is never free.

Always the Kingdom was in my mind – its vivid colours and spontaneity, its people driven more by emotion than logic. Forsaking such things may seem of no significance compared to the life of degradation I had escaped. But I could never escape my yearning for the gaudy exuberance of the place I had left behind.

It is ironic then, that on the very day I most clearly felt my love for my new home in the Republic, when its careful seemliness had reached out and gathered me in, I should also understand that the Kingdom was about to claim me once more.

The community of the cut felt more like a family that night than it ever had. They enfolded me in their care and protection. I assured them that my attackers would not return so soon, but they set up a rota all the same, taking turns to watch until the sky paled.

The coal boatman's wife washed and bandaged my feet. Then I was put to bed alongside two of her daughters, squeezed in top to toe, our bedroll laid out next to a pot-bellied stove. With my mind full of new understandings, I thought I would stay awake until dawn. But once the candle was snuffed, I quickly fell into a dreamless sleep. When I woke in the morning, the coal boatman's daughters pressed up for warmth on either side, it was with a calmness and clarity of thought I had not felt since I first met the Duchess of Bletchley.

The Sleepless Man did not try to hide. Rather, he sat in plain sight some fifty yards distant, a fishing rod resting over his knee, a red and yellow float bobbing on the rippled surface of the canal. He did not turn his head to look, but I knew he watched me. I knew he would not try to take a knife to me in unforgiving daylight. He was gaoler rather than executioner, for the time being. He was a sentry left to police my house arrest. But the moment he saw me try to run, I had no doubt his role would change.

Therefore, I went about my business unhurried. When the dairyman's boy rang his bell on the lane, I climbed the path from the cut, swinging a tin jug in my hand, returning with it full a few minutes later. The morning being free of rain, I draped the soaked linen and blankets over *Bessie*'s roof to dry. One does not lay out washing when preparing an escape.

Then I was up the path again, observed in everything I did.

"I shall be going away," I told Mr Simmonds in a lowered voice.

"So soon?" said his wife, who stood next to him in the hallway. "You need to recuperate, Elizabeth. Your poor feet must have time to mend. And what of your brother?"

"He's out chasing the villains still."

She wrung her hands in front of her chest. "So brave. So brave."

Such was the transformation in her attitude towards me, I began to think I had missed an opportunity and should have hired actors to stage an assault on *Bessie* years before.

"And what of your boat?" Mr Simmonds asked. "She's not weatherproof. The portholes want for glazing."

"Your boathouse is empty," I said.

He scratched his head. "Ordinarily I charge..."

"But you shall not this time, Mr Simmonds," cut in his wife.

"You would have my gratitude," I said.

"The poor girl has had such a turn of misfortune."

"It's more for *Bessie*'s safety than for the rain," I said. "I fear the men who did this might return."

This last point seemed to convince Mr Simmonds. "Very well," he said.

In the second after they had turned to lead me from the house, I snatched a china dog of which I knew Mrs

Simmonds to be particularly fond, and, feeling a twinge of guilt, slipped it into the folds of my coat.

I watched Mr Simmonds and his man leaning back as they hauled the ropes, guiding my beloved *Bessie* into the narrow safety of the boathouse. My sodden bedding still lay on the roof. From his place on the canal bank, the Sleepless Man watched also, a slight tension in his posture as the oak doors swung closed.

"One foot longer and she wouldn't have fit," said Mr Simmonds, slotting the lock in place. "She's a fine boat, though. I saw her that time she ran London to Nottingham. Her paddles churned the water white. Broke the record by almost an hour. Never dreamed she'd be moored in my boathouse! Have you thought to get the engine working? She'd be a sight."

"It may be that someone will come looking while I'm gone," I said. "A man with a credit notice trying to seize her. I'd be glad if you could keep the boathouse locked."

It was noon when I finally walked the path to where the Sleepless Man sat fishing. He did not look up until I stopped next to him.

"Hello," he said.

"Are you here as warning to drive me away or as a watchman to make sure I stay put?"

"I'll kill you if you try to run."

"And if I stay?"

He turned back to stare at his float. The silence grew in the space between us.

"The fishing is clever," I said, at last. "Working men respect it. And I can't prove that you were one of my attackers. Not without telling them things I don't care to admit." I crouched down and opened his catch bag to look inside. "Nothing biting?"

"Where's your brother hiding?" he asked.

I closed the bag and stood. "He watches over me."

"Keep your nose out of men's business, little girl," he said.

"You'd be surprised what I consider my business!"

"The kitchen and the bedroom," he said. "That's where you belong."

I turned and stalked back along the path, past the boathouse and up to the coal barge where I had slept the night before.

The Sleepless Man did not know he was their target. The coal boatman and his sons approached along the towpath. Five more young men of the cut converged from the other side, each carrying some weapon – staves and axe handles for the most part. Mr Simmonds appeared at the top of the embankment, the musket clutched to his chest. Then the Sleepless Man understood. But too late. He scrambled to his feet but they were on him.

I hauled my travelling case out of the boathouse and started to make my way up the path away from the cut.

"You! Stand where you are!" ordered the coal boatman.

"What's this about?" came the Sleepless Man's reply.

"You, sir, are a thief!"

"You accuse me?"

The voices grew fainter as I clipped briskly across the courtyard towards the road.

"Search him, boys."

"No, I've not– I've never seen them before!"

"Strange fish you've been catching!"

I was too far by then to hear whether the Sleepless Man started to offer an explanation for the presence in his catch bag of the china dog from the Simmonds' house and a small painted milk jug that had until recently adorned the top of the coal boat. Either way, he was not allowed to finish. He cried out in pain as the beating began.

A rattling omnibus carried me down Melton Road through the sprawling suburbs of North Leicester. Though a shroud of mist hung low, turning the houses grey, yet I seemed to see every brick in vivid colour. A reluctant Republican I may have been, yet now, as I headed towards the border, perhaps never to return, the details were suddenly precious to me.

My fate, together with that of Mr Orville and Harry Timpson, had become inextricably tangled with a mysterious machine. I had seen through too many illusions to give credence to the claims made for it. Yet it had persuaded the great impresario.

I pondered the question of how a box could draw with light. In my mind I pictured a moth-hole in a curtain, through which the bright sunlight streamed into a smoke filled room. Such an arrangement could make a line appear to be suspended in the air. Perhaps Mr Orville's machine simply captured and reflected the sun. But if so, why did they believe it could unlock the secrets of alchemy? Could light burn into the essence of one element and transmute it into another? Or was this simply part of some greater illusion that Harry Timpson had designed? One final mystery. A grand display to puzzle great minds of the future and give immortality to his name and legend.

The only things I knew for certain were that Timpson was willing to sacrifice everything on this quest and that he now perceived me as an obstacle. The Sleepless Man had been left to keep me out of mischief's way until Timpson had the box in his possession. But once he had disposed of Orville and secured his heart's desire, I would simply be a person who knew too much. To stay on the North Leicester Wharf would be to wait for the spectres of death and financial ruin to battle it out for control of my fate.

I had never much liked waiting.

Crossing the border is easy but to do so unseen is impossible, as both sides teem with private intelligence gatherers. The trick is to cross anonymously.

At the official border post one must present identification and possibly a permit of residence. Lists of comings and goings are drawn up by the border guards on both sides then handed over to the constabulary and the secret services of the two countries, who file them away in warehouses of similar paperwork. Ask to see the lists and you will be told that the information is confidential. Unless you have perfected the art of passing money in a handshake.

Crossing at Gallowtree Gate would be like sending a pigeon to the Duke of Northampton informing him that I was on my way back to a place within his reach.

Therefore I headed for the Leicester Backs, with its warren of illegal crossing points.

Showing a callous disregard for my reputation, the taxi driver dropped me short of my destination, saying he would not risk his steamcar in that den of iniquity. Thus I was forced to haul my case the last two hundred yards on foot, enduring glances that were by turns accusatory and licentious from the rowdy girls and respectable gentlemen.

Not all crossing points are equal. Some emerge in alleyways so dark and overhung by roofs on either side that robbery or worse is likely. Some are controlled by fierce gangs. Others are too safe in that they pass behind police houses. Whichever route you choose, payment is required – though different amounts.

I had selected the Odeon Passageway for my crossing. Not the cheapest route, but one of superior quality according to those who knew. It exited the Republic via the back of a tattoo artist's parlour on Cank Street. Not the sort of shop a lady should frequent according to Republican morals. But I was walking though the Backs anyway and thought I might as well be hanged for a sheep as a lamb.

I pushed the door, setting a bell jingling, and stepped into the small shop, a corner of which had been cordoned off with a carved screen. Framed designs lined the walls – predatory animals, palm trees, crosses, stars and national flags. The pungent, sweet smell in the air I recognised as opium smoke.

I coughed politely and the proprietor ducked his head out from behind the screen. His eyes flicked from my bonnet to my travelling case. I held out two silver tenpences. His eyes flicked to a pot on the counter. I nodded and dropped the money into it. When I looked back, he had already disappeared behind the screen once more.

Though he worked with ink and needle, I had heard it said that this was his highest art-form – looking the other way. For a pound he could be blind to a gang of porters sweating under a weight of cloth or china or any other commodity that he never saw. And so skilled was he in his work that a whole regiment might pass unheard should sufficient funds be found.

I picked up my case and started making my way towards the rear of the parlour. Glancing behind the screen, I saw a bare-chested man lying on a couch. The proprietor was wiping a patch of blood and ink from above his breast.

A doorway led through into a small kitchen from which I exited the building into a yard of greasy flagstones. From there I followed a narrow passageway, at the head of which was a door with a hole where the handle should have been. It swung open to reveal a second courtyard, this one stacked with barrels and crates of empty bottles. The smell of stale beer hung in the air.

With every step I found myself wondering if I had crossed yet. But no line marked the border on the ground as it did on the map.

Sunlight shone through from a passageway ahead. Hurrying now, I rushed towards it and emerged, blinking, onto a bustling South Leicester street.

CHAPTER 31

Though you live and travel all the years of your life in the gap between that which is known and that which is not known, yet you will have explored but a fraction of that vast land.

THE BULLET-CATCHER'S HANDBOOK

Returning home should not be bewildering. It should fill you with peace and a sense that everything is in its proper place. It should be the smell of baking bread or the sight of sunlight through lace curtains.

Carriages and pedestrians in the Kingdom are supposed to keep to the left. In the Republic it is the other way around. Making this small adjustment might seem easy, but there is a deeper difference. Good Republicans follow rules meticulously. But Royalists are meanderers – whether they be walking, driving or paying their taxes. On the roads and pavements they sometimes pass to the left and sometimes to the right. I bumped shoulders with a young woman, elbowed an elderly man and collided full on with a boy. By the time I was making my fifth apology, my initial elation at crossing the border had begun to chill.

The streets were busier than I remembered them. I wanted to step out of the jostle for a few minutes, to sit quietly and get used to all the newness. I also wanted a chance to watch for anyone who might have been following. There were coffee houses here, any of which would have served my purpose. There were even bars which I could enter without causing a scandal. Here women could drink alongside men in a public house without an eyebrow being raised.

But before any of that, I needed money.

Dressed in an ankle-covering skirt of subdued purple and a charcoal grey coat, hauling a case and now asking directions to the money changer, I could not have looked more like a tourist. Though I had seen across the border from behind the customs barrier in GallowtreeGate, I had never set foot in the other half of the divided city. From the safe side of the border things had not looked so very different. The cultural mixing across this most permeable of national boundaries made sure of that. But now it felt as if I had passed through Alice's looking glass. All the things I could not see from the other side were altered and strange.

I progressed up Granby Street wide-eyed, eventually finding the Midland Money Exchange, a grand red-brick building fronted by a set of low steps. Trying my best to move around obstacles rather than cut a straight Republican line, I wove through the crowd that jostled in the entranceway.

Just inside the door, I paused to rest my travelling case on the floor. It was an act that would have caused confusion and collisions at a busy junction in the Republic. Here, people simply moved around me as river water flows past a rock.

Two great sandstone pillars lay ahead, and beyond them, the huge expanse of the trading floor, which seemed more like a hive of bees than a room of people. Light flooded down from windows in the cavernous roof onto knots of men standing in inward-looking groups. Everyone seemed to be talking at once. Those in the centre of each circle wore colourful bowler hats. I saw greens, browns, reds and even a soft pink. These men gesticulated wildly with slips of paper clutched in their hands, calling out numbers. Their shouts mixed, becoming a dizzying cacophony. A few feet back stood men in high top hats, who seemed disinterested by comparison. There were a few women here also, but these stood waiting around the edge of the trading floor.

Making my way between the columns, I skirted the room and took up position next to one of the women. She wore the same jewel-green colour that the Duchess had been dressed in when we first met. Her red and black striped stockings were visible to the calf.

"The trade's full steam today," she said.

"What do I do?" I asked.

She turned to look at me properly. "You'll be a Republican, then?"

I shook my head. "But I've been away. I need to change money."

"You surely talk like a Republican. And will you look at that skirt!"

"I'll be changing clothes very soon."

"Well, the world's ever yours if you've money to spend."

She took my arm and waved towards a knot of men on the trading floor. The intimacy of her touch took me aback. It was something that would only have passed between close friends in the Republic. Moments later, a trader wearing a russet bowler hat had spotted us and was hurrying over.

"She's from the Republic," explained my new friend.

I emptied my purse onto his hand. After picking up one of the coins and examining it in close detail, he did a quick count.

"I can do you a one to five exchange, Kingdom for Republic on a half hour turn."

I had no idea whether the rate represented good value, or what was meant by a half hour turn. But the woman next to me gave a small nod and an encouraging smile, so I offered my hand and we shook on the deal. It was all done so quickly that only as he left with my money did it occur to me that I might have been hustled like the greenest josser ever to walk onto a gaff. I looked down at the contract slip he had given me. The ink was green and the writing so spidery that I could hardly make it out.

The trader was lost in the crowd already. If the woman now made her excuses and left, I would know for sure that I had been conned. It would take only one such slip to seal my fate. The woman had let go of me already. Fighting my reserve, I took her arm as she had done mine a few moments before. She did not pull away.

"Thanks for the help," I said.

She squeezed my hand. "You Republicans are so polite."

"Are you changing money for a journey north?"

"I'm surely not!" she said, as if I had suggested something dangerous. "This is only my hobby."

Perhaps she sensed my confusion because she gestured to the crowds before us and explained, "Only men can work the trading floor. They're lords over us, yes?"

"I suppose–"

"Well you suppose too easily! As do they. But they see only the little things. The price of the Mark against the Pound.The Franc against the Dollar. Standing here, listening in, we can see it all. My hobby is to change money from one currency to another, then on to another still."

I felt a smile spreading across my face. I was not the target of her games. The traders were.

"How much money do you make in a day?"

She put a hand to her chest in faux shock. "My dear! I thought such questions were never asked north of the border."

"Like I said, I'm coming home."

"I'm beginning to see that," she said. "There's a Royalist underneath all that Republican grey. As to the money..." She nodded towards the men of the trading floor. "I make more than any of them."

My trader in his russet bowler returned before the half hour had expired. He took the contract slip, wrote down the time,then made me countersign it. I counted the thick bundle of paper money he had given me. One hundred and sixty-five Kingdom pounds. The man touched the brim of his hat then dived back into the chaos from which he had just emerged. As I wove away through the crowds, I took a final glance at the woman in the jewel-green dress. For all her instant friendliness, she had not bothered to take a final glance at me. Her focus was back on the money market, her arm held high, waving to attract the attention of another trader.

It was said that the house of a true Republican was narrow, ensuring that the frontage would not give away the wealth within. The house of a Royalist was wide by contrast, often with a high false wall at the front. "Wide and shallow" had become the phrase wherewith Republicans made fun of their southern neighbours. "Mean and narrow" being the standard reply.

As if to belie this cliché, the Turkey Cafe, which stood opposite the Midland Money Exchange, seemed too narrow for its height. Yet its frontage was as rich and showy as any Kingdom building could have been. The ornately curved windows might have come from the Kasbah of Algiers. Moulded plaster turkeys stood proud from the walls on either side of the front doors and a brightly coloured turkey emblem crowned the apex of the building.

Taking a table with a good view of the street, I ordered a cup of rose-flavoured chocolate and something the waiter described as the Turkey Special – a raisin pastry square, dotted with brilliant blue icing and what appeared to be tiny flecks of gold leaf.

I handed over a note and received a handful of thre'pences, crowns and shillings, none of which were familiar to me. I pretended to check the money. Then, none the wiser, nodded my acceptance of the waiter's arithmetic.

As I ate, I thought about the woman in the money exchange. She had found a way to make the world of men serve her own advantage. In that respect we were alike. Yet I felt uneasy. The signing of financial contracts in the Republic was hidden away in wood-panelled offices – a shameful necessity in the pursuit of higher goals. One would no more talk of it than discuss intimate medical complaints with a stranger. In the Kingdom, the acquisition of money seemed to be an end in itself.

There was so much that I did not understand. Though I had spent most of my life south of the border, I had never learned to be an adult there.

Rested, but with my mind buzzing from more sugar than I had eaten at one sitting for many years, I hefted my case from the floor and set off back into the afternoon sunlight.

On Rutland Street, I found a used-clothing shop. A man in a lilac and mustard check waistcoat jumped to his feet as I entered.

"Are you the proprietor?" I asked.

He nodded, his fingers dancing nervously over the edge of the counter.

"I need a skirt, blouse, coat and bonnet."

"We don't... that is, we do... but not..."

I began to rummage through the nearest rack, pulling out possibilities, holding them against myself then replacing those obviously too small. The double life I led precluded any possibility of training my waist down to fashionable dimensions.

"There is nothing – how should we say? – nothing plain enough to–"

"It will be a gift for a Royalist friend," I said.

"Will your friend... ah... be coming into the shop for... for a fitting?"

"We're two peas in a pod. If they fit me, they'll fit her."

As a child, I had shopped in places like this. I used to love the touch and smell of the fabrics. Only the poorest women in the Republic would wear second-hand clothing. In the Kingdom rummaging castoffs was one of life's great pleasures.

Having found a green skirt similar to the one worn by the woman on the trading floor, I moved on to a rack of puff-sleeved blouses. My shoulders being unfashionably broad, I was surprised and pleased to find several possibilities. Soon I was striding across the changing room, testing my new outfit for the freedom of movement it allowed. After years of wearing full-length skirts, I felt a thrill of daring excitement on seeing my boots and stockinged calves in the looking glass.

"You're surely not wearing them?" said the frowning proprietor as I emerged, money in hand.

"I surely am!" I said, trying out an abrupt Royalist tone of voice and liking the effect.

"But they're for your friend. Won't she–?"

"She likes me to wear them first," I said.

He nodded, accepting my words. It seemed that no amount of strangeness would be a surprise if it came from the mouth of a foreigner.

Noticing a rack of accessories, I picked out a straw hat with turquoise ribbon and flash of jay feather. The proprietor eyed the pile of subdued clothing in my arms as if he were examining an exotic creature. "I suppose... that is, you'll be wanting to hold onto your old ones... since you're buying for a friend."

"Not necessarily."

Clothes in the Republic are made to last a lifetime before being cut into squares or hexagons and stitched together as quilts. In the Kingdom, fashions change from one year to the next and clothes fall apart if worn for too long. Therefore, I had no illusions, knowing full well I was exchanging good for bad. But I had no more need of Republican clothes. If I succeeded in my quest, I would win the freedom to remain. And if I failed I would be permitted no return.

CHAPTER 32

Comfort comes from simple knowledge, whether the knowledge be true or false. Thus are fools so common and wars and lovers also. And thus will the audience know for sure that you caught a flying bullet with your teeth.

THE BULLET-CATCHER'S HANDBOOK

The low winter sun warmed the red brick and cream sandstone of London Road Coach Station, catching the words Arrival and Departure above the arched entrances. London Road – the very name sent a thrill of excitement through me.

A woman travelling in a group is always less conspicuous. Therefore it was my intention to catch up with Julia and her father *en route* and arrive in the capital with them. If things had gone to plan they would now be at an inn near the air terminus at Bedford, having made the journey from Market Harborough by coach.

The faster route to Bedford was priced at a premium. I counted out an alarming number of notes from my newly changed paper money and was soon clattering out of the grand station forecourt on the express coach. A team of six fine horses rushed me and a select group of well-to-do travellers south towards the air terminus at Foxton Locks.

The landscape through which we passed became more familiar the further we travelled out of Leicester. Gripping the leather strap to steady myself against the wild rocking of the carriage, I stared out of the window at small fields, thatched cottages and winding side-lanes as they whipped past. In a cut-off triangle of grass at the intersection of three fields, I saw a bow-topped gypsy wagon with smoke rising from its chimney pipe. Animal skins were stretched on three wooden frames planted in the ground. Fox and deer, I thought. Pressing my face to the window glass, I craned my neck to prolong my view of the small encampment as it receded behind us.

"Does their squalor unsettle you?" asked a gentleman in a green velvet jacket. He was sitting directly opposite and seemed to be taking an unwholesome enjoyment in the sight of my ankles. I remembered him wearing a wedding ring earlier in the journey. At some point it seemed to have disappeared.

I could think of no answer that would extricate me without seeming waspish. Therefore I turned my face to the homely looking lady sitting next to me. Noting her pallid face, I said: "You'll feel better if you keep your gaze on the horizon. Would you like the window seat?"

She accepted my generous offer and thus I left the man in the green jacket disappointed.

Foxton was an important staging point even before the signing of the Great Accord and the birth of the Gas-

Lit Empire. The famous ladder of locks allowed boats to descend towards Leicester, completing the canal route from the south. There being no other practical means to transport heavy loads, traffic increased every year. Eventually the canal was widened and a boat lift constructed – an engineering marvel that cemented Foxton's importance as a transportation hub.

Wide beam barges carry cargo from London all the way to South Leicester, where they are unloaded. The cargo is given into the hands of teams of porters, who carry it through the maze of the Leicester Backs to be loaded onto the same barges that have, in the meantime, slipped across the border, paying no duty. From North Leicester the boats can steam on to Nottingham and the north.

When the age of the airship dawned, it was natural for the terminus at Foxton to grow in importance. As Anstey is to the Republic, so Foxton is to the Kingdom. Along the fifteen miles that separate the two air termini is the best paved road in either nation. Thus I was at Foxton before sunset, had bought my ticket and seen my case loaded.

Once again I felt the unsettling lurch of take-off. Having never before been on a night flight, the view and experience were thrilling to me. Instead of seeing the fields and towns spread out below, the world appeared like a map of the heavens, the lights burning by roadsides and in windows seeming more like clusters of stars than the creation of man.

As with the coach trip that had preceded it, I found myself subjected to the unwanted attention of a male traveller. This time older and dressed in charcoal-grey.

A tourist, I thought, behaving disgracefully abroad. Excusing myself from his company, I took a seat near a husband and wife and was thus able to complete the flight unmolested.

The engine noise changed, the carriage began to tilt forward and I felt that fluttering in the stomach that accompanies descent. Soon the floodlights of Bedford Air Terminus came into view. We slowed. The landing lines dropped. The ground crew hauled and we inched into dock.

A fugitive sees peril in every stranger's face. Picking my way down the stairs from the alighting platform I scanned the waiting crowd below. Some waved and jumped on seeing their friends or relatives emerge from the carriage, displaying degrees of exuberance that would have drawn disapproving looks at an air terminus in the Republic.

Others in the crowd held up paper signs on which the names of people or corporations had been written: "Herrick Mathews" "Telford Castings Ltd" "Edgar Payne". Cabbies I spotted there also, furtively touting for business, keeping clear of any terminus marshals who might throw them out onto the street. Scattered through this throng a few men of nondescript appearance stood watching, drinking in all the details of the arrival hall. I picked out three of them, each wearing unremarkable clothing. There may have been more.

Just as they stood out to me, so must I have been conspicuous to them. Though dressed in appropriately colourful clothes, I could not yet walk through a crowd with the same fluidity as the women of the Kingdom. That I travelled alone made me even more unusual.

I clipped across the polished stone floor, not turning to look but certain that one of them had fallen into step behind me. I seemed to feel his eyes on the back of my head as I handed my chitty to a magnificently moustached baggage handler and received my battered travelling case in return.

"Will there be more arrivals tonight?" I asked.

The handler shook his head. "She's the last of them."

"When's the next London flight?"

"Nine tomorrow morning. You've got somewhere to stay?"

"Thank you, yes."

I gave him a warm smile then started off across the emptying passenger hall. With less noise than before, I could hear the footsteps of the person following behind me. They only stopped when it became clear that I was heading for the ladies' washroom. I slipped a Kingdom penny into the turnstile and pushed through, hefting my case over the top of it.

Inside were white and blue tiles, a row of porcelain hand basins smelling of lavender soap and a line of stalls along the opposite wall. Choosing the stall furthest from the entrance, I bolted myself in, put down the toilet lid and sat with my case resting across my knees.

It was going to be a long night.

CHAPTER 33

Why disdain the bullet-catcher who employs a stooge?
The illusion will amaze just as surely, unless the
method be guessed.

THE BULLET-CATCHER'S HANDBOOK

There are many ways to confuse a witness, change
of appearance being first among them. As I sat in the
ladies' washroom, I occupied myself by searching
through my travelling case for the elements of an
improvised disguise. The best I could find was a
change of clothes. I swapped the full-sleeved, puffed-
shoulder blouse I'd been wearing on arrival to one
with straighter lines. I pinned up my hair, exchanged
the straw hat for a cotton bonnet, folded my coat
away and was thankful he hadn't had a close view of
my face the night before.

The eye of the observer is not a scientific instrument
of brass and lenses. It perceives a greater picture, and
thus it can be distracted. Have a man walk through a
crowd and many will afterwards be able to describe
the things he wore and even the details of his face.

But if that man were to walk the same path carrying a parlour palm or a stuffed crocodile or any other unexpected object, all details of his person would be forgotten. Everyone would see the object, but no further. Thus he could not be identified without it. My travelling case was my crocodile, so to speak – too battered and conspicuous for me to risk carrying it out of the washroom.

Since I had not returned through the turnstile the night before, the intelligence gatherer who'd followed me must know he had found a story of interest. He would still be there.

By half past seven in the morning, women had started to come and go from the washroom with enough frequency to confuse anyone watching outside. Water flowed in hand basins. Cisterns flushed. It was time to make my escape.

I emerged from the stall to see the floor being cleaned by a hunched Negro woman with a wrinkled face. She was pushing her mop from side to side across the tiles, leaving them wet and shining behind her.

"Could you watch my case?" I asked.

"I'm no luggage service," she said.

I placed a two shilling coin in her hand and closed her fingers around it. "Twenty minutes."

"The men will be for you then," she said.

"I'm sorry?"

She flashed her eyes towards the exit. "The men that's waiting."

"How many?"

She showed me the five fingers of her hand.

"Private intelligence men?"

"Red coats. Men-at-arms."

"Did you see the badges they wore? Whose insignia?"

Shaking her head, she took the suitcase from my hand and put it back in the stall from which I had just emerged. Then she took a wooden sign from one of the capacious pockets of her housecoat and hung it on the door catch: CLEANING IN PROGRESS.

The cleaner had not spotted the sixth man, a private intelligence gatherer who stood leaning against an iron pillar, nursing the last inch of a cigarette. As for the other five, they were exactly as she had described. Red-coated men-at-arms, swords hanging from their belts on one side, flintlocks holstered on the other.

Stitched to each chest was a badge of office, the emblem of the aristocratic house from which they derived their authority. It showed a green oak tree below a blue sky in which hung an off-centre triangle of white stars. All aristocratic families might have seemed the same to the cleaning woman, but they were not the same to me. This was the house I had grown to fear and loathe. This was the emblem of the Duke of Northampton.

To my credit, I did not break step on seeing them, but pushed through the turnstile and stepped out into the passenger hall, holding my head up so that the private intelligence man could get a clear look at my face – something he would not have been able to do the previous night. He frowned as he stared at me, then made a small shake of his head, a signal to the men-at-arms who were tensed, awaiting his direction. Only when I was clear of them did I begin to gasp in lungfuls of air, trying with no success to slow my racing heart.

Julia and her father were waiting near the alighting platform, watching the unearthly sight of a large airship approaching the docking pylons.

Mr Swain saw me first. "Elizabeth!"

I rushed the last few paces, holding my finger to my lips in warning.

Mr Swain beamed at the sight of me. "Why, my dear, I thought you were to stay in the north."

I could not speak, but held my hands to my chest, trying to slow my breathing.

"What's wrong?" asked Julia.

"Don't... speak... my name," I gasped.

They guided me to a seat. Julia placed her hand to my forehead.

"You're perspiring Eliz–" She brought herself up to a sudden stop then whispered urgently. "What has happened?"

"Your luggage–"

"They told us to bring it to the alighting platform." Mr Swain gestured to a pile of bags by the window. Among them, I now saw Julia's travelling case, which we had packed together two days before. It was newer, bigger and definitely more expensive than my own. I opened my mouth to speak but then changed my mind and closed it again.

Julia clutched my hand. "What is it?"

"I can't ask it."

"If something needs to be done, you must!"

Mr Swain cleared his throat. "If there is some

danger, I should be the one to do it, whatever it is."

"You can't," I said to him. "This must happen in the ladies' washroom."

It was not the men-at-arms or the intelligence gatherer that disturbed Julia. Rather, it was the thought of her clothes being on public view as we emptied her travelling case. But still she did as I asked and soon her things were piled on the seat next to me. Mr Swain placed his coat over the top to hide his daughter's underwear from public view.

We watched over the balcony as she descended the stairs, suitcase in hand, and made her way across the passenger hall towards the women's washroom. As she approached the men-at-arms she slowed. My heart did a double beat as I realised she was heading for the intelligence man who still stood leaning against the pillar.

"No!" the word escaped my mouth as a gasp.

Her father stepped forwards and gripped the railing. His knuckles whitened.

Below us, Julia was speaking to the intelligence man. She put down her case then handed him something too small for us to see at such distance. He fished in his trouser pocket and passed her something in return. Suddenly I understood.

"It is a penny for the turnstile!"

"But him! Of all the people she could have approached!" exclaimed Mr Swain.

"Oh, but you should be proud of your daughter. Don't you see? When she comes out, he'll know she's not the one he's watching for. He'll know her face."

Blowing air through his lips like a deflating balloon, Mr Swain lowered himself into a seat. "And your brother does this for a living!"

Julia was emerging from the washroom. Too quick, I thought. She should have waited longer. And now she struggled with the case, where before she had carried it with ease. One of them would surely notice. If they searched hers and found mine concealed inside... the thought of it sent dread through my veins. Watching was greater agony than ever I had felt when my own life had been in danger.

The intelligence man stepped towards her and reached his hand for the case.

Mr Swain was on his feet again. "I must go to her," he said, and was ready to act on his word, but I reached out and gripped his hand.

"Wait."

Julia had placed the case on the ground. She was nodding, in conversation with the intelligence man. At last he touched the brim of his hat. She smiled, picked up the case again and was off towards the stairs.

Her father said something under his breath that could have been a prayer or an oath, I could not tell which. Then she was up with us again, cheeks flushed and wearing the broadest smile I had ever seen on her.

"That was such excitement!" she said. "He wanted to know if there was anyone suspicious waiting inside. I told him someone could have been hiding in one of the stalls."

Then her father hugged her and so did I.

• • •

It was the biggest airship I had ever seen. Four carriages hung below the vast envelope. Though my ticket had been for a different carriage from the Swains', a word with the conductor was enough to have me transferred. Thus we sat together at the very front, just behind one of the great engines.

Julia and her father took the window seats.

The front mooring rope had been tethered to a traction engine. This now began to steam forwards, leading us through the hangar doors much as a tug might guide a ship through the tight confines of a harbour mouth.

Never having travelled on a ship of such size, this ballet of machines was new to me. In other circumstances I might have drunk in the details as my companions were now doing. But my mind was occupied with the perplexing events of the last few hours.

All ports and crossing places have their spies. That one of them had chosen to follow me across the arrival hall presented no mystery. As a woman travelling on my own, I had piqued his interest. Doubly so when he realised I was spending the night in the washroom. He would surely have suspected me of being a runaway from a husband or a father. I imagined him casting around the crowds for sight of a waiting lover.

But the intelligence man had not simply waited and watched, collecting information to sell later. He had immediately sent a message to the Duke of Northampton, who had dispatched men-at-arms so promptly that they were waiting when I emerged in the morning. It had been five years since my flight from the Kingdom. If I was indeed the one they sought, it could only be because news of my crossing the border had reached the Duke.

"Will you tell me your thoughts?" said Julia.

I wondered how long she had been observing me. "You should be enjoying the view," I said.

"There is no view."

I looked through the window. We had climbed already and cloud swirled around the ship.

"In such conditions they navigate by compass and dead reckoning," her father said.

"Why didn't the soldiers enter the washroom?" Julia asked.

"You should know that from our reading," I said. "The warrant they carry doesn't allow entry into private places. And certainly not to a ladies' washroom. They have to wait for a regular constable. Then they can force entry if need be."

Mr Swain tutted. "The law of the Kingdom seems unreasonably complex."

"The aristocrats wouldn't give up their private armies," Julia explained. "It adds a whole layer of law enforcement."

"And the King?"

"It may be called a kingdom. But the Council of Aristocrats makes the laws."

"Your lessons haven't been wasted then," her father said with a wry smile. "But if the aristocrats have all that power, why do their soldiers need a constable at all?"

Julia frowned. "I don't know."

She and her father both turned to look at me.

"That's politics, not law," I said. "Why should I know?"

"You have a way of seeing under the surface of things," said Julia.

"Well..." I began. "I guess there've been enough revolutions around the world to give them warning. There aren't many monarchies left. Perhaps the Council of Aristocrats knows that if they push the people too hard it'll be the end for them."

"You're saying they rule fairly?" asked Mr Swain.

"Certainly not! But I'm suggesting there are limits."

A growing puzzlement on Julia's face told me that she had begun to think through the events of the morning. "How did the soldiers know where to find you?"

"Harry Timpson doesn't want me to reach London," I explained. "Nor does he want to waste his time trying to stop me."

Her puzzlement turned to shock. "But he wouldn't!"

"I'm afraid he would. He'll have sent a message to the Duke of Northampton telling him I've crossed the border. I guess they'll have searched the washroom by now. That means they'll know they've been tricked. They'll also have a good idea where I'm heading."

Julia reached across and put her hand on mine.

"You're surely safe," said her father. "You'll be in the capital and disembarked and lost in the crowds before news reaches St Pancras. Nothing is faster than airship."

"I wish that were so," I said. "But a carrier pigeon is faster still."

CHAPTER 34

Jossers want to be tricked. They pay for the privilege.
Do not feel remorse for fulfilling their desire.

THE BULLET-CATCHER'S HANDBOOK

The great airship inched its way to the mooring pylons under a rainy London sky. Ground crewmen secured the front and rear lines. Then a steam whistle blew outside and a juddering movement passed through the carriage as we began to move once more. The pylons themselves were being winched towards the hangar along a pair of iron rails. Soon we were brought to a halt under the cathedral-like iron and glass canopy of St Pancras International Air Terminus.

A smaller airship rested to our port side, its two carriages adorned with Cyrillic writing and the double-headed eagle of the Russian Republic. The alighting platform on the starboard side was empty. But further along, I could see passengers climbing up into the carriages of a distinctively elongated French airship.

Amid all this wonder, it was the forecourt that

had my fixed attention. Immediately before us were the officials of the air company, waiting to check our tickets. But beyond them, I saw a cluster of red-uniformed men-at-arms mixed in with the jostling crowd. I could not recognise the badges from such distance, except to say that they did not belong to the Duke of Northampton. The aristocratic houses looked out for each other's interests, however. Northampton's men would be on their way.

Sitting next to me, Julia's eyes were round with wonder. "You were right about the clothes," she said. "I couldn't have believed it, but I look dull in comparison to these people, even dressed as I am."

Mr Swain drew in his breath and I knew that he too had seen the welcoming committee. Then Julia followed our gaze.

"Stay in the carriage," she said, alarmed.

"That is impossible."

"You could fly back to Bedford," her father agreed.

"They'd be waiting."

"But–"

"Please look after my travelling case," I said.

"Of course," said Mr Swain. "But there must be more we can do."

"There is. Empty your pockets. Give me all the coins you carry."

We stood in line waiting to be allowed through the barrier. With four carriages disgorging all at the same time, several officials were kept busy checking tickets. A considerable throng had gathered outside. Shouts of greeting rose above the excited hubbub.

"Why do they check our tickets again once the flight is over?" asked Julia.

"They don't," I said. "Not usually."

Though the men-at-arms could not know what I looked like, I assumed my ticket number had been carried to them. Two men were being checked at the front of the queue. Between myself and them stood a woman in a peacock feather hat. I started to breathe deeply and tightened my grip on the coins in both hands.

"Swap tickets with me," Julia hissed.

"No!"

"You could slip away."

"And let you suffer my fate?"

The lady with the feather hat was being processed at the front of the queue. The official nodded her through and called, "Next please."

I stepped forwards and presented my ticket, filling my lungs again.

"Thanking you," he said.

I saw recognition bloom on his face as he read the ticket number. He started to turn towards the men-at-arms and was raising his hand to signal.

"Thank you," I said, stepping into the press of people then immediately cutting left.

"Stop her!" came a cry close behind me.

A tremor of agitation passed through the crowd. Something was happening but they didn't know exactly what. Turning side on, I started shouldering my way through. A barrel-chested man in a greasy cloth cap grabbed my arm. I tried to wrench myself free but he held on tighter.

"Stop her!" I cried, gesturing my balled fist in the direction I'd been trying to move.

He let go and started barging on ahead of me. I followed in his wake, quicker now, but we'd reached the thinning edge of the crowd. I glanced back and saw three red coats, the nearest but ten yards behind. I flung one arm forward, opened my fist and let the coins fly. The sound of spilled money rang out and suddenly everyone was moving. The nearest red coat took a shoulder in the chest and went sprawling.

Jinking right then left, I dodged, picking up speed as I reached the end of the crowd. Twenty yards ahead lay a narrow archway and beyond that the forecourt where coaches waited and beyond that again would be the London streets.

I gulped air, my throat and lungs raw.

"Stop that woman!"

Now out of the crowd, I couldn't fool anyone. So I hurled the second fist of coins up into the air and shouted, "Money!" Metal glinted as they spun. Then I was under the archway and the coins were landing around me.

It took only a second for that constricted space to become a mass of bony-limbs, rags, oaths and the stench of unwashed bodies. The beggars who habitually crowd outside such places had rushed in *en masse*. Station guards were laying about them with long truncheons in a futile attempt to force them back out onto the street.

I ran the cobbled forecourt, dodging between coaches and steamcars, then out into the thin sunshine and the crowds of Euston Road.

• • •

I did not fear discovery amid the city's millions. Yet wandering the streets at random would not bring me closer to my goal. From what Tinker had told me, Mr Orville must have fled to the Jewish quarter in Spitalfields – and more particularly to the close-packed streets where apothecaries and chemists were known to work. There he would hope to find the knowledge to unlock the supposed power of his machine.

Harry Timpson had surely followed. His men would be scattered through those same streets, watching, offering rewards, putting the word around. That is where I needed to go also. But being fresh in their memories, I could not walk into Spitalfields undisguised. Therefore my first stop had to be to reclaim my battered travelling case from Julia and her father.

On approaching their hotel, however, I saw three red-coated men-at-arms questioning the doorman. It seemed that the connection between us had been established. The guileless Swains would not have been hard to track from St Pancras. They would be tailed until I was finally captured or they had crossed the border back into the Republic.

One course of action was available to me. I must arrive at the courthouse when it opened its doors first thing in the morning and wait inside for Julia and her father. The building would be safe because its rules allowed no weapons to be taken inside or force to be administered – except by the executive of the Patent Office itself.

With most of my money folded away in my travelling case, I did not have the option of booking into a comfortable hotel and was forced to search the cheaper streets for a guest house in which to spend the night. But even the most rundown establishments proved too expensive.

Eventually, having walked a couple of miles south, I discovered the Tangiers, a dimly lit hostel with alarmingly green palm trees painted to either side of the entrance. In the mildew-smelling lobby, the cashier informed me that they specialised in renting rooms for short durations. He said he would do me a deal on the hours from two until six in the morning. We shook on it, his palm greasy with sweat.

Then, having no other choice, I walked until my feet were sore. And as I walked, I stared into the windows of those shops that were still illuminated, looking through glass at colourful displays of shoes and dresses, foodstuffs and books. The Republic had wealth, but its riches would never be displayed in such abundance. Just as disorienting were the people who passed me on the street. In their clothes, their expansive gesticulations and in the volume of their speech, they dazzled the senses.

My father had once brought me to London. I'd been dazzled then also, my small hand gripping his fingers, scared of losing him yet elated to be seeing the marvels of our nation's capital.

With my remaining money I purchased a small, sweet loaf and a bottle of ginger beer from a vendor. These I consumed as I walked, and such are attitudes in the Kingdom that I received no glances of disapproval. I would have sat but there were no benches and I did not wish to join the many homeless who huddled together on the pavement, palms upturned.

At last I could walk no more and stood leaning on a railing, watching river traffic ploughing up and down the grey waters of the Thames.

I woke to the sound of knocking. Opening the door of my mildew-smelling room, I was confronted by a woman wearing a burlesque combination of wasp-waisted corset and red pantaloons. My time was up, she said. I could either pay for another hour or get out. She had customers waiting in the lobby.

I stumbled out onto the dark street, still half asleep. The air had turned colder during the night. Somewhere nearby a clock struck the three quarter hour. I had been thrown out fifteen minutes early.

Knowing I'd freeze to death if I stood still, I set off in what I hoped was the direction of Fleet Street and the Patent Office Court.

Gradually the city started coming to life. Occasional coat-wrapped figures hurried past. Working men at first, then gentlemen also. The further I walked west, the grander the buildings became. After half an hour, a sickly yellow dawn began to spread across the eastern sky. Lamplighters trudged their rounds, extinguishing the streetlights one by one. By the time I reached Fleet Street the roads had filled. Cabs and coaches raced through, wheels and hooves throwing mud and worse over the legs of pedestrians.

The Royal Courts of Justice and the Patent Office Court stood next to each other, ill-matched neighbours on that great thoroughfare. Just as the Normans had constructed their most magnificent castles and palaces in the midst of the people they wished to awe and conquer, so had the International Patent Office chosen London as home to its central institution. The Kingdom had been the last major nation to add its name to the Great Accord. It was a reluctant addition to the Gas-Lit Empire. What better symbol of its capitulation than to have the frivolous spires and turrets of the Royal Courts overshadowed by austere masonry?

Climbing the steps, I craned my neck to see the top of the mighty columns before me. Taken by itself, the portico was of similar height to the Royal Courts. But behind the apex of the portico a mighty cliff of grey granite blocked out the sky, into which rows of identical windows had been set.

Four soldiers in blue German uniforms stood to attention in front of the great doors, which were not yet open. A different day would have seen the position of honour occupied by men from a different nation – China, Ethiopia, the Confederacy, Russia... It would be half a year before the cycle began to repeat itself. The perpetual rotation of the guard served as another symbol. The Patent Office belonged to no single nation but was served by all.

A small crowd of men and women huddled next to the wall to one side. Petitioners, I took them to be, here to plead cases before the court. A couple were dressed in the manner of the Republic. Three seemed African. Two were Middle-easterners, from Turkey perhaps. I caught snatches of French from the group nearest the door. None of us were at ease and none of us warm.

At half past eight I heard a low clunk and the doors began swinging inwards. One of the soldiers shouted something I could not understand. In perfect time with one another, the guards shouldered their muskets, stamped, turned on the spot and marched to positions on either side of the entranceway. Stamping and turning once more, they lowered their guns and resumed their motionless vigil.

The small crowd, which had grown whilst we waited, now started shuffling through the doors into a high, echoing hallway, where rope barriers funnelled us into something that resembled an orderly line. One by one, those in front were called forwards across the polished stone to answer questions at a high reception desk. Peering beyond it, I could make out corridors and staircases leading off into the building. The stone lintel above each entranceway was adorned with a different Greek letter.

If the intention of the architect had been to intimidate, he had succeeded.

"Next," called the man behind the desk.

I stepped towards him more boldly than I felt.

"Name?"

"Elizabeth Barnabus."

"Your business?"

"To observe an appeal by Mr Swain of North Leicester against the–"

"The court doesn't begin session until ten."

"Please. It's too cold outside."

He peered down at me, frowning. "Very well. Do you have on your person any firearms, blades, impact weapons, projectiles, pointed weapons, black powder or corrosive chemicals?"

He reeled off the list in a single, well-practiced breath. I shook my head.

"You need to say it," he explained.

"No. I don't have any of those things."

"Do you agree to submit, whilst in this building, to all instructions given by officers of this courthouse, under the powers and penalties of the International Patent Office, even in such cases as these instructions conflict with the laws of the Kingdom or any other nation?"

"Powers and penalties?"

"Just say yes."

"Then, yes."

"Then by the power of the International Patent Office, I grant you entry. Passage Theta. Up the staircase. Third floor. Turn left. You'll find the courtrooms at the end of the corridor. There's seating outside. I trust you'll find it warm."

Warm it was, with plush chairs and thick carpets that softened the distant murmur of activity in the building. I stared down the corridor, wondering at the number of people it would take to populate so many offices and so many courtrooms.

Then I fell asleep.

I dreamed I was having tea with Julia, sitting in the bay window of her house. First she was playful. Then agitated. Then she was gripping me by the shoulders, whispering urgently. Something about the Sleepless Man. She shook me.

"Wake up!"

"What?"

"Elizabeth!"

I opened my eyes to see her crouched before me. Her father stood by her side.

"My things?"

"We have them here," said Mr Swain, placing my battered travelling case at my feet.

Julia gripped my hands in my lap. "We were so worried about you. The men-at-arms–"

"Your coins saved me."

"But they were waiting for us outside the hotel this morning. I fear we've led them to you."

"They can't come into the building," I said. "The Kingdom's laws don't hold here."

"You must leave eventually," said Mr Swain.

I lifted the travelling case onto my knees. "When the time comes, I hope I'll be able to evade them."

Men in lawyers' robes had gathered outside a set of doors over which read a sign: "Court of Appeal 3 – Anglo-Scottish Republic". Others began to arrive – citizens of the Republic to judge by their clothing. The building seemed to have done its intended job, for they advanced as if each step might be a mistake. Compliant enough, I thought, to accept any judgement.

When he arrived, the man-at-arms was starkly conspicuous. Though stripped of his red jacket and insignia, he could not have been mistaken. He marched directly to me. Stopping a yard short of my chair he clicked the heels of his mirror polished boots.

"Your name please?" he demanded.

I stood but still had to crane my neck to look him in the eyes. "To whom am I speaking?"

"Are you Elizabeth Barnabus?"

"I see you have no sword or flintlock," I said. "By which I gather that you aren't an official."

Then I sat down again and turned my attention to

Julia, who had the chair next to mine. Her fingers were gripping the arm rests. Her face had turned pale. The lawyers were staring at us. One of the younger ones stepped closer, the better to hear our conversation.

The man-at-arms cleared his throat and tried again, addressing the space above my head as if I were still standing. "I gather I am addressing Miss Elizabeth Barnabus, even though you will not confirm it. You are a fugitive from contracted servitude to the Duke of Northampton. I am empowered to demand your presence at—"

"Empowered by whom?"

"By the Duke of Northampton, who demands your presence at his estate where you—"

"I see no insignia," I said, cutting in again.

"It…" His face had begun to colour. "It isn't permitted to bring them into the Patent Office Court."

"Then I'm not obliged to go with you."

The young lawyer chuckled. "She has you there," he said.

The man-at-arms knelt, bringing his face to my level, though it clearly offended his dignity. "Come willingly and I'll see you protected," he whispered. "Your new life will be pleasant. You'll be comfortable. My master's favourites are given the best food and clothing."

"My duties?"

"The Duke is an old man. He'll not bother you often."

"And when he dies? What happens to his property? Who would inherit me?" The pitch of my voice was rising.

"It'll be long before you're troubled by that. He's in good health. The old Duke, his father, achieved ninety-five years."

We both turned to look as Julia stood.

The man straightened himself. "This is not your business, Miss—" he began.

But Julia had brought her arm back and was now swinging it forward again. A soldier should have quicker reactions. For a fraction of a second he was staring, dumbly bewildered. Then Julia's palm connected with his face with a stinging slap.

Everyone was staring now. He got to his feet, his cheek blotchy, reddening where she had caught him.

"You wish to press charges, sir?" asked the young lawyer, his voice mocking.

The man-at-arms ignored the jibe. "At five this afternoon they'll close the building. You'll be thrown out. My men'll be waiting. *With* insignia. The crowds won't help you this time. They turn on a woman in chains. I've seen it before. They'll tear your clothes. Throw filth in your face. You'll be a stinking, ragged thing thrown at my master's feet. He's sure to treat you accordingly."

He wheeled and began to march away down the corridor. The young lawyer began to clap. Others joined in. Some stamped their feet and wolf-whistled. They kept up the din until the Duke of Northampton's man had turned the corner and was gone.

"Forgive me for intruding," said the young lawyer to Julia. "But the man was a cad. And that was a very fine hit."

"Can he do what he said?" she asked, her voice shrill.

"Outside this building, yes. You can appeal a contract of service, but it would take months. Years even. And in all that time, your friend would be in the Duke's possession."

The court doors opened and people started moving through. The lawyer seemed torn. "Duty calls, I am afraid." He offered Julia his name card. "In case you require legal representation. Or for any other reason." Then he bowed and hurried after his colleagues.

"Lawyers are born to take advantage," said Mr Swain grimly. "But I must follow him. Though I'd abandon my case if you thought my staying could help."

"Go," I said. "Both of you."

Mr Swain bowed to me, something he had never done before. Then he followed the lawyers into the courtroom. Julia gripped my hand and would not release it.

"I'll be safe," I assured her.

"I can't leave you!"

"Unless you do, I can't make my escape."

"You're still holding something from me," she said. "I can see it in your face. Is your brother to rescue you?"

"I believe I will escape. And in a manner of speaking, my brother will indeed help. But I can't tell you more."

She dropped my hand. We stood for a moment looking at each other. Then I picked up my case and hurried away.

Like everything in the International Patent Office Court, the ladies' washroom had been built on a huge scale. Thirty stalls faced thirty simple hand basins across a tiled room. The air smelled of bleach and carbolic soap, both appropriately austere. Large, frosted glass windows bathed the room in soft white light. Like the corridor outside, the washroom was empty – the only sounds a dripping tap and my own breathing.

Closing the stall door behind me, I opened my travelling case and began the transformation, stripping off the female layers, replacing them with the symbols of a male persona. Turn by turn, I wrapped the binding cloth around me, the familiar pressure across my breasts and release around my waist starting to do its work, the modification of shape that triggered a deeper change.

No need to rush this time. I intended to step out of the building in daylight. The disguise must be flawless. Using the small mirror on the inside of the case, I applied the facial hair, using the tips of my fingers to touch it down against the adhesive.

No doors had opened or closed whilst I had been working. The emptiness of the place seemed wrong. Perhaps this wing of the court was unusual in that respect. Other sections of the building might be bustling with activity. Or perhaps it was an unusual time.

I listened for a moment before opening the stall door. A man in a woman's washroom would cause a commotion if discovered. Then I listened again at the exit door and, on hearing nothing, stepped out into the corridor.

And there facing me stood Julia Swain, her eyes wide with shock.

CHAPTER 35

Hold this book at arm's length. At first it seems possessed of no weight. But slowly it becomes a brick of lead in your hand. Such is the burden of those who carry the secret of a great illusion.

THE BULLET-CATCHER'S HANDBOOK

I glanced up and down that long corridor. We were alone.

"Mr Barnabus?" Julia's eyes flashed to the battered travelling case. She stepped towards me and I retreated into the washroom. The tap still dripped. Our footsteps sounded suddenly loud on the tiled floor.

"Mr Barnabus?" she asked again, then cast around the empty room with her eyes. "Elizabeth?"

I knew the moment when understanding hit her because her face became brittle.

"I'm sorry," I said, using my deep voice out of habit rather than any desire to prolong the deception. "I wanted to tell you. It just…"

I could see her fingers trembling as she reached out her hand towards my face. "All this time?" her voice was a whisper. "You knew how I felt for him. All this time, and I..." She didn't touch me. Her cheeks had gone pale and she was backing away. Then she bolted for the nearest stall. The door clattered as she barged inside. She threw herself to her knees and vomited into the toilet bowl.

"No one knows this," I said, having to force myself to speak in my female voice. Everything about this was wrong. "Without this, I've no life. I'm so sorry."

She retched again into the toilet.

Despite the male clothing, when I fled from the washroom it was with the gait of a woman. But as I walked the long corridor my training took over and the pattern of my footsteps began to change. I tried telling myself that there had been no other choice. What was done could not be undone. I should put it from my mind.

Retracing my journey through the high-ceilinged hallway and past the rope barriers, I stepped out once more into thin daylight. Northampton's men stood at ease under the portico, musket butts resting on the stone floor. One of them carried an iron collar and manacles connected by a loop of chain.

None of them even looked at me as I brushed past. It should have been a moment of triumph but all I could feel was gnawing guilt.

When I was a child, my father devised an illusion that required the lighting in the tent to change on his command. In his mind's eye he'd seen the colour of the torches flicker from yellow to blue. Knowing no means to create this effect, he travelled to London's Spitalfields to consult the Jewish scientists who had colonised an area of shops and houses to the east of Petticoat Lane Market. Within those few hundred yards of brick and cobble, he said, lay more knowledge of chemicals and medicines than could be found in any other single place in the Gas-Lit Empire. That had been twelve years ago and I could now recall little but a name – Strype Street.

I asked a barrow boy, who said he had never heard of the place. Then a chestnut seller who scratched his head and said it might be south of the river, or perhaps north of it. But when I mentioned the colony of Jewish scientists, a kind of disgust spread across his face – which I took to be recognition. "That'd be east, then," he said.

I set off as he had indicated and soon found others to confirm and refine the directions. Fleet Street gave way to Ludgate Hill. The Great West Door of St Paul's Cathedral gradually emerged from the thin fog. Its towers and dome loomed as pale outlines in the grey sky. On another day I would have stopped to wonder at the grandeur of it. But so focussed was I on my goal that the cathedral was merely a way marker, as were the great banks of Threadneedle Street. Two miles of London's cobbles and uneven paving should have left my feet sore, but with my goal seeming close I hardly noticed.

Having deposited my travelling case at the Bishopsgate Coach Station and received a chit in return, I began to pick my way through the final few streets. I had already passed several Jewish shops and businesses. As I finally turned onto Strype Street I saw an apothecary with its window display of giant flasks – blue, red and yellow. A painted sign on the building next door boasted of laboratory glassware at wholesale prices. The street was shorter than I had thought it would be – little more than fifty yards from end to end.

Suddenly, I remembered gripping my father's hand. An image flashed into my mind of following close behind as he stepped through an entranceway sandwiched between two shops. Climbing a narrow flight of poorly lit stairs, we had come to a room of burners, stills and retorts. There we met a man with a beard so long that it rested on his round stomach. I sat on a high stool while they talked, my nose wrinkling against a strange smell – oily yet sweet. I kicked my feet as I watched a clear liquid heating over a spirit flame. Three glass marbles in the bottom of the flask jiggled and danced as it began to boil. When it was time to go, the bearded man told me I was a good girl and pinched my cheek. Then he took a jar of marbles like those I had been watching and tipped one into my hand.

The dislocation of exile had so separated me from my past that these memories, vivid and unexpected, felt like imposters in my head. It was as if they belonged to another person. Someone I loved, perhaps.

I had almost reached the end of the street now, and not found what I was looking for. Then I caught a scent in the air. I inhaled again, more deeply this time. It was sweet like over-ripe fruit yet somehow less wholesome. The same smell from all those years ago. I slowed, scanning the buildings to either side.

The entrance was like and yet unlike the one in my memory. There had been no door before. Now there was one, though it stood ajar. The position seemed the same, but the shops that abutted to either side had changed. In the memory I was safe, my father's warm hand engulfing my own. Now I stood tensed. Steeled against shadows.

The sound of wooden shutters clattered me back to the present. A Jewish man dressed head to foot in black was closing up the herbalist wholesaler across the street. Glancing around, I saw a thin scatter of people hurrying about their business. One figure in the distance was staring in my direction. I had been standing for too long.

The laboratory smell strengthened as I stepped inside. I pushed the door closed behind me and began climbing the narrow staircase, feeling my way. As I approached the top, one of the stairs creaked loudly under my foot.

"I hear you!" shouted a male voice, crackling with irritation.

But stepping into the laboratory, I found it untenanted. Eerily, the years did not seem to have changed the room. A gas lamp on the wall hissed quietly, though it was not yet dark outside.

"Hello?" I called.

"Don't touch!" The voice barked from a room beyond. "I'll know if you steal!"

"I... I'm sorry to disturb you," I said.

"Disturb! All day it's the same!"

A crash followed – a chair falling, I thought. Then words in a language I did not recognise, though so clearly swearing as to need no translation.

"I'm trying to find someone," I called. "I thought maybe..."

"Thought you'd disturb Daskal!"

"...maybe you'd be able to help?"

A series of thuds followed, metal on wood, getting closer. Then the man – Daskal, I assumed – limped through the entrance on the far side of the laboratory, wearing a scowl that matched his words. As he thumped towards me, I saw that his left leg was not a leg at all, but a jointed metal strut. Thin cables ran taut from the place where a foot should have been, passing around wheels at the knee joint, and disappearing up under his trouser leg, which he wore short on that side.

"Stop gawping," he said. "Come here and give me a hand."

He placed himself on a high stool, which could have been the very one I had perched on as a child. I stepped towards him and accepted the curved metal object which he held out. It seemed like a length of stiff spring with a socket on one end.

He lifted the metal leg towards me. "Haven't you seen a foot before?"

I turned the object in my hand. The gas light reflected from its polished surfaces. Lining up the socket with a pin on the end of the leg, I slotted it home. Two clips snapped shut, gripping it in place. Daskal stood, stamped the metal spring down as if testing the fit of a new shoe. Then he strode back out of the laboratory the way he had entered, quiet and smooth as if all his limbs had been flesh and bone.

"Don't touch anything," he shouted.

When, after a moment, he hadn't returned, I parked myself on the high stool. My feet rested flat on the planks of the floor, whereas years before they had dangled.

"I'm looking for someone," I said, speaking as loud as my male voice would allow. "A young gentleman. An aristocrat, though perhaps not dressed as one. He came to Spitalfields looking for help in... in perfecting a process. A month ago or less."

Daskal stepped back into the room, carrying a wicker-encased demijohn, which he placed gently on one of the workbenches. "I trade chemicals, not secrets," he said, though with less bite than before.

"My hope is to help him."

"Feh!"

"For which I will be paid – that's true. But it'll be for his benefit as well."

"See this?" he said, patting the demijohn, which I now saw contained a clear liquid. "Would you drink from it?"

I shook my head.

"Even if I said it was water?"

"You'd not carry water with such care."

He nodded, satisfied, as if I had proved his argument. "It's vitriol. Would've burned through your throat before you'd swallowed. So you're not a fool. And it saved your life. You say the man you're looking for is an aristocrat?"

"Yes."

"But not dressed as one? So he's no fool either. He doesn't want to be found. We're not spies here. No one's going to help you."

Daskal's expression was set firm. It suggested no compromise.

I stood. "Sorry to have wasted your time."

"How did you know where to find me?" he asked, as I turned to go.

"I didn't. That is, I was looking for a scientist. Not you in particular."

"But there's no sign on the door. How did you know what you'd find at the top of the stairs?"

"I came here once. Years ago. There was a man with a long beard."

Daskal nodded. "Old man Bulmer. That's the first thing you've said that's made any sense."

"He gave me a glass marble," I said.

"That's him."

An awkward silence followed, as if I had made some embarrassing confession. Then Daskal adjusted the lamp on the wall. The hissing of the gas stopped and the light went out.

"We've had strangers all over us for days," he said. "Watching. Asking questions."

"How many days?"

"Three. Four. Did you know you were followed here?" He nodded at the window.

I edged towards it until I could see the street outside. Dusk had fallen and there were fewer people than before. But one man stood leaning against the wall opposite, his arms folded across his chest, the glowing tip of a cigarette just visible. Though half his face was hidden below the brim of a dented bowler hat, I knew it was Yan the Dutchman, proud member of Harry Timpson's troupe.

Daskal waved me through the back room to a second set of stairs, even narrower than the ones at the front. "I'll not come down," he said, patting the top of his metal leg.

There being no light and no rail, I kept my hands on the two walls as I descended. Feeling blind, I found the handle of a rear door and let myself out into the cold. A passageway between high walls led me behind the buildings, then turned, bringing me back towards the street.

The shadows at the end of the passageway were deep enough for my safety, though I could see Yan clearly enough. As I watched, he sucked the last life out of his cigarette and cast the dog end to the ground.

Thinking back, it seemed likely that he was the person who had been staring at me in the moments before I stepped through Daskal's doorway. He would not have recognised me through my disguise. But caught in my memories, I must have seemed out of place. And since Orville was his target, he would have been keeping special watch for a young man who did not fit in.

Questioning the locals would not have yielded any clues – if Daskal was to be believed. Therefore, Timpson's troupe would have scattered through the streets, watching and waiting. Perhaps Orville was holed up in a room somewhere with his machine, gradually starving. He could not stay put forever.

It was another five minutes before Yan hefted himself lazily off the wall. I watched as he brushed down his long coat and set off along the street.

I could have chosen that moment to escape. But the thought never occurred to me. As soon as Yan turned the corner, I was out of my hiding place and running in pursuit. If I could find out which streets Timpson's men patrolled, I would have narrowed my own search.

At the end of Strype Street, I slowed to a walk and an imitation of casual relaxation. Turning the corner, I saw Yan striding out some thirty yards ahead. Too close. Slowing further, I let the distance increase. A sign on the house opposite read "Leyden Street". I fixed the name in my memory. On the other side of the road, a scarf-wrapped figure hurried past. In the distance I could hear the rattle of carriage wheels. If only there were more people out and about, my task would have been easier.

By the next junction, Yan's lead had grown to fifty yards. As he turned left, I saw him nod towards a doorway – an acknowledgment of someone standing in the shadow. To turn back now would be to reveal myself. And if they recognised me, a blade would surely be slipped under my ribs. They would drag me into a side passage and leave me to bleed out, unseen.

My pulse pounding in my ears, I turned left, following Yan.

"Evening," came a voice from the shadowed doorway.

I touched the brim of my hat and walked on without breaking step. Surely he must have seen my limbs trembling. But there was no sound of following footsteps. Realising I had been holding my breath, I exhaled through clenched teeth. I glanced at the sign on the wall: Cobb Street. How wide had they thrown their net?

A steamcar rumbled past, filling the air with noise and smoke. Fresh manure lay on the cobbles here, as if a drover had only recently passed through the street with his herd.

The next junction was with Bell Lane. Yan made no new gesture as he turned right. The colony of Jewish scientists had thinned to almost nothing. A row of food shops lay ahead – a haberdasher and a barber had the ground floor of a terrace of tenement buildings. Lamplight shone dimly in some of the upper storey windows.

I turned the corner to follow. Too late, I saw Lara standing in the doorway directly ahead. She jumped in front of me, palm upturned.

"Spare a copper, sir?"

I side-stepped but she followed my movement. So I grabbed her shoulder and shoved her out of the way. Behind me she swore – too loud and deliberate to be a natural reaction. A warning, I thought, alerting another watcher who would be waiting ahead. The panic was rising in me again. The street too empty. If I ran, they would catch me. I could hear the din of an approaching carriage behind. The wheel rims clattering on the cobbles, getting louder.

Down the road, Yan had turned to face me. A shadow shifted from the wall to join him. I knew it was Silvan even before I saw his face.

I jinked into the road, stepping into the path of the carriage. The driver shouted a warning. I could hear the horses' hooves sliding on the cobbles as he reined back. But I was across the road. I felt the whip of the air as the lead horse passed a few inches behind my shoulder. Then I was sprinting after it, using all the freedom of my male clothes. The horses had passed me and I was level with the carriage, accelerating as I ran, trying to keep it between me and my pursuers.

Pelting down the road until my lungs were burning and the horses began to pull away.

Still running, I snatched a look behind me. No one had followed. I slowed to a stop, gasping for breath, bracing my hands against my knees.

Seconds passed before I realised that I was not alone on the street. A man in a battered hat had set off, walking away from me, away from Spitalfields. He wore a long coat, frayed at the hem. Afterwards, I realised it was his gentlemanly gait that marked him out. It was a subtle thing, only of note because it mismatched his clothing. I would have missed it had my senses not been tightly strung.

I took a glance to check that the street behind us was still empty, then called out, "Excuse me, sir."

The man turned up his collar and quickened his pace.

I sprang into a light-footed run, catching up before he realised what I was doing.

"Leave me alone!"

But I was in front of him already and had looked into his eyes before he managed to turn away. Clean-shaven cheeks emphasised every angle of a face that might have been carved from marble. In this low light I could not see the colour of his eyes, but knew them already to be sapphire blue. I'd never met the Duchess's brother, but he could not be mistaken.

"Please wait."

Such was my excitement that my words came out high-pitched, as nature had intended. I tensed for his reaction, but he did not break step.

"Go away!"

I opened my throat, bringing my voice down in pitch. "Please wait."

"Lay a hand on me and I'll shout for help!"

"Mr Orville!"

That stopped him.

"Your sister sent me," I said.

"My... sister?"

"I'm to find you and bring you back to her."

A confused frown was creasing his forehead. "I have nothing for her."

"She loves you."

"You're wrong," he said. "And what is it to you anyway?"

"She's paying me."

"In advance, I hope. Because I'll not go back."

"I think you've misjudged her."

"If she's sent you here, it'll be by some motivation of her own. I'd never have consented to live in the same house with her but for the Duke."

His words made no sense. I'd seen the look of love in the Duchess's eyes when she spoke of him. And her desperation when she thought I had given up.

"You stole from the Duke," I said.

He turned to look back up the road. We had put a good distance between ourselves and the place where Timpson's men had been waiting.

"The machine," I prompted. "You stole it."

Orville's back and shoulders had been upright and rigid as oak beams. Now they began to sag. "The Duke wanted rid of it. Didn't it occur to you that my sister might want the machine for herself?"

"No."

"She's a passable actor when the need drives her."

"I believe you have her wrong."

He breathed the sigh of a defeated man. "We'll never know one way or the other. The machine's lost now. Or at least unreachable."

"How so?"

"The landlord told me that strangers were snooping about asking questions. So I hid the machine and went out to look for myself. There was a certain dwarf from Timpson's troupe skulking at the corner of the road. He saw me but I ran. If I return now, they'll follow and find my lodgings."

"But you hid the machine."

"Not well enough."

"How long have you been out here?"

"This will be the third night. My money's all but gone."

I examined his face again, now noticing the fatigue and the shadow lines under his eyes. "If I could help you reclaim your machine, would you at least come with me to see your sister?"

"It's impossible."

"Getting to the machine will be easy. Getting away with it may be harder. But I believe I can help you."

"To retrieve the machine..." he seemed to turn the thought in his mind. "Yes. For that, I'd suffer a meeting with my sister. Though it'd be a brief one."

"All I ask is that you see her. Then I'll be paid. Afterwards you can go – if you still want to."

He nodded. "Very well."

"But to do this, I'll need to tell you something. And you must promise to keep it secret."

He took my hand and we shook on the agreement.

"You have small hands," he said.

I swallowed, tightening my throat so that my voice would return to its feminine pitch: "That's what I need to explain."

CHAPTER 36

Do not trouble yourself over what the audience can see.
Only worry on what they will think they have seen
when they walk from your pitch at the end of the show.

THE BULLET-CATCHER'S HANDBOOK

The first five houses yielded nothing but confused expressions and scratched heads. At the sixth we were confronted by a man so muscled it seemed his head rested directly on his shoulders with no neck between. I asked my question and instead of a blank "no" he bit his lip and glanced anxiously back into the rooms behind.

"We'll pay double the price of a new one," I said.

Thus we walked away from that house and back towards Leyden Street, pushing a small perambulator before us.

I'd been spending the Duchess's money with reckless abandon. Little now remained. Soon there would be insufficient to cover a journey back to the Republic. Not that I was planning on returning. One way or another, I was in the Kingdom to stay.

The revelation of my true gender had not surprised Mr Orville as much as I had expected. The equilibrium of his world being already deranged, one more strangeness added little to the confusion. Indeed, I think he had already begun to see through the disguise.

I had reverted to my female persona now, and was wearing the green skirt and coat purchased from the used clothing shop in South Leicester. My hair was pinned up under the hat. It was not a disguise as such. If Yan or Silvan or any of them looked me in the face, they would know.

Our hope lay in the dim light and in the confusion of context. Timpson's troupe were searching for Mr Orville, a clean-shaven young man. Perhaps they also kept an eye open for me, a single young woman. But walking together, pushing the perambulator in front of us, we seemed for all the world a young married couple, not worth a closer look. That had been the plan. But making our way back from Bishopsgate Coach Station to the Jewish quarter, it was brought home to me how little Mr Orville understood about disguise and how short a time I had to teach him.

He raised his hand to his chin again.

"Stop that," I said.

"Is the hair still in place?"

"It's glued. It'll not shift until you pull it free. And then you'll feel it ripping at your skin."

"They'll know me."

"They won't look closely enough. But you must walk more freely."

"My walking isn't correct?"

"You walk too stiffly upright, like an aristocrat. Let your shoulders roll."

He made an attempt.

"Better," I said. "But I'm supposed to be your wife. Let your arm touch me. And your hip."

"It doesn't seem... right."

Wondering whether it was my virtue or his that he hesitated to sully, I slipped my hand around his arm and pulled him in closer. "Don't lean away! You must enjoy the contact or others will think it strange."

"I'll try."

"We're only pretending," I said, though partly for my own benefit. Through the coat, I could feel the pleasant firmness of his muscles. I hadn't touched someone of the opposite sex with this manner of intimacy since I was a girl. Beneath clothes and soap every person's skin has its own scent. My reaction to Orville's had taken me aback.

More must have been known of the science of fire in those few streets than anywhere else in the Empire. Yet the corporation had chosen to set the lamps there low, as if the inhabitants were less deserving of illumination.

The wheels of the perambulator clicked over the paving stones as we walked.

"Relax yourself," I whispered. "You love me, remember." I looked down into the place where a baby should have rested and favoured my battered travelling case with an affectionate smile.

Yan was even more conspicuous now that the street was empty and the shops closed. He peered from the other side of the road, leaning forward as if about to set off to intercept us. Any closer and he would recognise me. I found myself tensing, ready to run. But after a moment he leaned back against the wall once more and I began to breathe again.

Steering by the arm, I guided my pretend husband across the roadway to the other side. "Gentle with the baby, dear," I whispered as he pushed the front wheels of the perambulator up the kerbstone.

Thus we arrived on Bell Lane opposite the place where Lara had intercepted me earlier. Knowing where to look, I spotted her without difficulty this time.

Bending forwards and reaching into the perambulator, I made as if to adjust a blanket. When I straightened myself, Lara was already behind us and my knife was in my hand, half tucked into the sleeve of my coat. I counted twenty paces more, then steered Orville's arm, bringing us back across the roadway. Tension had tightened his muscles so that they felt like bundles of cable under strain.

"Which entrance?" I whispered.

"A little further."

But every step brought us closer to the place where Silvan had been stationed. The blade of my knife rested against my hand. I moved my fingers across the edge, reminding myself of its sharpness.

Then, behind us, Lara whistled. A single shrill blast.

Orville started to quicken his pace, but I gripped him tighter and pulled back.

Fifty yards ahead, Silvan stepped out into the middle of the pavement.

"Which door?"

"Just a little further."

Forty yards away, Silvan began to walk towards us.

"This one."

"Slow," I hissed, taking the handle of the perambulator and turning it towards the entrance. Orville went to the front and lifted the wheels over the step. We were inside a bare hallway. Doors with peeling paint lay to left and right. My heart sank as I saw the stairs that lay ahead.

"You didn't tell me they were so steep!"

"I'll take most of the weight," he said.

We began to climb, Orville ahead, bent low, me following, holding the handle of the perambulator at face height. The front wheels bumped on every step.

I could see Orville's fear, but it wasn't until I reached the first corner that I saw Silvan standing in the doorway below. He stepped inside, but I was quickly around the turn and he was out of sight again.

Another gaslight hissed on the first landing. We pushed on past it into the welcoming gloom of the stairs, which creaked ominously under our feet. The smell of damp pervaded.

On the second landing there was no gas lamp. I gestured to Orville and we stopped, both poised, listening. I could hear the muffled sound of a man and woman arguing, perhaps in the rooms below. Quieter than that was the murmur of life in countless close-packed households – people talking, children playing, dishes being stacked. Outside in the far distance I could just hear a poorly tuned piano plonking out a sing-song tune.

We held each other's gaze. The stairs below us remained silent. If we abandoned the perambulator on this landing and Silvan were to find it, he would know for sure we were not what we had seemed to be. So we lifted it once more and set out, trying to be quieter on the final flight of stairs.

On the third landing, we found ourselves standing under the angle of the roof. The only illumination came from a skylight above our heads, and that but a dim reflection of the city's gaslights from the low clouds. Orville turned his key in the door and I pushed the perambulator into his small room. I caught the impression of an iron bed frame and small table in the darkness. Orville scrabbled about on hands and knees in the corner. Furniture scraped on the bare floorboards and he was standing again, a small square box in his hands.

"That's it?" I asked.

"Yes."

It seemed an unremarkable thing – a box barely big enough to contain a gentleman's top hat. I reached out to touch it and saw him flinch.

"I'm sorry," he said. "I've been hiding it for so long."

Then he held it towards me and I ran my fingers over the lid, feeling the ridges and lines of an inlaid pattern which I could not make out with my eyes.

"Is it heavy?"

"The perambulator will hold it easily."

"That may be a problem. Silvan isn't a fool. If we try to leave the same way we came–"

"But there isn't another door!" Alarm had raised the pitch of his voice. "These tenements are built directly onto each other. Back to back."

"There is a way," I said. "But you may not like it. Do you have any rope?"

• • •

I unpacked my battered travelling case one final time and secreted about my person those small, tell-tale items that might have given away the truth of my double existence. Then, boosted by a high stool from Orville's room, I reached my arms through the skylight window and braced them on the slates. "Push me," I hissed. But having taken one look up and caught sight of my pantaloons and perhaps more besides, Orville turned his head away and would not come close again. I dangled for a moment, before finding the strength to haul myself out on the steep incline of the roof.

He followed, climbing out easily enough. But when confronted with the drop he became distressed and clung tightly to the lip of the skylight. We had cut strips from his linen sheet to form a makeshift rope. This I now hauled, pulling the precious box up behind us.

"I don't have a good head for heights," he said.

"You tell me this now?"

He closed his eyes and took in a shuddering breath.

"Will you abandon your treasure?" I asked.

"I will not!"

"Then you must climb. At the ridge tiles it'll be easier."

I made him go first, steadying his foot with my free hand as he inched upwards, his body pressed flat to the slope. When he reached the apex, I let go and lowered the skylight glass, following him up on hands and knees.

Though sat astride the roof and thus having no risk of falling, Orville became yet more agitated by the vertiginous exposure.

"There is nowhere to look," he said.

"You don't have to look. There's only one way you can crawl!" I snatched a glance over his shoulder along the central ridge, taking in the chimney that stood like a wall some ten yards ahead, coal smoke rising from three of its pots.

I followed behind him as he inched forwards. A fine rain now drifted in the air, making the slates more slippery than they would have been. My clothes began to feel heavy with moisture. Orville's hand reached the base of the chimney and he stopped. Standing and climbing onto the top of the stack and across would have been the safest way to go. But judging by Orville's reactions so far, I did not think he could cope with such exposure.

"Hold this," I said, handing him the end of the rope. Then taking the box under one arm, I lowered myself onto the slick incline. Had I slipped, I doubt the strip of cut linen would have helped me. But even with the flimsiness of the cord and Orville's vertigo, I felt safer knowing he had hold of the other end.

Spreading the fingers of my free hand for a better grip, I descended, then crabbed across to the other side of the chimney and was quickly back at the ridge line where I anchored myself. Orville seemed emboldened by the length of linen in his hand just as I had been. Soon he appeared around the masonry and was climbing back towards me. But as his free hand reached for safety, one foot slipped and he fell heavily, knocking a slate free. I lunged, grabbing the sleeve of his coat to steady him. But the slate was skittering away down the roof, accelerating as it went. It shot out from the edge.

I clenched my teeth as it smashed in the street below. A second passed before the shouting began. Silvan's voice to start with: "They're on the roof!" Then a shrill whistle, Lara's I thought. Other shouts followed in the distance. The pounding of running feet.

I looked across the next stretch of roof, searching for a skylight, finding none. Orville's coat sleeve was still in my grip. I stood, one foot on each side of the ridge and hauled him up after me. We wobbled together for a moment, then I started walking towards the next chimney, leading him by one hand, clutching the box to my chest with my free arm.

I heard a clatter behind us. The skylight had opened. They had found the stool and must now be clambering out onto the roof themselves. I stepped down the slope and around the next chimney. Orville followed, not waiting for me to reach the other side.

At first it seemed there would be no escape from this stretch of roof either, but as I hauled myself back to the top, I saw another skylight window directly below. I was already sliding down towards it before Orville had reached the ridge. Slipping on the wet slates, I threw out my free arm and grabbed the edge of the frame to stop me.

Bracing my feet as best I could, and praying for luck just this once, I dug my fingers into the crack and heaved. The skylight lifted. In a second, Orville was with me. I gave him the box and climbed in through the opening, hanging for a moment before dropping onto the dark landing below. The box came next and then Orville.

"They're on the road," he gasped. "We can't go out."

"But don't you see?" I said. "We've come down on the other side of the ridge. This house empties out at the back of the tenement. If we run..."

He grabbed my hand and we were off down the treacherous stairs. I took them two at a time, praying they'd all be there, for there wasn't light enough to see. Hoping also that the rickety rail would hold me if I slipped.

Then we were out into the night once more, our feet sliding on wet flagstones. The poorly tuned piano that I'd heard in the distance was suddenly loud. I could smell stale beer and smoke. Bottles clinked. We scrambled over a low wall and dropped into the rear yard of a bustling pub.

"Is it done?" he asked, catching his breath.

"We'll know in a moment."

CHAPTER 37

A man may learn to lie on a bed of nails for the amazement of his audience and yet he will remain a fool until he knows what drives him.

THE BULLET-CATCHER'S HANDBOOK

It felt as if I had been running all my life – across rivers and woodlands, roofs and alleyways. The rain had set in now. It slanted through the air, lit by the feeble gas lamps of Spitalfields, and bounced off the cobbles and paving stones over which we ran. Behind us, keeping easy pace, loped the Sleepless Man.

He had been waiting outside the pub when we came through. With the two of us together, he could not attack. Nor could he run back to tell Silvan and the others where we were – for then he would lose sight of us and we could disappear into the labyrinth of London's streets. So he followed like a jackal waiting for its prey to fall from exhaustion.

"Your part... of the... deal," I said to Orville between gasps.

"I honour it," he said, "But my money... it's in my room."

"I've still some left."

By the time we reached the coach station our run had slowed and the Sleepless Man had closed the distance. When I turned to face him and brandished my knife he backed off a few paces, but always to draw closer again, keeping our nerves wound tight, wearing us down.

The food stalls in the coach station had closed for the night but a few late travellers stood around the forecourt waiting for departure. I handed Orville the knife. He turned to keep our pursuer from rushing us as I knocked on the kiosk window. I would have bought tickets to some other place to throw him off our trail. But there was only enough in my purse to cover two singles to Bletchley.

I did not notice the moment when the Sleepless Man slipped away. It must have been after we had boarded but before our carriage pulled out of the station.

We were the only passengers. Packages and parcels filled the left half of the coach. Orville and I sat facing each other on the right with his precious machine wedged on the seat next to him. With each streetlamp we passed, light swept from me to him, causing the inlay on the box to shine for a second. It was silver, I thought. Precious stones glinted at the corners of the design. Whatever it contained had driven Orville and Timpson to take extraordinary risks.

"They'll guess our destination," he said.

"But we're a step ahead."

He shook his head. "How long can I exist like this, hunted from place to place?"

I thought again about my own flight from the Kingdom. Here I was, running once more. Perhaps we weren't so different.

"I'm beyond the protection of the law," he said.

"Then give up the machine. Let Timpson take it. Or give it to the Patent Office. Isn't life worth more than wealth?"

"You think I did this for money!" He laughed. It was a cold sound. "What is money? Only a means to an end. If it can't achieve what you desire, then it's worthless."

"If your machine creates gold, there's nothing you can't have."

"You're wrong," he said.

"Then why not give it up?"

"Because I wish to change the world."

"By creating gold?"

"By destroying it."

At first I thought I had misheard him – his words barely louder than the clatter of iron on cobbles as the outskirts of London whipped past the carriage window.

"Are you joking, sir?"

He leaned forwards. His eyes fixed on mine. "Gold is precious only because it's rare. Make it as common as lead and it would have as little value. The poor sweat away their lives for the promise of a few coins. But when those coins are made worthless by this machine... then the poor man's labour will be the only thing of value. The idle rich won't be able to rest. The treasures they've stored up... they'll be worthless."

"You are an anarchist?"

"I'm sickened by a world in which class can be a barrier that even love can't break. If that makes me an anarchist, so be it. You think my dear sister, buried in all her riches, could share my aim?"

I had taken the Duchess's brother to be many different things along this road. First he was simply a runaway aristocrat, then a foolish adventurer. When I had seen his picture for the first time, his impossibly perfect features, I even felt the attraction a woman feels for a man. But it was only now that I saw his tragedy. He was kind and intelligent but had been hollowed out by his own high ideals. It was a kind of madness.

"Destroy the machine," I said. "Before it destroys you."

"For this, I've abandoned things I love more than life. I won't give it up now."

The road became bumpy and the carriage began to sway more violently. I gripped the strap to steady myself and sensed that he pulled the box more closely to him.

"Would you let me see it?" I asked.

He hesitated before unclipping and lifting the lid. "You've earned a look," he said. As the light of another streetlamp passed across us, I saw the contents of the box to be no more than a sculpture of laboratory glassware and mirrors. Three reagent bottles were held snug in pockets on one side. Across the centre lay a glass tube, mirrored at both ends. He pulled a small crank handle from another pocket and fitted it into the side of the box, giving the apparatus the appearance of a gramophone player.

"How can this thing make gold?" I asked.

He gazed fondly at the machine, as if it were a small child. "That I still don't know. But if we're still alone at the next stop, I'll show you something marvellous."

The route of the night coach zigzagged up the country with scheduled stops in many small towns. Thus I did not have long to wait. Soon we rolled into the courtyard of an inn. The driver jumped down, calling to us that we had ample time to use the privy should we require it. Then he strode off in the direction of the stables.

Orville unclipped and opened the box once more. He tapped the three flasks in turn. "Distilled water in this one. Active reagents in these."

I watched as he turned a dial between the bottles. "This alters the ratio of water to the other chemicals. I'm setting it low. A dilution of one to a thousand."

"What is the meaning of this process?" I asked.

"The chemicals will mix in the central reaction tube. The papers we found with the machine spoke of its capacity to change the essence of things. But all you see me doing now – this we discovered by trial and error."

As he spoke, he began to turn the handle in the side of the machine. I could hear the mechanism whirring within the box, the pitch and volume increasing as it turned faster. I was thinking of the similarity with Timpson's lightning machine when, quite suddenly, Orville stopped. A smile had broken on his face.

Then I saw it – a line of light the colour of garnet, straight as a ruler's edge suspended in the air. It seemed to originate in the reaction tube, but was reflected up by an angled mirror, and came to rest on the carriage roof. I moved my hand through the line, expecting to feel the touch of it, for it appeared to be of substance. Yet there was nothing. Only a slight warming, as though a spot of sunlight had fallen on my skin in a darkened room.

"I... I don't understand."

Orville swivelled the mirror, sending the line lancing upwards at a different angle. "From the workshop we aimed the beam at the stable door," he said. "That would be a distance of thirty yards or more. The spot of light it cast remained just as small as this. Then we became bold and aimed it at the wall of the mansion three furlongs away. The result was precisely the same. A dot of light no bigger than a child's fingernail."

"Who made this thing?" I asked. "And how can light change metal?"

"Who made it, we don't know. It was one of many curiosities in the collection. As to the changing of metal – it was mentioned in the papers, as I've said. But I took that to be a fancy. Harry Timpson isn't the only man to have made spurious claims of alchemy.

"We saw the machine as an invention in want of a purpose. A curiosity. But having painted a spot of light over a distance of three furlongs, we realised it might be used as a kind of heliograph or Aldis lamp – flashing messages over very great distances in perfect security.

"To increase the range of the beam, we tried setting the concentration of reagents higher. But when we did this, we discovered that the duration of the beam decreased. All the energy contained in the chemicals was thus concentrated into shorter and shorter times. At last we turned the dial full up and tried sending the beam clear across the estate, a distance of some three miles, to paint a spot of light on the gate at the head of the main drive.

"The duration of the beam was so brief, it deceived the eye into believing that nothing had happened. And its power... Until then I'd not believed that light could change the nature of metal. But in the place where the beam had touched the iron gatepost, we found a hole; pencil thin and perfectly smooth."

"Then it had melted the iron?" I asked.

"If it had melted, there would be traces – droplets congealed on the gatepost like wax on a candlestick. The iron had gone. Completely. And in an instant. Iron had changed into air."

The light from the machine had faded now. I could no longer see the beam and, as I watched, the spot on the roof dimmed to nothing. I thought of all that light being concentrated into a second. A fraction of a second. The power of it would surely be intense. But to make iron disappear?

Orville opened a valve in the machine and I saw the spent liquid emptying from the reaction tube. I could hear it trickling but could not see where in the machine it went. Then he closed the lid and snapped the brass fasteners in place.

Wiping condensation from the window glass, I looked out to the courtyard and the stables beyond. We had been stationary ten minutes at least and I was nursing a growing impatience. The Sleepless Man must have reported back by now. Silvan would be setting off towards Bletchley at the greatest possible speed, or, worse, he might try to intercept us on the way.

"A watched pot never boils," said Orville.

I sat back and pulled my coat closer around me. "The man who helped you, was he called Zoran?" I asked.

"How did you know?"

"Putting small clues together for the most part," I said. "I had some of it from Tinker also. Don't be angry with him. He loves you like a father."

"I didn't want to leave him behind," Orville said. "But this isn't the journey for a boy. Is he safe?"

"Yes," I said. "Last time I saw. He told me of an aged conjuror..." I held up my right hand with the two middle fingers down, as the boy had done. "My father used to tell me of the exploits of the Great Zoran. I knew about the accident. How does he make his living now? Surely no longer as a bullet-catcher?"

Orville's face lengthened. "He and his daughter have rooms at the post house next to the hall. He helps to maintain the steamcars. She cleans and carries."

"This saddens you?"

"I didn't plan to abandon them. They deserved better."

"I'm sure you were a good employer."

He turned his face away, but not quickly enough to hide his pain. When he spoke again, his voice dripped with self-loathing. "Everything that happened was my fault," he said. "Zoran had failed to make gold so I asked if there were others who might help. He knew how to contact Harry Timpson but wisely refused to do it. I pressed him, saying he should act – if not for his own sake then for his daughter's. At last he relented. The letter went but we received no reply.

"I had no patience for waiting. I tried new experiments with the machine. By angling the mirror upwards, I sent the beam into the night sky. It seemed to disappear at a great height above the hall. That was not enough for me. I tried again and again, consuming the reagents in an attempt to touch the heavens. Do you see the tragedy of Icarus in me?"

"Your strange light brought the Patent Office?" I asked, fitting his story into the jigsaw puzzle I had already assembled.

"Three days later. Yes. But Harry Timpson reached me first. We showed him what the machine could do. He was greatly excited. He couldn't keep still, but walked up and down, moving freely despite his age. Ideas poured from him.

"He saw that our first goal must be to identify and replicate the reagents. Unless we could make fresh supplies, the machine would soon be useless. Then he said we could combine the light beam with various substances mentioned in the notes of past alchemists – of which he'd assembled a great collection. He kept reaching into the air as he spoke, grasping it and pulling it back to him, as if he were trying to catch the essence of life. Together we would defeat poverty, he said. Such was the force of his personality, I couldn't help but believe him. He shared my goals, I thought. We would do all this together."

"Timpson can be persuasive," I said. "And when the Patent Officers came, you hid with the Laboratory of Arcane Wonders?"

He covered his face with his hands. "Yes. I abandoned those I loved."

"This machine is a terrible thing. It's consumed you and Harry Timpson both."

"It's the only thing I've not destroyed. You've helped me regain it. I'll honour our agreement and face my sister once more."

"I do believe she loves you," I said.

"Then you're cruelly deceived. Once I've seen her I'll be gone. I won't return."

Orville brooded over the box that had destroyed his life. I brooded over the delay, seeing in my mind's eye Silvan riding northwards as we sat waiting in the stable yard. At last my frustration pricked me into action and I stepped out in search of our driver.

I found him sitting in front of a fire in the snug of the inn. He jumped up on seeing me and flustered an excuse that made no sense.

"Is this also a post house?" I asked.

"Yes, miss."

"They have a pigeon master then, and a loft?"

When he flushed red, I knew the truth of it. Silvan had sent word of a reward should our journey be delayed.

"What would happen if the coach company learned of a bribe paid to a driver such as yourself?" I asked.

"I... that is... we are ready to be off. If you–"

"There will be no more delays."

"No, miss."

"You'll drive the horses hard."

"Yes, miss."

I thought of all the pain that Orville's machine had caused. It seemed certain that it would destroy him utterly. I thought also of Silvan and his men, armed and willing to do murder. I held all this in my mind, whilst the coach driver stood in front of me, clutching his hat in his hands, trembling with tension and the prospect of the workhouse. It had never been my desire to choose the fate of others. Yet here I stood, weighing each person and each possibility.

"Very well," I said. "But I'll need to see the pigeon master before we go. I have two messages to send."

CHAPTER 38

*All bullet-catchers are alike. Therefore take yourself
to be your yardstick and never trust another with the
secret of your illusion.*

THE BULLET-CATCHER'S HANDBOOK

We rode through the night. The driver, more afraid of
me than I had realised, missed three of the scheduled
stops. We changed horses once and kept up a good
speed, our path more or less direct.

"What did you do out there?" Orville asked me
when he saw the driver's haste.

"A little threat," I said. "And I sent a message ahead
to the Duchess, your sister. I hope she'll be waiting for
us when we arrive."

But when the coach put us out on the roadside,
we found ourselves alone. The sound of wheels and
hooves receded into nothing in the pre-dawn. Before
us rose a magnificent iron gate, emblazoned with the
Bletchley arms. High stone walls stretched away into
the distance on either side. I shivered.

The dark cloud of self-loathing that had hung so

heavily over Orville during the journey seemed to have lifted. With the box under his arm, he pointed to one of the iron gateposts.

"This is what I spoke of."

I lowered my head to look through the hole that his machine had cut. Everything was as he had described.

"Couldn't your machine be used as a weapon?" I asked.

He shook his head. "We know this because of an accident."

The image of a hand flashed into my mind – a small hole punched through between the thumb and first finger. A sword wound, I had thought. "Fabulo?"

"The same. He had his hand in the way when a powerful beam fired. There was no blood. The wound was perfectly cauterised. And no pain, he said, though it itched afterwards. Any musket ball would do fifty times the damage."

I stroked a finger over the ironwork. Despite Orville's assurance, I felt certain of the machine's capacity to destroy.

The gate swung open, smooth and silent. The dark forms of three great monkey-puzzle trees stood to one side of the long drive. Lying directly ahead, the hall seemed to be more a castle than a stately home. The self-confident affluence of the aristocrats still shocked me. I wondered again at Orville's dream. If gold were suddenly worth no more than lead, would the meek at last inherit? In my meetings with the Duchess, I had felt a surprising kinship. Did I want to see her brought low?

"They must have woken your sister when my message came."

"First we go to the workshop," he said. "There's something there I need."

Cutting across the wet grass, he began to lead the way towards a cluster of low buildings at the rear of the hall.

"Our agreement–"

"I'll honour it. But once my sister's seen me, she'll likely have us thrown off the grounds. This'll take only a few moments."

"This obsession has warped your judgement," I said.

"She won't hide her true colours when I'm in front of her. You'll see."

We were both whispering now, for the buildings loomed close.

The workshop towards which we were picking our way must originally have been built as a set of stables. I could see where doors had been bricked. Chimneys had been added also, lending it the appearance of a small factory.

"I hid two large bottles in the fireplace," Orville explained as we approached the door. "That's all that's left of the reagents. The Patent Office won't have found them. They had no reason to search."

We slowed as we approached, stopping a couple of paces short. A large padlock hung from a hasp on the door. A bill had been pasted at face height.

THIS BUILDING IS SEALED
BY ORDER OF THE INTERNATIONAL PATENT OFFICE

"I'll break it," said Orville.

"Too noisy. You'll bring the men-at-arms. Why not use that?" I pointed to the box he carried. "Your machine can turn the metal of the lock into air."

A smile broke out on his face. "You should have been an inventor."

I watched as he opened the box on the doorstep and began turning the handle. When the light appeared he angled the mirror so that the beam touched the lock. "This is to get our aim," he whispered. "Then we turn the dial up full and set it off again."

But when he reached out to shift the lock a fraction to one side, the hasp from which it hung fell free of the door.

"It's been forced," I said.

He pushed and the door shifted.

I hissed a warning but he was already moving. "It'll take only seconds."

As the door opened, I darted my hand to the mirror, shifting it so the beam of light did not enter the darkened room. Then I ducked to the side.

Though I was braced for action and fully expected it, the sound and flash of the gunshot made me flinch. A woman screamed within. Then someone must have lit a gas lamp, for a steady yellowish light spilled out of the door, casting a rectangle on the uneven grass next to me.

"Let her go!" That was Orville's voice, fearful, outraged.

"Where's the machine?" Timpson this time.

"First release her!"

"We don't have the luxury of time, Orville. The gunshot will have woken the household. I'll kill you both if need be. The box can't be far. You have five seconds. Save her if you will, or the machine. One... two..."

I picked up the box with both hands. The mirror now directed the beam of light directly out in front of me, as if it were a line emerging from my chest.

"...three... four..."

I stepped around the door and into the workshop. Orville stood in front of me, frozen. To the left, backs against a workbench stacked high with machinery, stood Silvan, Fabulo and Harry Timpson. On a stool between them sat the Duchess of Bletchley, dressed in the clothes of a working woman. Her eyes flashed from Orville to me.

Silvan gripped a cocked pistol, the muzzle pointing at the Duchess's chest.

"Stop!" My voice cried out into the silence.

In a blink, everyone was staring at me and at the box I carried. Timpson stepped forwards.

"I'll drop it!"

He stopped dead.

The line of light vibrated in the air in front of me, betraying my heartbeat.

Timpson looked from me to Orville and then back, nodding slowly, his opalescent irises seeming almost to glow in the dim workshop. "Drop it then. I'll mend it. Your time is up anyway."

I knew Silvan was going to shoot the Duchess. I could sense the tightening of his grip on the pistol. Orville must have seen it too, for he leapt across the room, clearing the space in two great strides. I saw the knife flash in his hand. Then it was thrust into Silvan's chest. The pistol clattered to the floor as Silvan fell.

A gunshot flashed, half deafening me. Orville looked down to his own chest, blinking rapidly. Then he dropped to his knees. From somewhere Timpson had pulled a second pistol.

For a fraction of a second the Duchess's scream seemed to come from a long way off. Then all the sound rushed back at me.

I swung the box around, aiming the beam at Fabulo's eyes. He recoiled and swiped the air, as if batting away invisible hornets. Timpson was coming for me now. His hands went to the smoked glass goggles hanging around his neck. But I shifted the beam before he could put them on. When the light touched his eye he screamed, and fell to the floor clutching his face.

"Enough!" the shout came from Fabulo, who squinted like a man looking into a stinging gale. "This is enough! Who will have this marvel now? A dead man? Or a prisoner? That will be every one of us if we wait. Miss Barnabus, you must run fastest. The Duke of Northampton knows you're here. We sent a message."

"I cannot see!" cried Timpson. "You've blinded me!"

Fabulo knelt by Silvan's lifeless body and pressed his stubby fingers to the man's neck.

The Duchess was on her knees next to Orville. She ripped open her brother's coat to reveal a red bloom, like a poppy, spreading out across the white of his shirt. His eyes stared up at the ceiling.

She collapsed onto his chest, her body heaving with unvoiced sobs of pain.

Fabulo was trying to help Timpson to his feet, but the old man batted the dwarf away. "Get the machine, you idiot," he hissed.

The beam of light had faded to nothing. I placed the box on the floor. Men were shouting in the distance, heavy feet closing at a run. "Duchess," I said. "I'm sorry for your loss. But I did as you asked. Protect me now."

Still she could not speak, but clutched the dead body to herself and rocked it in an agony of sorrow.

Then the door crashed open. The men-at-arms poured in. Fabulo lifted his hands above his head. A gun jabbed me in the back and I did the same.

"Call them off," I pleaded.

The Duchess looked at me through her tears. "I'm sorry," she said.

In that moment I understood the riddle that had been in front of my face for so long. The brother who said his sister loved him not, who never wanted to see her again, and yet gave his life to save her from a gunshot. The way she held him, clutching his head now to her blood-stained breast. I was not looking at Orville's sister. I was looking at his lover.

How simply I had been trapped. Too proud of my own detection, I hadn't entertained the thought that the clues I'd followed might have been laid as an illusion. The watermarked notepaper, the aristocratic hand, the place of postage – all would have been simple to arrange.

"I'm sorry," she said again, as the dreadful realisation took root in my heart.

"You are Elizabeth Barnabus," said one of the men behind me. It was not a question. "You are fugitive from a contract of indentured servitude held by my master, the Duke of Northampton." He gripped my shoulder and turned me to face him. The other men-at-arms bore the badge Bletchley, but he wore the oak tree and stars.

"That woman will pay the debt," I said, though I knew already she could not.

"She?" laughed the others. "She's a village girl! She mops the floor at the post house, or did before she went on the run. You thought her a princess?"

"She said–"

"She's the bitch daughter of an old gypsy called Zoran."

"Aye, and she's wanted for thieving here at the hall."

There it was. The whole illusion laid bare. Simple, like every good trick.The theft of a purse of gold – my advance.Theft of notepaper also, no doubt. One foot in the post house to intercept any letter or message I sent, stopping them before they reached the real Duchess.

Another man entered the workshop, an armful of chain and iron in his hands. "This do you?" he asked. Northampton's man took it with a nod. He turned me again so that I was facing away from him. I felt the cold weight of iron as he snapped the collar in place. Roughly, he grabbed my right hand and manacled it to the collar. Then the left. I did not resist.

"That should hold her," he said.

The laughter of the men mixed with the sound of more footsteps approaching along the path.

"Make way," ordered a new voice.

The chains clanked as I turned to face the door.

"I am an agent of the Patent Office," said John Farthing, holding up his warrant paper. "This workshop is under investigation. Who is authorised to be here?"

No one answered. One of Bletchley's men took the paper and examined the stamp of office on the bottom before handing it back.

"The door was sealed," said Farthing. "Who is responsible?"

"A crime was being committed," said the man-at-arms. "The seal was already broken."

"Indeed?"

"There was murder here."

Farthing strode into the room, stepped around the bodies of Orville and Silvan, turned slowly and looked down on Harry Timpson, now kneeling on the floor. The impresario still held a hand over his eyes. "This man is wanted for questioning by the Patent Office," he said, "in connection with various suspected infringements. Unfortunately I have no warrant here with me."

He reached down, grasped Timpson's free hand and pulled it up to smell the fingers. "He's fired a gun. Perhaps you'll need to question him. What's your analysis of the murders?"

"One killed by gun, the other by knife," said the man-at-arms.

"Then it seems you have your culprits. The knifeman killed this unhappy fellow and was then shot by the famous Harry Timpson."

"What's your name, madam?" Farthing asked.

"Florence May," replied the fake Duchess, still kneeling on the floor.

"Her father was once a bullet-catcher," said the man-at-arms. "Was helping Mr Orville – that's this dead gentleman before you – helped him with these machines."

"A bullet-catcher's daughter in a workshop such as this? It seems more than a coincidence. Tell me how you came to be here, madam."

Orville's head was still cradled in her lap. She looked up, from face to face, eyes red and tears still streaming. "I fell in love."

"I'm sorry for your loss," he said, then turned to Fabulo. "You, sir. I've seen you before. You're a long way from home."

"Harry Timpson *is* the Laboratory of Arcane Wonders," said the dwarf. "That's always been my home."

"Knife throwers and acrobats are of no interest to me. Go, if these guards will allow it."

"I stay with Harry."

At last, Farthing stepped across to me. "And this is Elizabeth Barnabus."

"She's the property of my master," said Northampton's man. "Indentured servitude in lieu of family debts. Fugitive in the Republic theselast fiveyears."

"So she must have been... fifteen?"

"Fourteen, sir."

"I'm sure the Duke will be anxious to exact his five missing years."

Two of the men-at-arms sniggered.

"However," Farthing continued, "For Elizabeth Barnabus there is a yet more daunting fate. I have here a warrant for her arrest. She's wanted in connection with patent crime. She'll be accompanying me."

"But she belongs to the Duke."

"Indeed you are correct. And once I've finished with her, if she is to be released, I'll inform you of the place and time, in accordance with the relevant laws and treaties. But the Patent Office has precedence over the individual laws of any nation. I'd be grateful for the loan of the irons. You wouldn't want her to escape any more than I would."

Farthing accepted the key from Northampton's man, then pointed to the machine, which lay on the floor where I had left it. "One of you take this to the carriage."

Chains clanking, I followed Farthing towards the door. Behind me, the woman I had known as the Duchess of Bletchley called out.

"Elizabeth, I'm sorry."

CHAPTER 39

Gold is the only measure of your art. If your purse is heavy, then the illusion was good.

THE BULLET-CATCHER'S HANDBOOK

We sat in silence as the carriage carried us along the main drive, away from the hall, and out through the gates. Dawn was spreading across a sky that promised rain. Orville's machine lay between us on the floor.

Farthing caught my eye. "We're clear of the Duke's lands," he said.

I rattled the iron manacles. "And?"

He raised a hand to his mouth and coughed. It was the same gesture he had used to cover his amusement on our first meeting.

"You're enjoying my discomfort," I said.

"A little," he confessed. Then he reached forwards with the key and slotted it into the iron collar, which released with a sharp click.

I threw it off, letting it drop to the floor. Then I rubbed my wrists and neck, trying to be rid of the feeling of it. "I take it my message reached you."

"Thank you. Yes. The pigeon master woke me."

"So you have your machine. And you agree to my deal?"

"Your 'deal' has no basis in law. But my office wouldn't benefit from your imprisonment."

"When did you get the warrant for my arrest?"

"I've been carrying it since Sleaford."

For a moment neither of us spoke. The carriage swayed. I watched the fields and trees passing outside the window.

"From the start I thought you honourable," he said. "I'm happy to be proved right. But I'm still not sure why you chose to help."

"Honour had nothing to do with it. I knew Timpson would tell Northampton where I was heading. It came to me that I could play the same trick on him – by telling you."

"We're no one's toy, Elizabeth."

"Your faith amazes me."

"And your attitude..." He sighed. "Can't we talk of something else?"

"Very well," I said. "What of Harry Timpson?"

"When we reach the next post house, I'll send word for a warrant to be drafted. Though I fear I'll be too late on that score. I don't think Bletchley's men are up to the job of holding him. There aren't many locks he couldn't pick."

"The machine blinded him," I said.

"The dwarf will be his eyes. But don't worry. He'll be too busy lying low to give you trouble."

I stared at the box on the floor, wondering that something so small could cause so much sorrow. Or perhaps it was not the thing itself, but what people believed it to be. Orville and the bullet-catcher's daughter had fallen in love. Such was the gulf in station that divided them, they could never have married. That was what had driven him to try to overturn the social order.

It was a long time before Farthing spoke again, but when he did his words carried a weight that made me meet his eyes. "Agents of my office are supposed to be detached from emotion," he said. "But I must confess, I've failed in that respect."

After everything that had happened in the last few hours, I was unsure whether he was speaking some great truth or merely having fun at my expense. "What feelings?" My words sounded harsher than I'd intended.

Whatever he had been trying to express, the moment seemed to have passed. He turned and stared out of the window. "Many different feelings. My distaste for Timpson is one example."

"I have feelings also," I said. "An agent of the Patent Office destroyed my family. I want you to know that."

"The Duke of Northampton destroyed your family."

"The corrupt agent was his tool."

"If you have proof–"

"Five years have passed. There's no chance."

"I'd help."

But I could see from his sadness that he knew the truth. No organisation relishes the prosecution of its own. The Patent Office would bury my claim in a mountain of paperwork, even with the idealistic John Farthing as my advocate.

"I want you to destroy this machine," I said.

"That's all I've been trying to do since we first met."

"Then search Orville's workshop again. The chemicals that drive it are hidden in the fireplace."

"Thank you," he said. "Perhaps our goals aren't as different as you think."

We crossed at a small border post west of Leicester, the guards lifting the barrier as soon as they saw the Patent Office emblem that Farthing held out of the window. I was not mentioned, nor were my papers asked for.

I made him stop the coach half a mile short of the wharf.

"You don't wish to be seen with me?" he asked.

"Bad for business," I said.

"I thought it was your brother's business."

"I help out from time to time."

"So I've seen. I'd very much like to meet your brother."

"He wouldn't show himself."

Farthing seemed affronted. "With the recovery of the machine, there's no active investigation into his case. His troubles are over."

"Indeed his troubles are not over!" I said. "The Duchess wasn't a duchess, so there was no money. Her advance is all used up. And if we don't make payment our boat will be taken."

His face flushed then, and he began to feel in his pockets. "I don't carry enough money to–"

"Stop! I wouldn't accept a hand-out."

"I'm sorry that you–"

"But," I interjected, "I would ask if the thing your office was so bent on recovering is only the machine?"

"The... the machine. Of course."

"Then anything else, you will have no power to impound."

"That's true."

"In which case, I'd like to take the box."

"The box?"

"The box the machine sits inside."

Clicking the catches, I opened the lid and lifted the mechanism out. He turned the empty box, knocked on its side panels, its lid and its base, checking for any trick or secret compartment.

"The inlay is silver," he said at last. "And I fancy the stones may be diamonds. It'd sell for a good price. But if you tell me it belongs to you–"

"It does."

"–then there's no power that I have as an agent of the Patent Office to stop you taking it."

CHAPTER 40

*It is in our faults and failings, not in our virtues, that
we touch each other, and find sympathy. It is in our
follies that we are one.*

EDGAR ALLAN POE

At first I imposed on the hospitality of Mrs Swain. She
told me that the appeal at the Patent Office Court had
found in her husband's favour. Then she questioned
me for many hours about the fashions of London
and the architecture and the food and all the other
important details Mr Swain had thoughtlessly omitted
from his message.

Julia and her father returned two days later. It was
a reunion I had been dreading. At first she would not
meet my eyes but gave polite greetings to me and
hugged her mother.

"It's time I was heading back to the wharf," I said.

Mr Swain coughed meaningfully. "See your friend
home, Julia."

Neither of us spoke on the path back towards the
cut. We reached the boathouse and I was about to step

inside when she said, "Your brother was real to me, Elizabeth. You'll think me foolish, but I'd imagined... I'd imagined a future with him. I understand how it happened. And it wasn't your fault. But when I knew the truth it felt like he'd died."

"I'm so sorry," I said.

Then I hugged her. She was crying. And then so was I.

"I'll promise to tell the truth – if that's what you want."

"Why wouldn't I?"

"Knowing things and not being able to tell – it's a burden. The bigger the secret–"

"But I want to know!"

"Then we should start as we mean to go on. I've something to tell you."

She broke the hug and stepped back to search my face.

"Tomorrow I have a risky venture," I said. "If I get it wrong, I'll lose my home. It's a wager of sorts. Would you care to help me?"

I was not present on the afternoon of January the first, when Leon arrived, accompanied by a magistrate and a crew of five strong men armed with axe handles and crowbars. Seventy foot of empty space on the wharf marked the place where *Bessie* should have been.

Leon threatened. The magistrate invoked the powers invested in his office and told everyone who would listen of the penalties that could be visited on those who obstructed the law. No one hindered. Nor did they cooperate. Thus it took an hour for Leon to find the locked boathouse, where Julia stood barring the way, her arms folded.

The magistrate rumbled through his speech again, whereon Julia demanded that Mr Simmonds be shown the warrant papers. Leon accused her of trying to waste time – which was precisely true. But the magistrate informed him that Julia's understanding of the law was correct. No entry could be forced without the owner having had the chance to read the papers.

Then, with Leon's blood pressure rising and his men looking dangerous, she demanded that a copy of the original contract be produced. No sooner was this in her hand than Leon shoved her out of the way. The small crowd of boat families that had gathered hissed and booed at this. But Leon had his eye to the edge of the boathouse door and could see *Bessie* through the crack.

He ordered his men forward, crowbars at the ready. They were about to wrench the hinges when Mr Simmonds produced the key.

None of this I saw for myself. While Julia had been pitting her bravery against Leon's threats, I had been running from the road where a steamcar had just dropped me. Disguised and dressed as a man, I could take the direct route, scrambling down the embankment.

On approaching the wharf, I could hear the shouts of protest from the crowd. Then I saw the boat families being pushed aside as the thugs forced their way through. Leon turned and saw me. His choirboy face broke into a grin.

"January's here," he said.

"Wait–"

"You lost the wager."

The magistrate cleared his throat. "Mr Leon, are you invoking clause nineteen of this contract of sale?"

"I am."

"Is it your assertion that Mr Edwin Barnabus, being the second party mentioned therein, is in breach on the grounds that he has failed to pay your company *Leon and Son Holdings Limited*, the sum of one hundred guineas that fell due at noon on this day?"

"Yes."

"And do you further assert that this is the boat named in the contract?"

"I do."

"Then I, standing witness to your statements and to this contract, forbid any here present to interfere with your seizure of said boat."

Leon stepped heavily onto *Bessie*'s aft deck and tested the padlock. Then he grabbed a crowbar from one of his men and slammed the end into the hasp. There was a splintering of wood and a squeal of metal as he wrenched the hatchway open. "The boat's mine," he said.

I gripped the boathouse door to steady my dizziness. "No!"

Everyone turned to look at me as I began to advance. I felt blindingly aware of every movement. The crowd parted to let me through.

"Do you have a complaint?" asked the magistrate.

"I do."

"You dispute the contract?"

"No."

Leon jeered. "Losers always whine."

I pulled out a receipt and passed it to the magistrate.

"I made payment today. Five minutes before noon. He'd left the office already but his son was there to receive it."

"This does seem to be in order," said the magistrate, examining the signature and stamp on the bottom of the paper.

Leon swore. A woman in the crowd covered her ears.

"There's always next year," he said. "Or the year after that. You've not won."

Julia held the copy of the contract above her head. "Excuse me," she said, her voice coming out as a squeak.

I heard because I had been waiting for her to intervene. But it took a moment before other heads started to turn towards her.

"Mr Leon isn't correct," she said. "He broke into this boat under a false claim. He said the payment hadn't been made, when it had." She passed the contract to the magistrate. "You were a witness to that."

The magistrate glanced from the document in his hand to the crowd of onlookers to Leon and then back to the document again. "I... yes. That is technically–"

"Mr Leon has broken the terms of the contract." Julia's voice was becoming stronger as she grew in confidence. "That means Mr Edwin Barnabus, being the second party, owes nothing more. Not now. Not ever. The boat belongs to him!"

"Clause nineteen," said the magistrate. "I'm afraid what she says is true. It cuts both ways."

I'd never seen a face turn truly purple before that day. Indeed I thought Leon might be having a heart attack as his men helped him up the embankment. I could not find it in myself to hope otherwise.

Within a week *Bessie* was out of the boathouse and moored on the wharf once more. With new curtains tied back and a pleasant smell of linseed oil from the glazier's putty still hanging in the air, I carried the teapot to the table and sat myself opposite Julia.

"I received a kind letter yesterday," she said.

"I trust all the letters you receive are kind."

She pulled a face, but I could see she was pleased about something. "Who was this letter from?"

"Do you remember the young lawyer outside the courtroom, who so kindly offered his help?"

"How did *he* find your address?"

"I... that is, I'd felt it proper to write thanking him for his kindness."

"Did you indeed? And what does he say in response to your thanks?"

Blushing now, she pulled a folded sheet of paper from within her sleeve. I opened it out on the table and read.

"He admires you, Julia."

"No. You think?" Julia was stirring the milk into her tea so vigorously that some of it slopped into the saucer. "When we met him, I was so preoccupied with anger that I... I may have acted in an unladylike manner."

"You mean you slugged a man-at-arms?"

"Is it possible," she asked, "that having seen me behave in such a muscular fashion, a gentleman might still think kindly of me?"

"To judge by the letter, I believe the way you acted may have made a very favourable impression indeed."

A brisk knocking on the hatchway broke into the pleasant silence that had settled on us after our tea.

"Miss Barnabus? Are you home?"

It was the voice of Mrs Simmonds calling from the steering platform. I felt so happy and at peace that I called for her to come in and join us.

"A package has arrived," she announced. "It's addressed to you, not to your brother. You must open it directly."

Having prised the small parcel from her grasp, I turned it in my hands. My name and address were written in that aristocratic hand I had once thought to belong to the Duchess of Bletchley.

When my guests were seated, I unpicked the knots and flattened out the brown paper with which the parcel had been wrapped. A book lay within, its leather binding wrinkled and distorted as if by great age. A sheet of notepaper rested on top of it:

Dear Elizabeth. In payment of my debt, I am sending this, an heirloom of my family. It isn't the gold I promised, but I've been told it has a hidden value. I hope you may unlock it, where I have failed.

"What is it?" Julia asked.

"It's a mouldy book, for sure," Mrs Simmonds said.

Certainly, a musty odour rose from it, but it was not entirely unpleasant. I could smell cinnamon as well as old parchment. Undoing the brass fastener, I opened the heavy cover and laid it flat. On the frontispiece, the title had been hand written in an archaic script: *The Bullet-Catcher's Handbook.*

I turned the first page and started to read aloud: "There was once a line marked out by God, through which were divided Heaven and Hell..."

"What a curious book," said Mrs Simmonds.

"My father used to quote to me from it. But I've not heard this part before." I flicked through some more pages, the parchment smell wafting up as each leaf fell.

"What does the note mean?" asked Julia.

"That," I said, "I do not know."

SELECTED ENTRIES FROM

A GLOSSARY OF THE GAS-LIT EMPIRE

THE ANGLO-SCOTTISH REPUBLIC

The northernmost nation formed by the partition of Britain following the 1819 armistice. The city of Carlisle is its capital, the seat of its parliament and other agencies of government. It is a democracy, with universal suffrage for all men over twenty-one years of age.

THE ANSTEY AMENDMENT

An amendment to the armistice signed at the end of the British Revolutionary War. The border had initially been drawn as an east-west line from the Wash, passing just south of Derby. However, when news started to spread that Anstey was to be controlled by the Kingdom, new skirmishes broke out. The Anstey Amendment was therefore drafted, redrawing the border to include a small southerly loop and thereby bring Ned Ludd's birthplace into the Republic.

The border had originally been drawn so that it would pass through sparsely populated countryside. An unforeseen consequence of the Anstey Amendment was the bisection of the city of Leicester between the two new nations and its subsequent flourishing as a centre of trade and communication.

ARMISTICE

The agreement which brought the British Revolutionary War to a close. Britain had been depleted of men and resources in the stalemate of the Napoleonic Wars. Three further years of civil conflict reduced it to economic collapse and the population to the point of starvation.

On January 30th 1819, the leaders of the opposing armies met in Melton Mowbray and signed the armistice document, which was later ratified by the two governments. (See also: The Anstey Amendment.)

AVIAN POST

The name given to commercial services in various countries that rely on pigeons to carry messages rapidly over great distances. The breeding of specialist night flying birds greatly increased the efficiency of the Avian Post, though it remained too expensive to be of significant use to the general population.

THE BRITISH REVOLUTIONARY WAR

Also known as the Second English Civil War and as the Luddite Revolution, it ran for exactly three years from January 30th 1816 to January 30th 1819 and resulted in the division of Britain into two nations: the Anglo-Scottish Republic and the Kingdom of England and Southern Wales.

The untamed lands of northern Wales cannot be said to be a true nation as they are ruled by no government.

BULLET-CATCHER

One who performs a bullet catch illusion. The term is also used to describe stage magicians known for other large-scale or spectacular illusions.

THE BULLET-CATCHER'S HANDBOOK

The Bullet-Catcher's Handbook is a collection of sayings, aphorisms and technical knowledge accumulated by travelling conjurors. Being the product of many different authors in different centuries, the entries vary widely in style. Some seem to be transcriptions from an early oral tradition, possibly medieval in origin. Others belong to the Golden Age of stage magic.

Though extracts have been reproduced in scholarly works, the book itself has never been printed or distributed among the wider population. Not all the sayings known of by academics are present in every copy. Travelling people believe in the existence of an authoritative and comprehensive manuscript, which contains even such portions of the text legitimately expunged from other copies by the Patent Office. However this belief is not shared by experts in the field.

THE COUNCIL OF ARISTOCRATS

The highest agency of government in the Kingdom of England and Southern Wales. It meets in London and has authority over the general population as well as the monarchy.

THE COUNCIL OF GUARDIANS

The highest agency of government of the Anglo-Scottish Republic. Sixty per cent of its membership is appointed. Forty per cent is elected by universal suffrage of all men over the age of twenty-one. Its meetings are held in Carlisle.

ELIZABETH BARNABUS

A woman regarded by historians as having had a formative role in the fall of the Gas-Lit Empire. Born in a travelling circus, and becoming a fugitive at the age of fourteen, with no inheritance but the secret of a stage illusion, she nevertheless came to stand at the very fulcrum of history.

No individual could be said to have caused the collapse of such a mighty edifice. Rather, it was brought low by the great, the inexorable, tides of history. Yet had it not been for this most unlikely of revolutionaries, the manner of its fall would have been entirely different.

THE EUROPEAN SPRING

The period of revolutions and utopian optimism in Europe that began with the overthrowing of the French monarchy in 1793 and ended with the execution of the King of Spain in 1825.

THE GAS-LIT EMPIRE

A popular though inaccurate phrase coined by the Earl of Liverpool to describe the vast territories watched over by the International Patent Office.

The term gained currency during the period of rapid economic and technical development that followed the signing of the Great Accord. It reflects the literal enlightenment that came with the extension of gas lighting around the civilised world.

Though ubiquitous, the term Gas-Lit Empire is misleading, as no single government ruled over its territories. From its establishment to its catastrophic demise, the Gas-Lit Empire lasted exactly 200 years.

THE GREAT ACCORD

A declaration of intent, signed initially by France, America and the Anglo-Scottish Republic in 1821, which established the International Patent Office as arbiter of collective security. Following revolutions in Russia, Germany and Spain the number of signatories rapidly increased until it encompassed the entire civilised world. The most famous portion of the original text is reproduced below. Subsequent amendments, together with the charter of the powers and responsibilities of the International Patent Office extended it to twenty-three pages:

> *When men of high ideal and pure motive devote themselves to the establishment of an agency and of laws that will surpass the jurisdiction and sovereignty of the nations, it behoves them, out of respect to the opinions of others, to state the cause which impels them so to act.*

Whereas some sciences and inventions have manifestly secured and improved the wellbeing of the common man, We hold it self-evident that others have wrought terrible suffering. Never has it been the way of science to separate the seemly from the unseemly. Therefore has the good of all been offered up for sacrifice on the altars of egotism and narrow self-interest. Since the nations have failed to rein in their scientists and inventors, it has fallen to Us to establish, through this Great Accord, a supra-national sovereignty adequate to the task.

In adding Our signatures to this declaration, We are not embarking on a campaign of military conquest; rather it is our intention to subdue recalcitrant nations through the evident truth of Our cause. But should any nation rise up against this Great Accord, We hereby pledge to combine all the strength at Our disposal into one mighty army and reduce the aggressor to abject submission.

We also pledge to offer up such funds as are necessary for the establishment and maintenance of an International Patent Office, whose task it shall be to secure the wellbeing of the common man. This it shall achieve through the separation of seemly science from that which is unseemly, through the granting or withholding of licences to produce and sell technology, through the arbitration of disputes and through the execution of whatever punishments are deemed fit. In creating an agency of such sweeping powers, We are minded also to put in place the means for its dissolution. Thus, should two thirds of the signatory nations agree, the entire accord will be deemed null, the Patent Office rolled up and its assets divided equally between all.

With these high aims and clear safeguards established, We, the representatives of the republics of France, America and Anglo-Scotland, together with whatsoever nations may hereafter voluntarily append their names and titles, freely enter into this Great Accord on behalf of Our peoples. In doing so We hold ourselves absolved from all previous alliances and treaties.

THE INTERNATIONAL PATENT OFFICE

The agency established in 1821 and charged with overseeing the terms of the Great Accord. Its stated mission and highest goal is to "protect and ensure the wellbeing of the common man". This it does through enforcement of International Patent Law.

Agents of the Patent Office have wide powers to investigate, prosecute and punish patent crime by individuals and organizations. Were the Patent Office to judge any nation guilty, it would issue an edict calling on all other signatory nations to reduce the transgressor to dust.

Though investing them with sweeping powers, the Great Accord and its amendments also subject agents of the Patent Office to certain restrictions of personal freedom.

THE KINGDOM OF ENGLAND AND SOUTHERN WALES

The southernmost nation formed by the partition of Britain following the 1819 armistice.

With its capital and agencies of government in

London, it would be easy to mistake the Kingdom as merely the rump of the older, larger Britain. However, with the rule of the country passing out of the hands of the monarch and parliament and into the control of the Council of Aristocrats, it must be regarded as a revolutionary nation in its own right.

NED LUDD

Inspirational figurehead of the Luddite movement. A weaver from Anstey in Leicestershire, Ned Ludd inspired the Luddite movement by smashing two mechanical knitting machines in 1799. He was posthumously named "Father of the Revolution" and "Father of the Anglo-Scottish Republic".

NED LUDD DAY

The annual celebration of Ned Ludd's life. It takes place on 21st March, though there is no reason to believe this was his actual birthday. It is traditionally marked by the presentation of gifts and the symbolic destruction of models of the "infernal machines" by the head of each household. Bank Holiday in the Anglo-Scottish Republic.

PATENT CRIME

The production, sale or use of any technology judged by the International Patent Office to be "unseemly" or otherwise lacking a patent mark.

POLARI

The cryptic vocabulary that makes up a private language used by travelling showmen, circus people and other sub-cultures throughout the Kingdom and the Republic. Polari words and phrases include:

Gaff – The fairground
Jal – To arrive or leave
Josser – Non circus person
Rum Col – The boss. Literally, your best friend.
Scarper – To run away
Tober – The fairground lot

THE RATIONAL DRESS SOCIETY

An organization dedicated to minimising the harm caused to women by excessively restrictive clothing.

REVOLUTIONARY NATIONS

Those nations established during the European Spring.

THE SECOND ENLIGHTENMENT

The long period of relative peace that followed the establishment of the Great Accord. Though nations had engaged in border skirmishes and imposed trade embargoes on each other and used their economies as a weapon, there had been no pan-European conflict since stalemate and exhaustion ended the Napoleonic Wars in 1815.

WILD EIGHTS

A gambling game typically played for low stakes by working men and travellers. Though sometimes viewed as a simplified version of poker, Wild Eights may be the game from which poker emerged.

ACKNOWLEDGMENTS

I would like to express my warm thanks to the following people for their help and encouragement in writing this novel: Stephanie Maude, Ed Wilson, Chris d'Lacey, Rhys Davies, Terri Bradshaw, Dave Martin, Liz Ringrose and the other members of LWC. Also to Marc Gascoigne and Lee Harris for having faith in the Gas-Lit Empire.

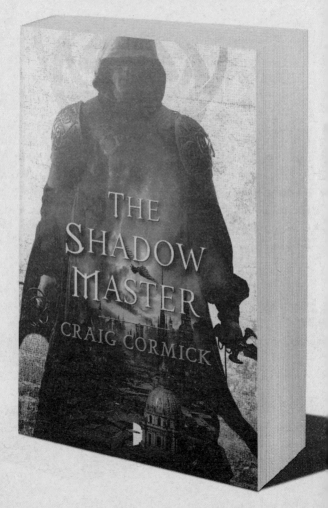

**Knowledge is power, and power must
be preserved at all costs...**

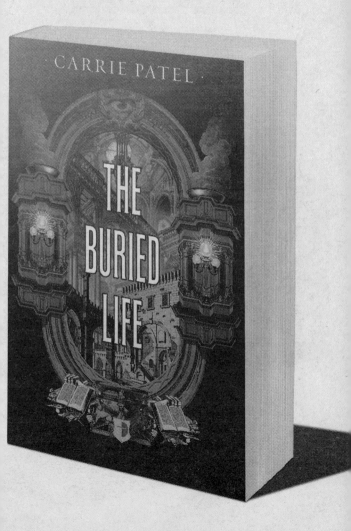

CARRIE PATEL

THE
BURIED
LIFE

War is the only reality.

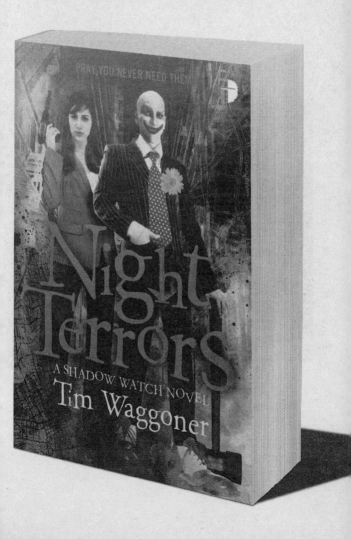

It's *Supernatural* meets *Men in Black*
in a darkly humorous urban fantasy
from the author of *Nekropolis*.

PEACEMAKER

MARIANNE DE PIERRES

"TWO LINE AUTHOR SHOUT ABOUT THE FANTASTIC PEACEMAKER WILL GO HERE."
AUTHOR NAME

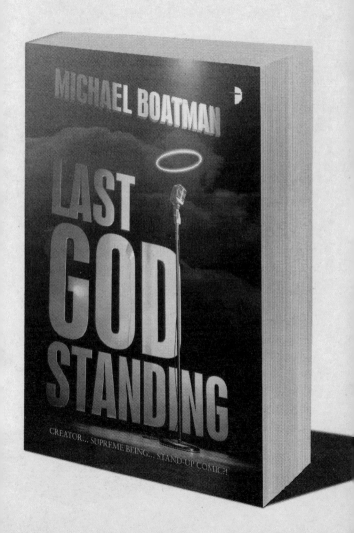

The quest for the Arbor has begun...

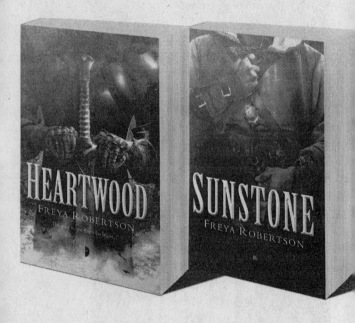